Stubborn Love

A MURPHY BROTHER STORY, BOOK 5

JENNIFER RODEWALD

WORDS THAT EDIFY
Rooted Publishing

ROOTED PUBLISHING

Contents

Be joyful always; pray continuously; give thanks in all circumstances, for this is God's will for you in Christ Jesus.

I Thessalonians 5:16–18

***

No duty is more urgent than that of returning thanks.

—St. Ambrose

CHAPTER ONE

(in which Becca flies)

TYLER MURPHY WAS ABOUT undone. Today was the day! He'd planned. He'd saved. He was entirely prepared. And after three years he was certain...

This was it. Rebecca Colson was everything—his whole world and all that was good and beautiful. She was his future, and nothing could ever sever what they had together.

Energy coursed through his body as he sat on the back deck of the Murphy home, gazing at the eastern horizon. He gripped the mug in his hand, the coffee's warmth working against the mild morning chill of that early June day. To him, it seemed the sun was taking its sweet time cracking over the pine tops to chase away the lingering darkness. The cruel tease. *Come up...come up!* Alone against the rail, Tyler chuckled. He was like a seven-year-old on Christmas morning, all impatient and ridiculously eager. He wouldn't apologize for it though. Wasn't every day a guy had plans like his.

As a cool breath of pine and mountain swept against his freshly shaven face, he shut his eyes and imagined how it all would go one more time. Everything was in place—he'd set up the finishing touches the night before and confirmed their reservations at the adventure park, and Mom had helped him arrange the gazebo at the end of the zipline so it was perfect. Stunning, actually. Again, Tyler laughed as his mom's teary expression resurfaced in his mind.

"Any woman who would say yes after this setup might be able to keep up with you, my Tarzan," Mom had said.

Tyler agreed—and Becca wasn't just any woman. She was the love of his life. Waiting to propose until they had been this close to graduating from college had seemed like torture. But he had, because he knew how her parents felt about it. Her father had been perfectly clear—reason enough not only to wait to propose until the summer after their junior year, but also reason enough for him to stay in school until he earned that business degree he'd promised. If not that, he'd have ditched school to climb roofs and pound nails after leaving CalTech his freshman year. But Mr. Colson had concerns about him dropping out of college entirely. Specifically, how Tyler intended to take care of his daughter in the future.

Frankly, that had been a rub. Not only on Tyler, but also between him and Becca, as she'd defended her father's position. Hadn't mattered that *his* dad was doing quite well without some expensive paper from some school telling the world he was "qualified." Dad had found his niche in building and had the mathematical aptitude and the experience gained from an apprenticeship to do what he did with precision.

Both facts that were true of Tyler—and had been *before* he'd even gone to college. That hadn't carried much weight with Mr. Colson, and Tyler had felt pinned into earning a college degree. A bit grudgingly, he'd dropped enrollment at CalTech and enrolled alongside Becca at Sacramento State.

But whatever. That was in the past. At least he and Becca had each other there. And there was the added bonus of Brandon joining them. More importantly, Tyler's degree was in sight, the waiting coming to an end. Tyler had bent to Mr. Colson out of respect (a point encouraged by Tyler's own father) and out of love for Becca. She was worth it.

Looking for the sunrise again, Tyler mindlessly sipped his coffee. Soft light pushed against the gray sky, touching the low, wispy smattering of clouds with variations of oranges and pinks. A beautiful start to the perfect day.

Thanks, God.

He took the quiet, glorious display as a blessing, as a heavenly nod. "Every good and perfect gift is from above, coming down from the Father of heavenly lights." The verse rolled easily off his tongue—it was one of his dad's favorites and had been quoted often. Tyler lifted his mug in salute, then turned to go back into the house.

His future looked like that sunrise—perfectly beautiful and blessed by God Himself. He couldn't wait.

***

A hot rush of panic flared through Becca as she quadruple-checked the carabiner attaching her harness to the zipline. The platform was more than fifty feet above the river coursing below, a sea of green pine tops on either side of the swath of water waving at her from the distance. Her heart kicked hard as her vision blurred. But she'd not chicken out. Not when Tyler stood there at her side, grinning like a man who'd just won a gold medal.

Three, two—she swallowed hard, drew a deep breath—*one*. Squeezing her eyes shut, she pushed off the platform. For a moment, there was the terrified sensation of free-falling, and she let out a yelp. But then the slack caught. She bounced against the harness, and the sound of air rushing and the carabiner gliding against the zipline filled her ears. Opening her eyes, she gripped the union of harness and line, watching while the earth flew beneath her dangling feet.

Don't miss these moments. She repeated her mantra in her head.

Rebecca Colson hadn't always been this adventurous. Frankly, she'd been the kind of girl who would rather try out a new cupcake recipe than launch herself into the vast space between platforms on a zipline course. She liked solid ground, predictable outcomes, and smaller thrills that didn't involve life-risking adventures.

But she loved Tyler Murphy. With every inch of her less-than-adventurous heart, she loved this crazy, Tarzan-esque man. Because of him and his insatiable thirst for the next adrenaline rush, not to mention his endless supply of high-energy enthusiasm, Becca had learned to embrace some daring adventure. And it wasn't so bad.

Granted, these risk-taking, high-flying, crazy-guy stakes weren't her lifeblood, but being with Tyler, feeling his life pulse in everything they did, was worth pushing through her comfortable, feet-on-the-ground life. And if she wanted to have a life with this guy, she needed to up her capacity for risk.

Becca definitely wanted a life with Tyler.

Hadn't taken her long to know it, either. She'd suspected it from their first date—one that involved a morning climbing rock walls, followed by a drive out to some falls for a hike and a picnic. He'd mixed his drive for high-octane adventure and challenge with the calming beauty of nature and ease of a picnic so perfectly that she'd known he was no ordinary guy. By their next date—one in which he'd volunteered them as helpers for a youth day camp for a basketball tournament—she'd been dead gone for Tyler Murphy.

The landing platform zoomed in close, and Becca prepared herself for the stop. Using an extended arm, the guy at the end helped her break momentum as she trotted across the wooden slats. As soon as she was stopped and steady on her feet, he asked if she was good—she was—and radioed an "all clear" back to the worker at the start. That would be Tyler's cue.

Becca's safety harness was detached, and she turned to watch her boyfriend's incoming.

"You're shaking a little bit," the zipline worker said. "This your first time?"

"No." Becca laughed nervously. "Actually, I've been here a couple times. Just never get used to it, I guess."

"Ah. Nervous or exhilarated?"

"Both?"

The guy chuckled, and Tyler came into view. "Did he talk you into the first time?"

"Not really." Becca gripped the railing that surrounded their high-rise deck. "He sort of just took me, and I didn't want to chicken out."

"Hmm..."

Becca wasn't sure if that was disapproval or a general *hmm*. Didn't matter much, as Tyler whooped into the landing zone, unhitched the carabiner that hooked him to the zipline, and dropped an arm around Becca. "Epic, right? Doesn't get old."

She could live without her whole body trembling. But his pure-delight smile and the gleam in his eyes didn't get old. Becca smiled up at him, and he dipped for a kiss.

"You're my girl, Bec. No one like you."

She wasn't sure about that. Truth be told, Becca was pretty sure she was fairly ordinary—and these risk-loving outings were never her idea. There was no one like *Tyler* though, and she'd take him, even while shaking in her tennis shoes, every single day of the week.

Leaning back, she grinned up at him. "You go first this time."

"Heck no." Tyler tapped her nose. "Then I'd miss that cute little yelp you let out at the start."

Becca squinted at him as if irritated but couldn't hold the false expression long. "There's cheesecake waiting for me at the end of this, right?"

"I told you what waited at the end of this day was a surprise. Don't try to spoil it."

"But not like a hang-gliding sort of surprise, right?"

His gaze softened, even while his eyes still gleamed with electrified anticipation. "It's an epic surprise. That's all I'm saying."

The wobble in her legs was definitely from nerves. "Tyler..."

He caught her hand and cupped her jaw, drawing her in for another kiss. "Promise you'll like it," he whispered.

Oh, that tone. Soft and low, and so...so...just for her. Becca melted in the middle.

"Off you go." Tyler spun her around and clipped her harness to the next zipline.

After he backed away, the guy working the take-off zone stepped in to double-check every fastener. Becca went through her shut-eye ritual countdown again, and then she was off, flying through the air, attached to a suspended wire from raised deck to raised deck, with a mix of terror and thrill pulsing through her veins. Mostly, if she was being honest, terror.

As she zipped away, she overheard the worker say something to Tyler about being lucky, and that she was pretty shaky, and maybe there was *brave* in there. Tyler laughed and said, "That's my lady."

Tyler's pride in her buoyed her heart above the shallow waters that felt like resentment toward him. As the cool mountain air whisked by her face, whipping her braided hair beneath her helmet, she prayed, *God, please erase my fears. Let me be the girl Tyler thinks I am...*

The whole landing and taking off was repeated two more times, Tyler insisting Becca go first. Neither takeoff came easier, but his evident thrill in this activity, and his building excitement for whatever surprise he had set up, kept her moving forward. After the final landing, they descended the ladder and Becca breathed a sigh of relief to have her feet back on terra firma. Tyler hopped down, skipping the last four rungs of the ladder and landing beside her, not entirely unlike an ape in the jungle.

"Thanks, Becs. That was a blast, don't you think?"

"As soon as my heart rate settles back to a normal rhythm, I'm sure I'll agree."

He locked an arm around her and tugged her close, pressing a kiss to her temple. "You're the best, beautiful. Ready for your surprise?"

"Does it involve harnesses and helmets? Because the answer is no if—"

Her words stalled.

Tyler took her hand and led her down the pathway to the end of the adventure park. There the company had built a gazebo that overlooked the class-three rapids of the river curving into a deep canyon. Actually, the adventure company hadn't built that gazebo—they'd hired Tyler and his dad to do it the year before. It had been one of Tyler's favorite projects ever.

But that wasn't what had stopped Becca short. Her steps came to an abrupt halt fifteen feet before they reached the overlook. The gazebo had been dressed up. Twinkle lights outlined the structure, casting a soft white glow against the gathering dusk. In the middle of the covered structure, a small table for two had been set up. A long white cloth draped from the tabletop and spilled onto the floor. Candles—likely powered by LED bulbs and batteries—flickered in the midst of an evergreen and wildflower arrangement centered on the table.

"Tyler..."

His warm, rough hand surrounded hers, and he drew her close again. "How about an early dinner, love?"

With a hand on his chest, she looked up at him, meeting his dark, glittering eyes and turning to melted butter all over again. "What are you up to?"

His mouth brushed her lips and lingered. "Surprise."

Anticipation zinged throughout Becca's body, and suddenly it seemed she was out of breath. She shut her eyes, her world spinning in the most delightful, amazing way ever. This was no ordinary date, no ordinary dinner... "Tyler?"

He moved, leaving her chilly without his body heat infusing her, and when she opened her eyes, she found him going down to one knee.

Breathing was no longer necessary, and flying seemed like a total delight. Becca wasn't sure her feet were truly on the ground at all.

"Rebecca Grace Colson"—with tenderness that summoned tears from her eyes, Tyler took both her hands in his—"I've been in love with you from the first day. I'll be in love with you until my last breath. Will you marry me?"

Becca sputtered a laugh-sob. "Yes!"

Somewhere in that euphoric moment, Tyler stood, placed a diamond on her ring finger, and hauled her into his arms.

She was flying again, only this time, it was only thrilling. No fear at all.

CHAPTER TWO

(in which there's a setback)

TYLER TUGGED METAL SHEETING one at a time from the trailer attached to the quad. The off-grid build he and Dad had been on for two weeks was nearing completion. Usually Tyler was glad for another successful build, but other than that was fairly indifferent about getting back down to grid living. That day, however, anticipation about getting home filled his mind.

Two weeks away from his fiancée proved to be two weeks too many. His *fiancée*!

"You've got that goofy grin on again." Dad clapped his shoulder with a gloved hand and nudged him forward. "If Becca thinks half as much about you as you've been daydreaming about her, I'd say you'd best just move up the wedding and get'er done."

A self-conscious heat tinged his cheeks, but Tyler chuckled. Man, he hoped Becca was missing him the way he was missing her. Actually, amend that. He'd been having a hard time focusing on his work, and that wasn't necessarily a good thing. Becca hated when she made mistakes—they'd chase around in her head into the deepest part of the night, not letting her sleep. She didn't shrug things off the way he did, and he didn't want her to have to stew about things not done right. So he hoped she missed him but that it wasn't disrupting her summer job at Sugar Pine Treats.

"I wouldn't argue with you at all, except Becca's dad is still pretty insistent we graduate first. Even reemphasized the point when I asked if I could propose."

Dad laughed quietly, slid another roofing sheet onto the pile, and looked at Tyler with a knowing glint. "Patience is not one of our strong points, is it, my boy?"

"No." The word fell from Tyler's mouth like a brick, and he knew Dad understood the tone. While Dad had encouraged Tyler to abide by Mr. Colson's wishes over the past few years, even stating that there was wisdom in it, Tyler knew Dad understood the struggle. After all, he and Dad were so much alike. Driven, a little impulsive, and not ones to stand around waiting for...well, for anything. They were doers and go-getters. They were decisive in what they wanted and intense when it came to going after it.

And Tyler had wanted Becca for his wife. Three years of waiting, of doing school when he really didn't want to, hadn't changed that.

Eleven more months...

Little less than a year, and he'd get to call Becca his wife. Mrs. Murphy. Man, did he like that thought.

"Maybe this job would have been easier if we'd found a spot with cell reception after work." Dad carried the final sheet toward the tiny house they'd erected in the middle of nowhere.

The owners would be around in the next thirty minutes to do what they could to help. Sometimes that was useful. Other times it set their progress back. Teaching took time, and he and Dad worked to a rhythm that had been established between them over years' worth of experience. But Tyler couldn't begrudge the homeowners their wanting to participate —and learning started somewhere.

"I don't know if that would have helped or not. I'd still miss her." Tyler strapped on his tool belt, checked the battery on his power drill, and then pulled the heavy-duty collapsible ladder from inside the small dwelling. Once unfolded and propped against the structure, he scrambled up the rungs and launched onto the plywood sheeting they'd nailed to the rafters the day before. His boots slid, and he gripped the apex of the roof to regain stability.

"If you're not gonna have your mind on what you're doing up there, maybe you'd better strap on the harness."

Righting himself, Tyler waved off his father's concerns. "I'm good."

Dad shot him a wry grin. "Be present, son. That's a pretty steep pitch."

"Got it."

"No showing off for the owners either."

"Do I ever?"

Yes. Every single time. Dad didn't answer though. Just shook his head and grabbed the top sheet of metal to shimmy up to Tyler.

Grinning, Tyler reached for the nearest edge and pulled the roofing material onto the plywood. The work was familiar enough to let him rely on muscle memory. Reach, tug, place, line up, tack down with a few screws. Repeat.

Not hard. Nothing mentally challenging at all. Which meant that he shouldn't have missed tacking down the fourth sheet he placed.

It was a stupid, stupid mistake.

***

Becca looked at the name on her caller ID. Actually, it wasn't a name, but a number—a local one.

"This is Becca."

"Becca. It's Kevin Murphy."

Her heart stalled, and something heavy and hot drained through her limbs. Not only did Tyler's dad never call her, because that'd be odd, but Kevin didn't sound normal. At all. "Mr. Murphy, is everything okay?"

"No, hon." His voice frayed with emotion. "There's been an accident. Tyler fell from a roof. We're finally back to the road, and I'm heading toward the nearest hospital. Can you get there?"

Panic clawed her chest as her pulse didn't just kick back into gear but leapt to a frenzied pace. "Give me a location. I'll get there."

The line held for an agonizing moment.

"Mr. Murphy? Is he okay?"

"I don't know, kid. His leg is broke—that much I'm pretty certain about. He hit a tree on impact—hit it hard. It took us over an hour to get out of the bush. He passed out before we reached the truck. He's been in and out of consciousness, and the swelling is pretty bad."

Good heavens. *Oh, God, let him be okay!*

"I'm leaving now. Can you send me a location pin?"

"Yeah, as soon as we get in the ER, I will. For now head northwest."

"Got it."

"Becca."

The catch in his voice nearly provoked Becca to a sob.

"Yeah?"

"Pray, hon. Something about this seems much worse than a broken bone."

***

By the time Becca reached the ER, Tyler's leg had been x-rayed, and it'd been determined that the break, which was in the femur right above his knee, was complicated. The doctor had also declared the injured area too swollen to cast. They'd moved him out of the ER and into a room, and Mr. Murphy had ensured the hospital would grant Becca access to it.

Tyler remained in a severe amount of pain, and that was concerning. Becca arrived minutes before the nurse administered an IV pain medicine that would likely knock him out. Witnessing this vibrant, daring, and typically tough man she loved writhe against the pain shook Becca to her core.

Steeling herself, she slipped to Tyler's bedside and took his hand. "Hey, Ape Man."

His grip on her fingers squeezed too tight, and he grunted. "Hi, babe."

She'd thought to drop a teasing comment about him breaking his *I never fall* promise to her, but that wouldn't lighten the moment. Instead, she leaned down and kissed his brow. "Hurts pretty good, huh?"

"Naw." His groaned response said the opposite. "Just a broken bone. Not my first."

Nope, it wasn't. Mrs. Murphy had shown Becca several pictures of Tyler with a cast. One on his arm. One on his foot. *He never stays down for long*, his mom had said, chuckling. *Can't keep a monkey out of the trees and off the roofs.*

Becca was willing to bet those other breaks hadn't left him breathless and sweating for hours on end the way this had. This was bad. If Tyler's pain level wasn't indication enough, the furrowed brow of the nurse and the serious set of the doctor's jaw was a sure gauge.

Whatever the nurse had pushed through Tyler's IV took hold. His dark-brown eyes went glassy, and his harsh grip on her hand eased.

"Better?" Becca asked.

"No. I don't like feeling..."

And then he was out.

Becca looked first to Tyler's dad, and then they both looked at the nurse.

"Hopefully, that'll hold him for a couple hours, because I can't give him any more. Cross your fingers, by the time he wakes again, the swelling will have let up and the pain lessened."

"We'll do more than cross our fingers." Mr. Murphy stepped toward Becca and laid a tender hand on her shoulder. "We'll pray." He looked back to the nurse. "Thank you."

Concern still furrowed the young woman's brow, but she pushed up a smile and nodded. "I'll send your wife in as soon as she arrives. In the meantime, if he wakes or you're worried, push the Call button. I'll be right in."

She left, and for several moments, Becca stood as if stunned, her gaze pinned on the man she was going to marry. Tyler was pale, and even in the medicine-induced sleep, agony lined his handsome features. The hand on her shoulder squeezed.

"What happened?" she asked.

"I'm not sure—he's done that job a hundred times at least. He's never made a mistake like this."

"What mistake?"

"He didn't tack down the metal sheeting. When he came to get another sheet from me, he stepped on the loose one, and there was no time to recover. The pitch of the roof was steep, and that sheet acted like a sled on an icy hill. They both slid off the roof before I could even move."

Tyler didn't tack down the material? Mr. Murphy was right. That didn't sound like Ty at all. He was a monkey for sure, but he was also meticulous in his work. What had he been thinking? And why hadn't he been wearing the harness?

She knew why. Tyler didn't work with a harness. Ever. "Do you see Tarzan wearing one?" he'd responded once when she'd asked him why.

"You wear them on the ziplines."

"Different. Completely different." With a kiss to her hair, he'd grinned. "No worries, babe. I never fall."

As those memories played through her mind, Becca covered her face with both hands, pressing her fingers into her forehead. *Dadgum, Ty. You did fall! All you had to do was strap on the stupid harness!*

A strong arm wrapped around her shoulder and tugged her close. Cheek pressed to Mr. Murphy's brown flannel, Becca released a shuddered breath.

"God, You see us here, and we're worried. Lord, we are so worried about this young man we both love. You love him too, and You know what's causing the excessive pain in his leg. Please ease it. Please give the doctor wisdom." There he paused, as if he too needed to regather his emotions. "Lord, please let Tyler be okay."

CHAPTER THREE

(in which life changes)

TYLER TRIED TO BLINK away the fuzzy blur of not only his vision but of his mind. How long had he been out this time? What day was it by now?

Both questions faded to the recesses of his mind as what had transpired streamed into his recall. *God, no!* Why would a good God allow this? Didn't He know all that would be lost? One slip! One freaking misstep, and his life was ruined. *Why?* It was a raging shout to the heavens. A fist lifted to the sky.

"Ty..." Her voice soothed the outrage boiling within, her gentle touch to his forehead a calming balm.

"Bec." Tyler lifted his hand, ignoring the sting of the IV in his arm.

"Hey. You're back." She pressed the softest kiss to his hairline, her breath warm on his clammy skin. "How are you?"

Angry. So, so angry. Suddenly, tears threatened to brim. Their sting felt hot, volcanic. He blinked to clear the moisture away so Becca wouldn't see, and to focus his vision. "Did they..."

Heartbreak scrawled over her features, a sheen in her eyes. "It's done, hon."

A bitter curse pressed in his mind, threatening to escape his lips.

"I'm so sorry, Tyler."

Not as sorry as he was.

Becca leaned in again, her mouth brushing his. "It's going to be okay though. I know it, babe."

No. No it wasn't going to be okay. "They took my leg, Bec. How am I gonna..." His throat closed, and he turned away from her, focusing his glare at the recovery room wall. It was daffodil yellow—he knew because Mom had a thing with colors.

It wasn't fair. Mom got to pursue her passion in floral arrangement and all things homey. Dad spent his life building stuff—a love they shared, he and his father. One they had planned to pursue together once Tyler graduated. Now?

Now he was irrevocably broken. He'd never climb again. Never scale a ladder to set trusses. Never be anywhere close to the man he'd been three days before. He'd be useless, someone to pity. To work around. Bile churned in his gut.

Compartment Syndrome. A condition he'd never heard of before. Two words he'd come to loathe in the past forty-eight hours. Opening the length of his leg, a procedure called *open fasciotomy*, hadn't worked—the severe swelling had gone on too long. His leg, from just above the knee down, had died.

The only option had been to amputate. That, or risk further necrotic flesh, acute renal failure, and possibly, death.

One stupid mistake! Why hadn't he secured the roof sheeting? Why hadn't the doctor opened his leg sooner so it didn't die? *Where's the grace, God?*

Resentment and rage boiled again, and though he curled his fists and set his jaw, trying not to let the volcano erupt, the ugly words that pounded in his mind flew from his lips. Curses aimed at the accident, at the doctors.

At God.

Becca didn't try to stop his tirade. She simply waited until his fury was spent, and then her hand cupped his unshaven jaw, her thumb smearing the wetness of his cheeks.

He'd cried in front of her. Damn that too.

She leaned in, pressing her head to his. Her feathery kisses to his eyes, his cheeks, his lips, worked to bring him back, and he gripped her elbow, slid his hand up her arm, and then held her shoulder.

"We'll get through this, Tyler. I promise."

He squeezed his eyes shut. "You can't still want me. You can't want to do this with me..."

"I wasn't in love with your leg." Her fingers rolled into his hair. "I said I wanted to do life with you, Ty. I still do. Did you think I was a wimp? That I'd give up at the first hard place we ever encountered?"

He remembered their zipline adventure before he'd proposed a few weeks back. One of the workers had commented to him about how Becca was pretty scared up there, that she was trembling hard—and that Tyler had found himself a rarely brave sort of woman who would take on her fears just to be with him. He'd been so proud in that moment. She was *his* girl.

"You're the bravest person I know." Tyler found her mossy eyes and searched them. "But this wasn't what we planned. You don't have to—"

"Stop." Her gaze turned fierce. "Stop this now, Tyler Murphy. You lost a leg. That's all."

"That's all?" His whole life had been dumped upside down. That was all?

"That's right. That's all. You're tough and determined. Strong and fearless. You'll go into rehab, they'll teach you how to use a prosthetic, and we'll get on with our life together. It's just a setback, not the end of everything."

"Not the end of us?" He sounded so pathetically vulnerable, and he hated it. But there it was.

"No. I love you." She winced and then blinked. "You'll have to do a whole lot more than lose a leg to scare me off."

Tyler gripped her hand and drew her back, wrapping her shoulders with one arm and holding on as if she was his lifeline. He couldn't hold back the wave of emotion anymore. He knew he quaked with the cries, and felt ashamed of it.

But Becca held on.

The anger didn't die there, but he put down the defeatist attitude. If she could be this brave, he would be too.

They'd move forward, plans unchanged. He'd find a way, no matter what.

***

Becca paused just beyond the door separating the surgical recovery room from the hallway that would lead, in just a few short steps, to the waiting room. Kevin and Helen Murphy sat out there, anxious and wanting to see their son.

It'd been kind and generous of them to send her in first, alone. And a good thing too. She hated thinking of Tyler's parents witnessing him the way she just had. The thought of it made her shiver. But who could blame him? Not her. And with all her heart, she'd meant what she'd told him—she wasn't about to shrink away from their relationship, had no intention of calling off their engagement. She'd be with him every difficult step of the way. As would, she was certain, Kevin and Helen Murphy.

She should go out there, let them have their rightful place with Tyler. And she would, after a moment of composing herself.

Suddenly she couldn't. Under a crushing wave of grief and fear, Becca wrapped her arms around herself and gave way to a course of trembling sobs. She couldn't decipher what had been the worst point. Going in to see the man she loved lying on a hospital bed, tubing running from his arms and mouth like California freeways, looking pale and nearly dead? Seeing the lump of his right thigh shaped beneath the blankets that unnaturally fell into total flatness where the rest of his leg should have been? Or hearing him give up on life, himself, and them?

All of it had been awful.

A hand warmed her arm. "It will get easier."

Wiping the streams that wetted her cheeks, Becca looked up, finding the weathered, solemn face of Tyler's surgeon aimed at her. His eyes looked sad but compassionate. "I promise. It will get easier."

Fumbling around for any wispy remnants of courage, Becca tried to cut off her tears. And failed. "He tried to call off our engagement."

"Not really that shocking, my dear. Men are prideful creatures." He squeezed her shoulder. "And women are equally determined, I'm sure."

She sniffed and attempted a chuckle. It came out as a sputtering mess.

"I am sorry that it came to this," he said. "I wish I could have saved the leg."

Shaking her head, she looked toward the floor. "We know you did what you could."

A moment of silence passed. Then he spoke again, his tone low and grandfatherly. "May I offer you some advice for the near future?"

"Of course." She lifted her face to him again.

"It will sound harsh. But know that it comes from years of doing this. Years of seeing my patients wrestle through all the hard things yet to come."

"Okay..."

"Don't pity him." He held her with a serious look. "Don't make it easy for him to feel sorry for himself. Expect him to rise up, to live life fully. Never expect less from him."

Swallowing, Becca nodded, not entirely sure what the doctor meant.

"I mean it, young lady." His expression shifted to something determined and insistent. "It will be tempting to soften blows and give him excuses. You won't be doing him any favors, nor yourself. He can be every bit the man he wanted to be before this, but he will have to choose to do it for himself. You can't do it for him."

Mind and emotions on a roller-coaster ride she'd like to get off of now, thank you very much, Becca nodded. "Yes, sir. Thank you."

He again and gave her arm a gentle squeeze. "It's a lot to take in right now. You've both been through some trauma. So just tuck that away for later and go find some rest."

Nodding, she tried on a smile she wasn't sure actually worked and nodded. The doctor moved around her and into the recovery area, and Becca made herself shuffle toward the waiting room. Toward Tyler's worried parents.

Helen stood first, seeing the moment Becca rounded the hallway that dumped into the small, comfortable waiting space. Kevin remained seated, his hands locked together, head bowed.

"How is he?" Helen moved toward Becca, hand outstretched.

"He's..." Becca bit her lip and swallowed, taking Helen's extended hand.

"Is he more aware of things?" Lines furrowed into Helen's brow.

"He knows what happened. He knows his leg is gone."

Tears dripped from Helen's eyes. "Is he—"

"Helen." Kevin strode behind his wife and stopped at her back. "We can go see him for ourselves. Let Becca process."

"Right." Tyler's mom tried to smile. Her lips trembled, and another tear rolled instead. "I'm sorry, sweetie."

It was so overwhelming to all of them. Becca squeezed her hand. "Thank you for letting me see him first. He's upset. You probably should know that. He's really, really upset, and..." Dare she tell them of their son's angry outburst?

"It's okay, Becca," Kevin said. "We've seen the worst out of all our boys. We won't be shocked and appalled."

Nodding, Becca released Helen's hand and moved toward the chairs along the wall. Kevin caught her elbow as she passed. "Are you okay?"

She nodded. And began to cry.

Kevin pulled her against his flannel alongside his wife, and the three stood there for a quiet, grieving huddle, unsure what the future held. Uncertain how to chart these unknown waters. But knowing for certain they loved the man whose world had changed, altering theirs along with him.

Becca had a feeling she'd have to dig deep into that love in the coming months. Find a strength beyond what she'd ever had before. Likely even a stubbornness. There was comfort in being held by both of Tyler's parents right then.

Even so, she'd never felt so scared.

CHAPTER FOUR

(in which Tyler makes up his mind)

S WEAT DRENCHED HIS HAIR, trickling down his neck and running from his forehead into his eyes. Tyler shrugged his face into his shoulder, wiping the moisture with the sleeve of his T-shirt. How could this be so blasted hard?

Icy-hot pain shot from his foot, through his calf, and clear through his residual thigh. Wait. He no longer had a foot or calf or knee. Just the stupid stump.

Not a stump. Don't call it that.

Blast it all to— Tyler gripped the parallel bars with his sweaty palms with a strength that seemed able to bend metal. With a shout of frustrated pain, he shook the contraption he was bracing himself with and let out a string of words Becca would most certainly disapprove of.

"Deep breath, Ty." Renee, his physical therapist, spoke calmly, as if not at all put out by either his failure to complete a simple ten-foot walk or his angry outburst.

"How can I feel pain in a foot I don't even have anymore?"

Renee squatted on the floor, outside of the parallel bars and in front of him. She gripped the calf portion of his prosthetic. "Does this hurt?"

A burning current ran the length of his leg.

"Yes, dang it. Why the heck should it?"

"You had some severe trauma before the doctor amputated. Sometimes the nerves in our spine and brain remember that pain, and with this section of your leg gone now, your body knows something isn't right—the signal for that is pain. But it also could be that there's something in your residual leg that isn't settling right in the prosthetic, and that's signaling the problem."

"So it's all in my head?"

"No. It's in your nerves. It's real pain, Tyler."

"How can we make it stop? I need it to stop!"

Renee stood, placing a hand on his trembling forearm. "I know. We'll try some different approaches, and I'll call the doctor after our session here to see what he thinks. There's a fairly new therapy developing, using virtual reality. If you're a candidate and you agree, it might be that we can give that a try. Today though, let's start with acupuncture. I can do some dry needling in your residual limb, in case that's the source of the problem, and then we'll work on your back."

"Wait. Go back to virtual reality. How would that work?"

"We give you a very realistic image of your leg intact and unharmed. The idea is to replace the memory of the trauma your leg went through with something painless. It's hoped that replacing that last painful memory with something else will allow your brain to cease firing pain signals."

"So it is in my head."

"Not in the way you're thinking. The nervous system is complex, and we don't understand all of it yet. But you don't need to be ashamed of experiencing phantom pain—it's not something your conscious thoughts control."

Tyler gulped in a staying breath, realizing that the agonizing pain had eased and that his body had stopped shaking. He stood straight again.

"Ready to give it another go?" Renee stepped back, fully expecting he would try again.

It was so humiliating. He'd been the guy who had never met a tree he couldn't climb. He'd never embarked on a challenge he couldn't master. And now he was staring at ten feet of a line—five steps. Just five little normal, nothing steps, and he didn't think he could gut it out.

"One step, Tyler. That's all we need right now. Take one step, and then recover."

"That's pathetic."

"It's a start." Renee's expression was firm. Chin set, eyes challenging. She didn't give him the luxury of pity, even though that was what he wished for.

He knew then he wasn't leaving this facility until he did exactly as she said. She wouldn't help him to his crutches until he completed this task. Renee Bristol was every bit as stubborn as he was, and someday—though not in that exact moment—he'd be grateful.

As he prepared himself to push through the difficulty and the pain, a memory flashed through his mind. *That girl is braver than you know. You're a lucky guy.* At the time, up there among the swaying treetops, Tyler had chuckled and congratulated himself on having such an amazing girlfriend—hopefully fiancée by the end of that day. But he hadn't fully appreciated what the guy on the zipline had been saying.

Becca did hard, scary things. For him. Not because there was some kind of adrenaline-inducing thrill in it for her. She did them to be with him.

That wasn't just courage. That was love. And Tyler fiercely loved Becca back. He'd promised her an amazing life together, starting the following May, just a week after graduation. If he intended to keep that promise, he needed to get himself upright again. He needed to get through PT and back in school. Regardless of pain—phantom or otherwise.

They had plans. He'd made promises.

Tyler adjusted his grip on the bars and gritted his teeth. One step? No way. He'd do five. Right now.

He didn't have time to let the pain hold him back, and if Renee wasn't going to feel sorry for Tyler Murphy, then he wouldn't either.

He'd find a way to get it done.

An hour later, Becca had him home, his mom had brought him water, and he'd told them both he just needed a quick nap. He'd gotten it done all right. Frustratingly, Renee had warned him not to push too hard too fast, not to ignore his body's signal to take it slow.

"Don't quit," she'd said, "but don't blaze through this either. Give your body a chance to rebuild. Be intentional about everything we do."

Could be that she'd said those things because he had again broken into a sweat worthy of a whole day's work in the hot summer sun and couldn't control the violent trembling rattling his entire body.

Man, it hurt. His leg—all of it, killed. It was impossible not to let that fact take over his whole mind.

Pushing him into a wheelchair, Renee had taken him into a room where she then administered the dry needling and acupuncture treatments. They'd helped. Some.

But now at home alone with the memory of both his pathetic progress and the excruciating sensations electrifying his leg, suddenly it crashed on him again. The pain! It burned, it sliced, and it wouldn't let up. Rolling his fists, he pressed them against his forehead and focused his energy into those fists and on not yelling.

Meds. He needed meds. Now. And one would not be enough.

***

"Two more appointments, and Renee will cut me loose." Tyler hobbled around his bed to grab a prescription bottle off his dresser. He'd been packing, getting ready to go back to school with Becca the following week.

With every step, he winced. With every wince, Becca wanted to beg him to ease up a bit.

He was pushing too hard. Everything in Becca screamed a warning about Tyler's near-manic drive to make sure he was walking and strong enough to go back to school on time. He refused to even consider holding back a week or so, let alone an entire semester.

That would be fine—Becca might even feel proud of him and impressed, except she could tell by the ever-present dullness in his eyes and tightness around his mouth that he was in pain. The only time he wasn't, he was glassy eyed and snarky. If Becca was brave enough to voice her suspicions, she'd say those were the effects of his narcotics. Drugs he'd been prescribed since his accident and had taken with increasing regularity for weeks on end.

Wasn't that dangerous? Didn't the medical community worry about the opioid epidemic these days?

She watched him toss one back and swallow. There had been only one in his palm, hadn't there? Becca lowered onto his mattress, her movements as cautious as her voice. "Tyler, maybe we need to revisit this plan."

"We've discussed this, haven't we?" His dark-chocolate eyes pinned on her with a stern heat. "Nothing's going to change. I'm going to senior year with you. We'll graduate together. And then..."

"We'll get married." She lifted her chin, trying to match his stubbornness. "Ty, you're not hearing me. We. Will. Get. Married. I promise. You don't have to kill yourself to make this graduation deadline you have in your head to marry me."

"Yes I do." With that, his back was turned, his posture stiff. Unrelenting.

The questions about the drugs nagged at her, especially as she watched this hard edge sharpen in the man she loved. From the accident? From anger? From pain? Or from narcotics? Maybe all of them.

But it seemed that she was the only one concerned. Tyler's surgeon had prescribed the hard-hitting drug, with refills. Renee, Tyler's PT, whom Becca liked, didn't seem concerned. Not about the pills anyway. Becca's occasional visits with Renee led her to believe that the therapist shared Becca's concerns that Tyler was pushing too hard and steaming toward a hard crash in the near future.

But it didn't seem those worries stemmed from the pills. At least, it was never worded that way. Renee voiced concerns that they hadn't completely vanquished the phantom pain, and perhaps that was tied to pain in the residual leg, which Tyler was determined to harden off and make useful. If so, his continual, stubborn pursuit to "make deadline" wasn't helping—not the way he was going about it.

Sitting there in his room, because she'd said she'd help him pack, Becca felt helpless. She didn't know what to say or do, and it didn't seem to matter even if she did. Tyler was determined.

Resolutely obsessed with making his deadline, no matter what it took.

An uneasy wave moved within Becca's chest. The sensation another warning: his determination could come with a steep price.

CHAPTER FIVE

(in which hope surfaces)

TYLER STARED AT HIS computer screen, unable to focus on the data spreadsheet in front of him. It shouldn't be this hard—this was basic accounting stuff. Material he'd mastered freshman year. Man, though, he was tired. And achy.

A shiver ran over him, and he reached for the hoodie he'd discarded fifteen minutes before. The chill that hit his body felt like ice against his sweaty back and neck. Great. Now was a great time to get sick.

Was he sick?

This chain of events—exhaustion, sweating, chills—was an awful lot like the flu. But he'd had these symptoms several times before in the past couple of days. Yet he really wasn't sick. It wasn't the flu.

Groaning, he reached for his thigh and massaged the dull ache just above where the socket for his prosthetic leg met what remained of his thigh. The lingering pain irritated him for more than one reason.

He'd made a trip back to his physical therapist to talk to Renee about the continuing throb there, and she'd examined the area. She'd made space for him in her schedule because the prothesis had been a new version from what he'd started with. He'd been in it for a week. "I don't see signs of tissue damage. It really looks like the socket is a good fit."

"It still hurts," he'd said. "Holding me back. I don't think this new one is right."

She'd scowled, her mouth a grim line. "Are you keeping to the wear schedule we laid out?"

Tyler shifted his gaze left, suddenly finding the late-summer flowers bobbing outside the huge windows fascinating.

"Well, there we are then, Tyler. You're overdoing it." Renee crossed her arms. "Again."

"I have classes. I can't hobble my sorry butt to class and take off the fake leg. People will weird out. And putting it back on...that doesn't need to be a public event."

"We also discussed this. Tyler, it takes at least a good week of doing things right to see if a socket is a good fit and to acclimate the limb to it. And while we're talking about this, it takes most people a solid year to walk as if nothing had ever happened. You've given yourself, like, a day for the new socket and less than two months to be off at running break-neck speed. It's not reasonable, and if you continue to push too hard, you'll cause more damage. The socket fit looks right to me. Back off your need to prove that you're fine and stick to the schedule we created, and the pain might decrease. You might make progress instead of hitting walls you've created with noncompliance."

Tyler had ground his teeth and glared at those carefree blossoms outside. How dare they act like life was all happy and lovely. How dare they bob and sway in the breeze as if there wasn't a care in the world.

How dare Renee tell him to back off?

He had things to do. A life to get after. And he didn't have time or desire to wait around for his leg to adjust to a prosthetic attachment that wasn't a good fit.

"I want a new mold taken," he said.

"Go a full week, and revert to the week-one wear schedule we made. Then we'll talk."

He pinned his glare on her. "Do you know it takes almost two hours of drive time for me to come see you?" Time he'd asked Brandon to make for him, because he didn't want Becca to come this time. She'd worry. She was worrying about him a lot these days.

Unfazed, Renee slipped a single eyebrow upward. "I am aware. And I've given you a recommendation as well as a referral to a PT near your school campus."

"I went. Wasn't impressed."

"Why?"

"He was a..." *pompous windbag.* Tyler didn't finish his statement, because saying it would require an explanation. The bottom line of it would be that the guy wanted him to wean off his hydrocodone, switching to high-dose ibuprofen. Said he'd be contacting the prescribing doc about it after their next session. Like Tyler wasn't already having a hard time getting where he wanted to go *with* the narcs. He didn't go to the next session.

Renee stood mute, waiting for the rest of Tyler's answer. When he didn't deliver, she turned away, a knowing expression passing over her features before her back was turned.

The memory of that look, and the fact that the pharmacy had informed Tyler just that morning that he had no more refills on his prescription and the doctor denied a new script, flooded his veins with heat. The surgeon hadn't seen him in almost a month. How would he know if Tyler was ready to step down in meds or not?

Rolling a fist, Tyler pounded his stupid stump and growled at the spreadsheet open on his laptop. He'd taken his last dose earlier that morning. If he had another pill, maybe he could concentrate on this stupid account reconciliation assignment, instead of being distracted by the throb in his leg. Also, maybe he would stop feeling like crap—like he had the flu.

Pushing from the table, he stood up on his one leg with such force that the chair behind him soared backward and fell.

Fantastic. He reached for his crutches and then shoved the dumb thing out of his path, working his way across the small space toward his bathroom. Maybe he'd miscounted. Maybe there was one more pill in the bottle. Or a bottle he'd forgotten about?

Nothing. The only prescription meds in his mirrored cabinet was 800 milligrams of ibuprofen. No way was that gonna cut it.

He shouted and slammed a rolled fist against the wall just above the light switch. The impact on his knuckles didn't hurt as much as he was flat-out furious. After his outburst, the apartment rang with silence.

Silence.

Lenz. He had a housemate. Lenz had his own room and attached bath. Who knew what Lenz kept hidden in a sock drawer and the medicine cabinet?

It took less than a half second for Tyler to decide to find out.

***

Becca huddled against the chilly wind as Tyler's short text passed through her mind again. He'd cancelled on her.

Again. That made five times in the last two weeks.

Still not feeling great. I'm gonna go to bed. See you tomorrow.

It wasn't like she was high maintenance. She didn't think. But a phone call to say hi, to hear his voice at least once a day, seemed like a reasonable expectation. Especially when Tyler had called off all their evenings together the past week. And that confused her. He was tired, didn't feel great—she got that. But couldn't she bring him something hot to eat? Wouldn't it be nice to just snuggle on the couch and watch a movie? He could go to sleep for all she cared. She just wanted to be with him.

Used to be he felt the same way about her.

They were engaged—going to be married in a little more than six months. Did he think she'd shirk from him not feeling well? Or maybe it was the fact that he was still limping, and his therapist had told him repeatedly to stick to the wear schedule for his prosthetic leg—something Tyler hated. He hated not wearing it, hated that anyone, including her, might see that his right leg had been amputated.

Pride. That was what was going on here.

Well. Becca wasn't the kind of girl who would silently let things go unaddressed for long. If Tyler thought he was going to spend their lives pretending he didn't lose his leg, he had another thing coming. And if he thought she was squeamish about his residual limb, or anything that came with this new reality in his world, he was in for a new education.

After all, she'd braved heights and speeds that had terrified her, and she certainly wasn't afraid to face the altered future they now had together. Tyler could find some courage in the face of his fears too.

Resolved in her new thinking, Becca changed her direction from walking back to her apartment to moving toward the student association. She'd grab some takeout—Tyler loved the Chinese food—and make her way to his apartment instead.

Twenty minutes and about two thousand steps later, she was knocking on his front door. Lorenzo, Tyler's roommate, answered.

"Thank goodness." Lorenzo stepped back to give her entry. "He's a bear these days."

Concerned tightened Becca's mouth. "I'm sorry, Lenz. Where is he?"

"Sequestered in his room." He nodded toward the hall. "And good thinking bringing food. Maybe something besides chips and soda will snap him out of it."

"Chips and soda? Please tell me that's not all he's been eating."

"Can't say for sure. I'm not here to sulk-sit. But when I see him grabbing something, it's a bag of salt and carbs."

"Great." Becca slipped off her shoes and padded toward Tyler's room. "Wish me luck."

"With everything I've got, lady. I miss the old Ty."

Dread sank into Becca's stomach, pulling down her recently resolved courage. Truth be told, she'd been missing the old Tyler too.

But he'd bounce back.

She had to believe that the man she loved would bounce back.

Summoning strength, Becca knocked her knuckles against Tyler's door.

"What?"

Yeah, that sounded bearish for sure. Becca turned the knob and eased the door open anyway. "Hey. It's me."

Tyler lay sprawled out on his unmade bed, shaggy hair a mess, staring at a screen and holding a bag of—yep, Lenz wasn't wrong—chips. His residual limb was exposed.

Well, at least there was that. He hadn't been very good at letting his leg rest.

With a jerk, Tyler sat up and snagged his prosthetic from the end of his bed. "What are you doing here? I told you I wasn't feeling—"

"Knock it off, Ty." Rolling a tighter grip on the take-out bag, Becca stepped into the room and pushed back against the door so that it closed behind her. "I'm not some girl you met last week who you can just blow off."

"Never said that," he barked. Crimson seeped into his cheeks, and he busied himself with the socket attachment for his leg.

Becca strode forward and placed her free hand on his thigh. "Stop. Just stop."

He froze, every muscle in his upper body tensing and his jaw setting hard. When he looked up, his eyes blazed.

But Becca wasn't willing to back down. "Do you think it scares me?"

With a hard intake of air, Tyler looked away, but not before she saw his pressed lips tremble.

"Do you think I'm repulsed?"

He pushed her hand away. "How could you not be? It's—"

She wasn't sure what hung on the end of that bit-off sentence. But she guessed it was something along the lines of *horrible. Stupid. Broken.* Frustrations dammed against the pity she felt for him.

"I know you didn't used to think so little of me." She knelt in front of him, setting the bag of food on the floor. "I'm thankful you're alive, and I'm still looking forward to a future with you. But not like this."

His angry look swiveled back to her. "Like what?"

"You. Like this. In here hiding. Pretending this will just go away. If not that, then you're out there faking it, pretending like nothing happened or like if you ignore it long enough, this will all just disappear. You lost your leg, Tyler. You're not a lizard. It's not going to grow back. You and I have to face that reality."

"I know!"

"Do you? Then let's face it." Holding his gaze firm, she pulled her hand from the folds of the haphazard gray comforter, once again placing it on his thigh. The muscle beneath her palm spasmed. She lowered her voice, battling tears. "I'm not scared of this. I'm not repulsed by anything except the fact that you keep pushing me away."

Tyler pinned his lips shut, and yes, they were quivering. The sheen glazing those dark-brown eyes nearly broke Becca's heart. Keeping her hold on his thigh, she reached with her other hand to cup his face. The three-day growth of hair on his cheek bristled against her palm.

"Tyler," she whispered, her voice and heart cracking. "I'm not scared. But I do miss you."

Slowly, his hand lifted, the clump of blankets he'd been clutching falling from his grip. His fingers grazed her chin, her jaw, and then he palmed her neck. She stretched as he leaned, the brush of his mouth against hers warm and tentative.

"I'm sorry." Emotion made his low voice rough. Then he leaned his forehead against hers, his nose brushing her cheeks. "Don't give up on me."

"I'm still here."

She felt the warm moisture of his tears, the firmness of his grip, and the quaking of his shoulders as he drew her close and held her fast. And she felt hope surface once again. Tyler was going to be okay—he'd come out of this.

They would be all right.

CHAPTER SIX

(in which the light fades)

TYLER LEANED HEAVILY AGAINST the counter as he ran the quad razor over the hair smattering his face. He'd given his leg a full twelve hours of rest, and he did have to admit, the hard ache in the socket area had eased.

Last night couldn't have hurt either. After they'd eaten the Chinese Becca had brought, she'd stayed long enough to watch a couple of episodes of *White Collar*. It'd gone against every prideful impulse in him to leave the prosthetic off, but he knew that if he reached for it, she'd narrow a stern look on him and tell him to stop.

Wow. She could be a formidable force when she decided to be. Last night he wasn't sure how much he'd loved that about her. But he'd sure loved having her snuggled in his arms, tucked up against his chest as they watched his show. And that good-night kiss she'd left him with...

His lips tugged upward, and he had to school them into conformity as he finished shaving. Becca was his grounding point in this disaster. His reason to plow through the obstacles. And last night, he'd sure wished it was June, that they were married, and good night didn't mean she left his arms. If it was June, that'd also mean he'd have walking with a prosthetic down without a hitch in his gait and he'd be moving on with the rest of his life.

At that thought, chilled despair worked like a killing frost in late spring on his budding hope. Moving on with the rest of his life? What did that even look like now? Besides having Becca as his wife, which was an amazing thought, Tyler didn't have an answer. He'd spent his college years planning and working toward going back to Sugar Pine to rejoin his dad.

They'd schemed and looked forward to it—he and Dad—since Tyler had been eighteen. Tyler was Tarzan. The scaffold guy. The one to get up there and put together the awkward, trickier things, since Dad's arthritic back had set its own limiting boundaries.

Now? Now he was Tyler the one-legged liability. That was the last thing he wanted to be. Ever.

As his thoughts plunged into the realm of despair, his muscles tensed. With that tension, the familiar, persistent ache throbbed in his leg.

The stupid leg. Stupid pain. Stupid accident. Stupid everything.

He wiped his hairless face clean and tossed the towel against the mirror. Not caring where it landed, he spun away and limped toward his room, his thoughts narrowed on one mission.

Top dresser drawer. Right side, behind the supply of socks.

Ah. There it was. A little tan bottle with long white pills. Tyler ignored the prick at his conscience as he glanced at the label—the one that did *not* have his name printed on it. Like Lenz needed this stuff anyway. He'd had his wisdom teeth pulled over a year before. Shouldn't have even kept this stuff...

No more than Tyler should have swiped it. How much of a crime was it to steal hydrocodone from your roommate, anyway?

He cut off that question before it sank in too deep.

Maybe not soon enough. His hand trembled as his gut twisted.

Just stop. Why was Becca's voice in his head?

Tyler looked at the pill in his palm. He could slide it back into the bottle, slip into Lenz's bathroom, and replace the whole thing. He could...

No. He couldn't.

Hardening against the guilt, he popped the med into his mouth and gulped it back. With his face tipped upward, he swallowed hard again, drew in a breath, and let it go slowly.

It's just to take the edge off—the ibuprofen doesn't do it. Just this one last time...

His eyelids burned, and he mashed his lips hard together, shutting out the core knowledge that he was lying to himself.

He had a life to figure out and to get back to, and if he needed the meds to do it, then so be it. And he *did* need them, no matter what his doc or physical therapist said. That was the bottom line.

No one would have to know.

***

Tyler sat back against the couch, silently thankful that Brandon had come to his apartment for their weekly game night. They'd been at Ty's place for the past three weeks, but the thought of walking across campus to Brandon's dorm to engage in their PS4 game ritual actually provoked a heated throb in his leg.

When was that going to stop? Setting his teeth on edge, he refused the urge to growl and hoped the pills he'd downed before Brandon's arrival would stretch until his brother left later that night.

An hour into it, Tyler felt closer to himself. Strategizing and action proved to be a good distraction. That, and Lenz's drugs were exactly what he'd needed.

"Got a call from Big Brothers. Jack is still enrolled, so that's good." Brandon flashed a grin toward Tyler. "Talk to Cameron yet?"

"No." Tyler kept his focus on the action happening on screen. Why'd they have to talk about this? *Battlestar.* That was what they were doing right now. Not talking about real life.

"What do you mean, no? Cameron's gotta be excited that you're back."

"I withdrew from the program."

"What?" Brandon paused the game.

"I'm sure by now Cameron's been reassigned."

"You've been his Big Brother for two years, Ty."

"Yeah, well, I'm graduating this spring anyway, so..." Tyler unpaused the action.

"So? Are you serious? Come on, man. That's just cruel. You're not even going to call him, explain to him what happened?"

"Nothing happened. I'm just not up for it this year. They'll get him another guy. It's fine."

Tyler could feel Brandon's hard stare, but he refused to meet that challenging look.

"Look, I've got a full load of classes and a wedding to plan—a marriage to prepare for. I can't—"

"Bull." Brandon tapped Pause again, then tossed his controller onto the table and turned against the couch cushions. "That's a bunch of crap, and you know it. You've had the same class load for the past two years. Didn't stop you from being the first in line for Big Brothers and certainly didn't prevent you from talking *me* into joining the program. What was that you told me? 'We grew up with so much. There's gotta be something we can pay forward.'"

Jaw clenched, Tyler fought against the welling guilt that soured his gut. "I wasn't engaged then."

Brandon snorted. "Keep shoveling it, Ty. Like I don't know Becca has it handled. Like I don't know what is really going on." Pushing up to stand, he crossed his arms. "This is all about your leg and nothing more."

"Shut up, Brandon. What do you know?"

"I know when my big brother is having a pity party."

"Yeah? Do you know when your big brother has had enough of your mouth?"

Brandon held him in a cold silence, and then he shook his head. "You look bad, Ty. Worse, your attitude smells like a dumping station. Get some sleep." He strode across the room, stopping short of leaving before he turned around. "What does Becca think about you dropping Cameron?"

Hadn't told her yet. Truthfully, he was hoping the subject wouldn't come up because he knew she'd be disappointed. And suspicious about his reasons. For her, he needed to keep everything in orbit, as if nothing had changed. She needed to believe he was getting better, and all things were a go for June.

"That's what I thought." Brandon sliced into Tyler's silence. His scowl furrowed deep, and for the first time in his life, Brandon looked at Tyler like he was less than Tyler Tarzan, his hero. "You're not this guy, Tyler."

The door closed with a hard thud, leaving Tyler alone with the deep barb of Brandon's disappointment. It stung. It stung hard.

***

Becca slid her hand into Tyler's as they walked from the student union. "You okay?"

His jaw tightened. "Yep. Why wouldn't I be?"

Huh. Maybe the fact that he'd just snapped at the poor cafeteria worker about something menial and dumb—totally uncharacteristic of any of the Murphy boys. Helen had raised her sons to be respectful, and from what Becca had gleaned, their mama could lower the hammer when they weren't.

Apparently they were pretending that little sour fit hadn't happened back there. Good thing Helen hadn't seen it.

Becca chose to let that grumpy dog lie. "You're sweating."

"Walking around on two legs when I've actually only got the one is a bit of a workout."

Sheesh, there was that dry, irritated tone that had a way of grating. Ty needed a nap. Maybe a hibernation. "It's been close to four hours." She motioned toward his leg. "Time for a break?"

He shot her a glare.

Well then, she was done trying to be there for him for the day. Becca pulled her hand from his. "I've got that project for advance sales and marketing to work on..." She stepped away from their shared path, intending to split away toward her own apartment. Hanging out with

Tyler when he was in this sort of mood had become a strain on her stability. More, it didn't do him any good.

"Bec." His call was part repentant, part command.

Turning to face him, she tugged her windbreaker close. By the feel of that cool, humid breeze, they were in for a rainstorm. Maybe that was what had Tyler spinning into a dark mood fast? She wanted to groan—searching for excuses for him had grown old.

With a hobbled gait he'd kept constrained all day, he walked toward her. "I'm sorry."

"You're in pain, so..." Was this to be the common justification she'd give him every time he snapped for the rest of their lives? How long should she hand him that out?

"Yeah. Still, I am sorry."

After adjusting her backpack, Becca hugged her jacket against herself again. The pause between them lengthened, and in the midst of it, uncertainty began to sow. Quiet, subtle, but Becca felt its presence enough to alarm her heart. Three weeks ago, when she'd confronted him in his room, it had seemed like things had made a turn—both in Ty's attitude and in their relationship. It had felt like regaining firm footing after a slippery slope. But as the days passed, a fissure had opened in her surety that Tyler would come out of this...this blackness. That they would be okay.

Something still wasn't right. She couldn't pin exactly what was wrong— Tyler had been more careful about doing the PT he'd been given and going back to the wear schedule that he'd been assigned for his prosthetic leg...something that Becca suspected he wouldn't have to do now if he'd done it right in the first place—and really making an effort to participate in life instead of faking it all the time. All that as it was, she felt something just beneath the surface, and it wasn't good.

She'd also seen the strain in Tyler and Brandon's relationship. Just yesterday she'd run into Brandon at the store. It'd been the brothers' game night. But when she'd asked about it, Brandon's expression had hardened, and he'd glanced away with a shrug. "Ty's not up for it right now, and I've got a test to study for."

Things were sliding south, and Becca couldn't pretend otherwise.

But she did love him. So, so much. They had dreams and plans together. He wanted nothing more than to go back home and work with his dad—someday he'd even hoped to take over the company. And she had a solid line on the little cake shop two doors down from the Storm Café, where she'd worked summers for the past two years. The cake shop owner wanted to retire in five to seven years, and he'd taken on Becca as his apprentice. Everything had seemed to fall into place for them, and she and Tyler were excited to step forward into the future together. All they needed was to graduate, both with a business degree, and then begin their forever together.

It'd been perfectly idyllic and so attainable four months before. But now?

Becca shoved the depressing spiral of thoughts from her mind. Biting her lip, she looked back up at Tyler and fished for a smile and something happy to say.

Tyler beat her to it. "Maybe I'll just head back to my place while you go to yours. You can work on that project, and I'll take a nap. I'm not feeling awesome."

There was that. Again.

Sweating. Moody. A sort of illness that came and went. And snacking all the time like he was a junior high boy. Becca tallied these items in her mind, hesitant to tell herself to Google them later.

"I can work on my stuff at your place, if you want," she said, not wanting him to hole up by himself. He did that too much too. Again, she thought about seeing Brandon last night. Those two were best buddies. Brandon seemed to think Tyler could sprout a pair of wings and fly if he wanted to. They didn't cancel their game night. It just wasn't done.

Tyler looked toward his feet and then shook his head. "That's all right. Like I said, I'll just take a nap. Totally boring."

"Tyler—"

"I'm just gonna sleep, Becca. Let it go."

She drew back, and he shut his eyes. After cramming a hand through his hair, he shook his head. "Sorry."

"You said."

The look in his dark-brown eyes, heavy on her, made her want to cry. He *was* sorry. And he felt helpless against whatever this was that had morphed him into the moody, exhausted man who stood before her. He wasn't this man. Tyler-Tarzan, as his brothers often called him, was *not* this man. And it had nothing to do with his leg. Her frustration surrendered to the ache that pulsed in her heart for him. With a step forward, she closed the gap between them and welcomed the warmth of his arms as he wrapped her close.

"I just need a nap, babe," he rumbled near her ear.

"Okay." She threaded her arms around him, wondering when he would recover the weight he'd lost over the past four months. Maybe if she could make him eat decent meals more consistently, rather than him munching on garbage all the time. "Bring you something to eat tonight?"

He tucked his face into her neck and pressed a kiss. "You're not done with me for the day?"

"I'm never done with you, Ty."

His sigh was a slow, warm breath against her neck, his hold both determined and needy. "I do love you wildly, Becca. You know that, right?"

"I hope it."

With slow deliberateness, he straightened to find her eyes and held her with a deep and mesmerizing look. "Know it." He cupped her face, then slid his fingers into her hair, pulling her into a slow and soulful kiss. By the time he pulled back, her pulse throbbed with heat and his eyes blazed with something altogether different from his earlier ire. "Know it."

He turned and started away, his limp almost untraceable as he covered the distance toward his apartment. Becca fingered her lips, which still tingled, and shut her eyes.

She did know he loved her. As much as she knew she loved him. But there was that sinking feeling again, and now it was somewhat defined.

Their love might not be enough against the unidentified monster lurking in the shadows.

The thought shook her to her core and made her want to weep.

***

Stop this madness!

Tyler wasn't sure if the words screaming through his mind were a prayer directed toward heaven or a command aimed at himself. Gripping the countertop in his bathroom, he lifted his head just enough to see himself in the mirror. His hair had gone wild. Once again three days' growth smattered his face because he simply hadn't felt like shaving.

As he stared at himself, the scene he'd made at the cafeteria earlier that day replayed through his mind. The worker hadn't meant to spill his coffee, and the stuff really wasn't even that hot. He had no reason to bark at her the way he had, humiliating the poor girl and mortifying Becca in the process. His fiancée had shot him a disapproving look and then left him alone at the table to find the girl he'd berated, most certainly to apologize and to make sure she was okay.

When had he turned into such a beast? *This stupid leg...*

The leg? Did it have anything at all to do with his leg?

His gaze flicked from the sallowness of his skin just below his glazed eyes, to the bottle he'd smacked onto the counter. This time the label read *Vicodin, 10 mgs*. Double the strength of the hydro he'd *borrowed* from Lenz. Tyler had no idea who Arnold Spatz was or why he had a prescription for Vic. All he knew was that he'd paid $100 to obtain the bottle, and at the time that he'd done so, he didn't care about either the price or the fact it was stolen.

He'd purchased black-market opioids.

What did that make him?

With a jolt he stood, swiped the bottle, and hobbled toward the toilet, knowing deep within exactly what that made him but unwilling to acknowledge it. He popped the cap and then glanced at the bowl of water. And there he stalled.

Dump it.

He gripped the bottle harder.

What if I need it?

You don't. You're not even really in that much pain.

Yes, he was. He hurt everywhere. Tyler focused his mind on his residual thigh, examining every nerve there. It hurt, didn't it? There was the ever-present ache, right?

Once again he didn't allow the answer to that question to form in his mind. Instead, he shook a pill into his fist, pivoted on his good foot, and moved back to the sink. After tossing the Vic in his mouth, he replaced the open bottle on the counter and ran cool water. He splashed his face, ran a wet hand over the back of his neck, then looked at himself in the mirror again.

Just need a nap.

Using a hand towel he snatched from the hook to his left, he wiped the water away, then shut off the faucet and looked back at the bottle of Vicodin.

His attention bounced. Toilet. Bottle. Toilet. Bottle.

Dresser.

The cap replaced, he took it back into his room, nestled it with the two empty bottles he'd left behind his socks, and shoved the drawer shut.

When he could think straight—after his nap—he'd have the strength to do the right thing.

CHAPTER SEVEN

(in which everything becomes uncertain)

B ECCA SAT BACK AGAINST the heated seat of Tyler's Explorer, shutting her eyes and letting her consciousness drift. Christmas break had been a reprieve from several levels of stress. Finals had been exhausting weeks before, more so than they'd ever been. A combination of upper-level classes, a credit load exceeding twenty, and her pressing worry about Tyler over his continual slip in mood, personal upkeep, and energy levels had made the first two weeks of December brutal.

But then they'd loaded his vehicle and traveled to Sugar Pine for the break, following Brandon as he traveled on his own. Becca's parents had met her at the Murphys to drive her home to Idaho for the week of Christmas, and then drove her back to Sugar Pine the day before New Year's Eve so she could finish out her break working at the bakery where she'd spent her past three summers.

The time away from school seemed to have done Tyler a world of good, and it was easy to see that he and Brandon were back on good footing again. Relieved, Becca put her energy into creating delicious little confectionary treats. Seeing her customers enjoy them had recharged the empty stores of her ambition, and hope for the future she and Tyler had planned had renewed.

"I've missed that look."

Becca peeked, squinty eyed, at the man beside her. Tyler took her hand and brought her knuckles to his lips.

"What look is that?" She lifted her head to study his profile while he continued to drive.

He grinned, sending a spark of thrill through her. "The one you just had. Content little smile. You look happy again."

She twined her fingers with his. "I am happy."

"Break was good, right?"

"Yeah." Becca swallowed, wondering if bringing up his poor attitude the last semester was a good idea. She proceeded with caution. "Seems like it did you some good too."

He winced. "I've been a bear, haven't I?"

Biting her lip, she let that rhetorical question lie all on its own. He squeezed her fingers.

"I'm sorry."

"I know." He'd said so often. But this was the first time in weeks that she'd seen the angry clouds clear from his expression. The anxiety that had lingered in her chest softened, and she lifted his knuckles to her cheek. "It's good to have you back, Ty."

His attention remained on the road, and he swallowed visibly. After a lengthy silence that felt sadly like expanding distance between them, he worked up a small smile. "I worked with my dad in the shop."

"I know." She had been overjoyed to discover flecks of sawdust in his shaggy hair the day she'd returned. "You never said what you were building."

"Nothing. I was making cuts, bundling supplies for his next project. He goes to a little town somewhere north of Tahoe next week. We were getting things ready so the project will go up fast."

"Must have been good to play with power tools again."

He released her hand and pushed his fingers through the mass of his dark-brown hair. "Yeah." The glance he settled on her was both hopeful and resigned. "Maybe I can still work with him. Maybe everything we'd planned doesn't have to fall apart."

"I didn't think our plans were falling apart." At last he was talking to her, letting her see what had been souring in his heart.

Eyes settled again on the road ahead, he blinked, and his jaw tightened. "Becca, you were the one who said I needed to accept the fact that my leg is gone."

"That's true. But your life isn't. Our life isn't—it never was."

"I can't do what I used to do."

Pressing her lips together, Becca looked at her hands. Rolled in her lap, her fingers tightened, and she missed the connection of his fingers woven with hers. She didn't know how to respond to his statement. There were so many stories of amputees doing amazing things—and she had no doubt that this high-energy, determined man she was going to marry could do anything he set his mind to.

But he might also have a point. He'd climbed build projects like a monkey. He'd been the one to do the tricky work up high, saving his dad's knees and back. That had been his role in their partnership, and Ty had done it exceedingly well. Now, he was on the ground, regulated to doing precuts and prep—things he'd done before but hadn't been restricted to.

Construction was dangerous work—especially the way Tyler had done it. All scramble and free form and untethered. Did she really want to encourage him to strive after his old plans?

Tyler released a long sigh. "I'm still trying to accept it all, I guess."

And there she had her answer. Hearing the defeat in him broke her heart. "Tyler, you're barely six months out with this new way of life. I don't think it's fair for you to decide yet what you can and can't do."

"I've accepted this, Bec." By the slump in his shoulders, followed quickly with a hard shift in his jaw, Becca knew Tyler had neither accepted this life sentence nor appreciated her encouraging him to push past it. He pulled in a hard breath. "I'm trying to accept this. I need you to as well."

Wanting to let the sting in her eyes trickle down her face, Becca instead blinked and held her gaze on him until he glanced at her. "That's not what

I was saying all those weeks ago. You know that's not what I meant. Your life still can be whatever you make of it."

"I have to accept reality." His lips pressed hard, and he swallowed again. Then he reached for her hand, fingering the diamond on her fourth finger. "But I know that's not what you were signing up for. If you—"

"Stop this, Ty." Becca shifted in her warm seat. "I want you. I want to be with you, to marry you, and to build a life with you. Not wanting this life with you isn't why I'm arguing this point. I know you. I know you're not really swallowing the idea of being grounded, not in a way that will be stable for you in the long run. And more importantly, I *know* you don't have to. Ty, there are so many possibilities out there. Have you asked Renee about—"

"I'm done with PT." Irritation flared in his look. "Last session was almost a month ago."

"You could still ask."

"No I couldn't. I don't want any more doctors, no more therapists. I'm too tired to keep going with it all. I just want to figure out how to do life as it is."

"What is really going on here?"

"I just told you, Becca. I want to move forward. In reality."

"This defeated attitude isn't you. There's something you're not telling me."

"You said I looked like I was doing better. Literally just said that it was good to have me back. If you're still willing to have me, then this is it. This is me."

Becca turned, focusing her attention on the scenery slipping by but not really noticing it. She'd traveled down this road a dozen times before at least, already knew the transition from mountains to sea level, from rural country to densely populated regions. While once the variety had taken her captive, right then it only passed as a blurry, unimportant backdrop to the turmoil that brewed again in her soul.

They weren't even back to school yet, and the solace of the break they'd enjoyed had already begun to erode.

She wanted with everything in her to argue with him—this was certainly *not* him. And she knew with growing assurance that whatever was going on had less and less to do with his injury and more and more with the unidentified monster lurking in the shadows. More, she suspected powerfully that Ty knew whatever that monster might be, and he wasn't telling her. This wasn't him trying to move forward at all—this was him covering the truth.

He was lying to her.

That more than anything else—more than the mood swings, this defeatism, and his significant loss of energy and zeal for life—the intuition that the man she loved was hiding something important from her unsettled and angered her the most.

But Becca didn't know what to do about that. Lying wasn't one of those things a person could force another to confess. It was a secret, unformed thing, tucked into the space that could only be felt with fearful uncertainty.

***

Tyler hated when he disappointed people in general. When he disappointed Becca, he felt as low as grub.

Their conversation on the trip back to school stayed with him for days. He'd disappointed her. But this time, along with that dirty, crappy feeling of knowing he'd done so, a new bolt of frustration fastened in tight. He'd spent the days working with his dad, intentionally focusing on being happy that at least he could still do that much. Still could run the boards through the saw. Could measure, mark, and cut. Could go over plans and make suggestions and envision the plan come to life.

Did she have any idea how hard that had been for him? To be the sideline part of the program, the guy who had to keep both feet on the ground because only one of them was actually real? He'd tried, dadgumit. He'd freaking tried his guts out to be happy for that much.

And Becca had tossed it in his face, the fact that *no, blast it!* he wasn't going to love that life in the long run. He didn't love it now. But it was reality. And reality said he needed to figure out how to live, how to exist. How to support a wife, because Becca's dad expected him to do it well. And how to be content with what was.

With no longer being Tyler-Tarzan.

Flinging his pen to the tabletop, Tyler rolled a fist and pressed it to his forehead. He was supposed to be updating his business model for the entrepreneurship course. It was due for round-two grades in the morning. Looking at it made him want to bellow, and at some point while looking over all of what had been his ambitious ideas and plans for taking Dad's built-from-the-ground-up construction company to new levels, Tyler actually started seeing red.

It. Was. Not. Fair.

He reached down and squeezed his thigh, pressing on the knotted muscle that usually ached by the end of the day. Wasn't so bad these days, but if he pressed in just the right spot, with just the right amount of pressure...

Groaning, he bent forward. Right there. Hot pain zipped up his thigh into his hip, and he felt the sizzle race through the remainder of the leg that wasn't there. Ghost pain was bizarre, and truthfully it had become more and more rare. But right then, for that second, he felt it, and it was searing.

Tyler pressed against the table until he stood. Holding on to the impression of savage ache, he hobbled toward his room and shut the door behind him. Top drawer, to the right, behind his socks...

Stop this. You don't need it.

The heck I don't. It hurts.

Because you made it hurt. On purpose.

Did normal people have arguments in their heads like this? He swallowed, rifling through the bottles. Man, how many had he collected? Five now? He should get rid of all this—empty bottles as well as stocked ones. He was gonna get caught.

What would Becca say if she knew?

At the sinking sense of massive loss—greater than even losing his leg— Tyler pushed the bottle he'd grasped back into the drawer and shoved the thing shut. Clutching the sides of the dresser, he leaned in and shut his eyes while his heart hammered fiercely. Losing Becca was a risk he couldn't take. He needed her. Wanted her. Loved her wildly.

Enough to stop this?

Yeah. He loved her that much. Pushing up straight again, he walked to the door, opened it, and headed out.

A walk would work. He'd get out there and burn off this driving demand. And after, he'd come back and get rid of the bottles. All of them.

***

"Hey, Lenz." Becca smiled around the door at Tyler's housemate. "Is he here?"

"Was just a while ago." Lenz opened the door to let her in and shut it after she passed through. "I think he just went out for a minute. Maybe a walk? He was working on that big business-plan assignment and looked pretty frustrated with it when I left for class earlier. Maybe he needed to clear his head?"

"Frustrated, huh?" Tugging her backpack from her shoulders, Becca looked into Lenz's face to get a real read on the situation.

Lenz made a face that said *danger* and *leave me out of it*. "His fuse isn't what it used to be, is it?"

"No. I'm sorry if he's difficult to live with."

"You don't need to be sorry. And I wouldn't say difficult. Actually, I barely see him. When I'm home, he's usually holed up in his room or out with you. Kinda miss Catan nights with him, you know?"

"Yeah, I'm sure." She reached for his arm. "I'm sorry."

Lenz shrugged. "Life, eh?" Then his look settled heavier on her, and he gripped her elbow. "You doing okay? I mean, Tyler's not been himself..."

"Sometimes he is." Batting away that sad, yucky feeling of losing something precious, Becca formed a smile, hoping it looked bright. "He'll get through this. He just needs more time."

By the pull of his brows and the squeeze of his hands, Lenz wasn't so optimistic about that, and he was worried for her. A shiver trickled down her spine—a chill from the wet, chilly weather outside and the dreary sensation inside.

"Can I get you something hot while you wait for him?"

Becca shook her head. "No, I think I'll just go see if I can steal a pair of socks from Ty's dresser. I stepped in a puddle in the parking lot, and my foot is soaked."

Lenz nodded and moved around her toward the kitchen. "If you change your mind..." He tossed over his shoulder.

She waved and mumbled "thanks" as she stepped toward Tyler's room. Maybe he'd have a sweatshirt tossed at the foot of his bed or something. That would help smother the chill, and it wouldn't be a bad thing if it smelled all woodsy like Tyler.

Yep. There it was—his black *Murphy Builds* hoodie, just as she'd hoped. Scooping it up, she held the sweatshirt to her face and inhaled.

Mmmm...so Tyler. Warmth gushed through her as she tugged it over her head, making her smile. Grinning like the girl in love she was, Becca turned toward his dresser and cracked open the top drawer. Jackpot! Socks.

The top few were low-cut ankle socks. Not what her cold feet needed. She pushed them to the side, searching for the taller pairs she knew he owned. Finding a suitable set, she pulled them free and moved to shut the drawer.

Except, what was that? Something had moved in the back of the drawer, making a noise. A noise that sounded an awful lot like...

Becca shoved the barrier of socks away. One glimpse and her heart plummeted. Her fingers trembled as she reached into the back of the drawer.

One, two, three...five...eight.

She swallowed. There was no way his doctor had prescribed eight refills of Oxy in six months. No. Way. Not wanting to see what she knew she'd find, she rolled the nearest bottle—this one half full of pills—until she could read the label.

Vicodin. For someone named Lucette Gange. Becca stepped backward and dropped onto Tyler's bed. Tears slipped from her eyes as she covered her face.

Oh, God, what has he done?

CHAPTER EIGHT

(in which darkness falls)

TYLER WIPED HIS FEET at the mat in front of the door before he stepped in and turned to shut it. As he shook off his jacket, Lenz rounded the corner from the front room, a bowl of ice cream in his hand and a spoon full of vanilla halfway to his mouth.

"Hey, bruh."

Tyler lifted his chin. "'Sup."

"Becca's here."

"Yeah?" He drew in a breath—one of relief, because that walk hadn't completely stabilized his resolve against the compelling demand for one of those pills hiding in his drawer. "She in the living room?"

"Naw. She went to find some dry socks."

"Socks?" Something icy gripped his chest.

"Yeah. Said she stepped in a puddle or something." Lenz ate the bite of ice cream, then rubbed his bottom lip with the side of his hand. "Something wrong? You look..."

"Naw. I'm good." He was anything but good. His pulse pounded a rhythm that somehow felt like a death march. "So she's in my room?"

"Yep." Lenz lifted his bowl. "You two want some ice cream?"

Tyler strode for the hallway, not answering. Panic closed in, making breathing a chore, and heat throbbed against his temples. Since when did Becca just help herself to his stuff? *God, please don't let her find...*

Hand on the door to his room, he heard a sniff coming from the other side.

God, no! He was jumping to conclusions. Why would she dig all the way to the back of the drawer? She'd just snatch whatever was on top, and that was that. And the sniff? It was pretty chilly out there, with the cold winter rain and wind. A sniff didn't mean she was crying.

Swallowing, steadying his breath, he readied himself to smile at his beloved, snag a kiss from her sweet mouth, and put all his suspicions and guilt out of his mind. Mask ready, he pushed the door open and stepped into his room.

She looked up at him from the place where she sat on his bed, and his delusions shattered. Rivers ran down her cheeks, tears dripped from her chin, and she sniffed again.

Tyler's world came to a hard stop. He was barely conscious of gently pushing the door shut behind him, then stepping to the bed to sit down beside her. Fists rolled tight, he leaned his elbows onto his legs and waited.

Silence. Aching, disappointed, hard silence.

Becca waved a pair of his socks in the air between them, the movement limp and weak. "Mine got wet." She sounded lifeless.

It took a concentration of will to look at her. She didn't meet his gaze. With a shaking hand, he reached for the socks and slipped them from her grasp. Unrolling them, he offered them back to her. "You should change them. These are dry."

Taking them back, she nodded, the movement shaking a large teardrop from her chin. She didn't move to change her wet socks though.

Tyler still hadn't mastered kneeling with his prosthetic leg. Honestly, he suspected it would always be a jerky and awkward motion—the replacement joint wasn't as fluid in all motion as his natural one had been. But he made the effort, using the bed for support as he angled and cajoled his body until he was on the floor before her. Becca remained lifelessly still, even when he first lifted one foot, removed her wet sock, and replaced it with a his dry one. He started on the second, but when he went to take the other dry sock from her hands, he found her stare—chilled with betrayal—concentrated on him.

"Are there more?" Though her voice was soft, the words cut hard.

He could barely make his voice work. "More?"

"More bottles. More pills."

Tyler rolled his fists and then used them to brace himself against the carpet. "No."

"You've been hiding these from me for months. Why should I believe you now?"

"All I have is in that drawer."

"How often do you take them?"

He shrugged. Truly, he couldn't give her an account. He simply followed the drive and took one when the demand for it crushed his resolve to stop.

"They're stolen, Ty."

"I didn't—"

"It doesn't matter who did it! You have stolen narcotics!"

His residual thigh burned as the socket pulled against his muscle, and Tyler shifted so he sat on his backside. With both hands he covered his head, unable to think, unable to feel anything beyond the crushing shame and the rising anger.

With a jolt, Becca was on her feet—one socked and the other bare. With two steps she was in front of the dresser, jerking the top drawer open. Socks flew to the floor, and then bottles rattled. She returned to the spot in front of him, hands full of his illegal stash. Pushing them in front of him, she waited until he looked up at her.

"How many have pills in them?"

"Three." The word felt like knives against his throat.

She dumped the loot on the bed and then picked one up. "Who is Lucette?"

"I don't know."

"How do you know *Lucette* doesn't need her Vicodin?"

He could barely swallow, let alone answer.

Becca lifted a different bottle. "How about Spencer? Or..." She selected another bottle, and her expression froze on a new level of appall. "Lenz? You stole from Lorenzo? Tyler, how could you?"

Becca tossed Lenz's empty bottle back to the mattress and took one with pills in it. She marched to his attached bathroom, and it occurred to Tyler exactly what she intended to do. And he should let her do it—it was what he should have done earlier but hadn't had the strength of will.

And yet the demand that bullied within him had him scrambling upward, the speed of his movement sending a sharp stab into his residual thigh. *Ouch, da—* This! This was *why* he'd needed those blasted pills, because he couldn't do simple things a whole man could do without experiencing this bolt of pain in his stupid leg. With a sort of hobble run, he reached Becca's side and grabbed her elbow as she tipped the bottle toward the open toilet.

"No!" he barked.

With a plop, plop, plop, the little white meds slipped beneath the water's surface.

"No!" He snatched the empty bottle from her hand as if he thought she'd held back and there was something in there left for him to save.

Becca scowled, then reached to flush away his contraband. With a fierce grip, he crushed the bottle as he glared down at her.

"Stop." Tyler barely held on to control as he shook, and a curse slipped from his taut lips. The broken bottle in his grip bit into his palm.

"You're addicted."

"I need them." He shut his eyes as his words sank past his hearing. *I need them.* The response clear in his mind came immediately.

Because you're addicted.

Everything in him screamed that he *needed* these drugs. And almost as strongly, he wanted to shake the woman before him for flushing away what he needed. He wanted to beat his fists against the wall, smash the mirror over the sink, slam doors and break something...

God, help me!

A cool touch brushed his jawline. Her fingertips traced his stubbled cheek, and then her palm cradled it. "Tyler."

His name was broken breath, a cracked whisper, and hearing her shattered heart in her voice drew him back toward sanity, toward calm thinking. The tight muscles in his shoulders eased. The rigid hold of his fists unfurled.

"Ty..." Her thumbs traced the lines of his cheekbones, summoning the hot tears he'd dammed.

I'm addicted. With ferocious desperation, he pulled her into his arms, held her tight against his body, which still trembled. Tucking his face into the soft crook of her neck, he sobbed. "I'm sorry, Bec. I'm so sorry."

Her touch both destroyed him and offered him solace as she wove fingers through his hair, traced the line of his neck, and kneaded his shoulders. Held him while he cried.

"Help me." He wasn't clear if he was begging her or God. Possibly both. Either way, though he despised the shame coursing through his whole being, he knew relief that Becca had uncovered his secret. Because he needed help.

He needed her.

***

Becca felt crushed in his arms, but she was unwilling to pull away. Instead, she clung to him, her back now pressed against the wall and his hold desperate.

What on earth was she to do with this?

Now that unidentified monster had a name, but it felt more dark, more sinister than when it had been lurking in the shadows. Addiction was beyond her. And terrifying. *And so not Tyler.* A fresh crop of tears streamed down her face, getting lost in the thick shag of Tyler's dark hair.

"Help me," he choked.

Shutting her eyes, she tightened her hold on him. *God, I can't fix this. I don't know what to do.*

For many minutes, she prayed against their duet of muffled cries, feeling helpless and lost and frightened. And, truthfully, angry at the man she loved. If he'd done what his therapist had asked, if he'd slowed down and not rushed into *Everything's fine. I can do normal. Our plans will not change...*

If he'd been honest with her...

Well. They'd never know if all those *ifs* would have made a difference, would they? They only had this reality, in this moment.

"Help me." Ty's hold loosened, and she tipped her head back against the wall so she could see his eyes as he lifted his head. His hands moved from her back to frame her face. "Please, Becca. Don't give up."

She blinked, and a teardrop flicked onto her cheek. "Never, Ty."

He leaned his head against hers, shutting his eyes. "Good. I can beat this. With you, Becca. It's going to be okay."

A hollow ache opened in her gut, and with it a chilled warning. "Tyler, I think we need help. You need—"

Against her forehead, he shook his head. "No. Please, Bec. We can get through this, you and me."

"I don't think this is something that can be done like that."

"Becca." His fingers curled into her hair, and he pressed a hard kiss to her head. "Please. Please. I can't face my family like this. They don't need to know." He looked down at her, his dark-brown eyes so sad, so imploring. "Please be with me on this."

That pit of alarm widened. *What should I do?*

With his thumb, Tyler traced the bottom of her lip, and then he cupped her cheek. "I can do this."

Oh, but those eyes...that surrendered, desperate look...

"Flush them," she said. "Everything you have left. Flush them right now."

He held her gaze, gratitude softening the edge of panic in his face. "I can do that." He kissed her forehead again, then limped back into his room. A few seconds later, he returned with his stash. One after another he opened each bottle. If there were pills, he dumped them into the toilet. If it was empty, he gave it to Becca.

"That's it." With a sigh that sounded like relief, he flushed them away. And then with an expression of total vulnerability, he stared at her. Waiting for her to decide.

Becca licked her lips and swallowed. It still didn't feel right to her, but—"Tell Lorenzo what you did. If you can do that, then..."

Relief washed Tyler's expression, and he nodded. Then he pulled her head into his chest, and she slipped her arms around his waist.

"Thank you, Becca."

Her lips trembled, and she squeezed her eyes shut, fighting against the dark feeling that continued to gnaw and grow in her gut.

Tyler's hold was gentler this time, but still strong. Still needy. "I won't let you down."

Becca warred against the sense that she'd let them both down already. They were not okay, and she wasn't sure they were going to be.

***

Tyler stared at the last remaining bottle. He'd double wrapped the others in old grocery sacks and took them to a dumpster on the other side of town. Like a criminal.

Because he was. Was buying stolen narcotics a felony? He could be in so much trouble. So much more trouble than he already was. And he was sure Becca knew it. She was a smart, savvy woman—after all, she'd known something had been going on all along. Hadn't she asked him time and again to trust her with whatever he was dealing with? And he'd shut her out. Lied.

So that made him a felon and a liar. And an addict.

God, how did I get here?

Maybe more importantly, how was he to break free?

The name on the printed prescription label came into focus again. Lorenzo Gonzales. Tyler rolled his fingers around the bottle and pressed his closed fist to his forehead. Becca's stipulation was that he confess to Lenz. But that not only was humiliating, it was terrifying. Lenz could turn him in.

He could go to jail.

Had Becca realized that when she'd stated that provision? Surely not. She wouldn't want him in legal trouble, not on top of everything else, right?

Stop being a coward.

Tyler-Tarzan, a coward? Since when?

Standing from the edge of his bed, he pocketed the bottle in his zip-up hoodie and made his way out of his room, down the hall, and knocked on Lenz's door.

"It's open," Lenz called.

Tyler drew a quivering breath and turned the knob. "Hey."

Looking up from an open textbook spread in front of him on his bed, Lenz flashed a quick grin. "'Sup, buddy?"

Something in his throat grew to the size of a golf ball. Tyler leaned back on the doorframe, aiming for casual, and tried to swallow the lump back. "I need to say something to you."

Usually easygoing and happy, the furrowed scowl on Lenz forehead looked out of place. "Everything okay?"

"Yeah, um..." *Come on, man. Quit being such a willow.* "The thing is, I haven't been myself, and I—" *Snuck into your room and stole your hydrocodone.*

I'm a thief. A criminal. An opioid addict.

He couldn't do it. Tyler couldn't make the words come off his tongue.

"I'm sorry," he said instead.

His trademark easy grin smoothed Lenz's wrinkled expression. "No worries, buddy. I know you've been through a lot this year."

"Yeah." Tyler's heart felt like a drumroll, and it seemed his blood had turned to toxic slime in his veins. Hands tucked in his pocket, he gripped the stolen bottle. He was a criminal. A liar. An addict. And a coward.

But he couldn't force a confession from his lips.

"Good thing you have Becca." Lenz pushed off his bed and came around to grip Tyler's shoulder. "She's solid, and you two cuties are going to fight through this."

"Yeah." Apparently that was the only word he could force out of his mouth.

Lenz clapped his shoulder. "We're good, Ty."

"Thanks." Another word. How about that? Tyler dug deep for the strength to do what Becca had asked. But as Lenz turned back toward his bed to resume studying, Tyler found himself rolling off the doorframe and exiting the room.

Shoulders rounded in a defeated slump, he wandered back to his own room and shut the door. He went to the dresser and opened the top drawer.

Later. He'd try again later.

He glanced at the pile of socks, then shut that drawer. On the left, he kept his jockey shorts. On impulse that felt familiarly desperate, he rolled the condemning evidence of his crime, and now of his cowardice, in the folds of a pair of underwear and shoved it to the back.

Failure felt like cold sludge filling his gut. Awful.

Worse, he really wanted a pill. No, that wasn't exactly right.

He needed one.

***

The sun poked through the dreary gray clouds for the first time in days. Becca walked toward her first class feeling a touch of hope that she hadn't felt in a while. Maybe it was the gentle kiss of the sun. Or maybe it was because they'd gone a week since her discovery of Tyler's opioid stash, and so far, it seemed things were ironing out.

She stopped second-guessing herself. Tyler had flushed the pills, and he seemed so much better this week. Hopeful, kinder, more like the man she'd known him to be for these past three years.

A tiny smile pressed her mouth as she tugged open the door and walked the hall toward her class. She and Tyler had this course together, and she was anxious to see him, to say good morning, and to really smile into his eyes the way she hadn't felt up to in a week.

But Tyler's seat was empty, and it stayed that way throughout the ninety-minute class.

Doubt eclipsed the tender growth of warm hope, and as Becca made her way across campus again, heading toward Tyler's apartment rather than her next class, the warmth of the sun didn't penetrate the shiver that came from within.

Lenz met her at the front door, answering her knock. "Hi, Becca. Enjoying the sunshine today?"

"Yes," she answered automatically, glancing down the hall toward Tyler's room. His door was closed. Dread and anger mixed within her veins, making for a painful throb pulsing through her body. After stepping inside and shutting the front door, she looked back at Lenz. "Is everything okay with you and Tyler now?"

"Sure." Lenz shrugged. "He's been a bear, as I know you know, but it's understandable. He even came to my room a couple days ago to apologize for it." He gripped her elbow and gave her a friendly squeeze. "No worries, lady. We're big boys."

"He came to you to apologize?"

Again Lenz shrugged. "Yep. No big deal."

Tyler had told her yesterday that he'd talked to Lenz. The impression he gave was that he'd confessed. This conversation didn't really confirm that.

Becca eyed Tyler's door, and her hands shook.

"Becca? You okay?"

"Tyler apologized for...how he'd been acting?"

A scowl folded Lenz's brow. "Uhh, yeah."

"That's all he said?"

"What's going on?"

"He didn't apologize to you for taking your meds?"

Lenz drew back, his expression moving from confusion to shock to stone. "No. My meds?"

"You had a bottle of hydrocodone. Tyler took it."

"I had a— What?"

It should have been storming outside. Thunder. Lightning. Wind. That would be so much more appropriate to the moment than sunshine and birds chirping. Becca covered her face with both hands, clenching her jaw as she fought for self-control.

Somewhere in the screaming silence of that awful moment, Lenz had pulled Becca into a hug. "Man. I didn't know."

With a pounding head, Becca stepped back. "I'm sorry, Lenz."

"It's not your fault. Honestly, I forgot I even had those—they must have been somewhere in my travel bag. I think I took like three of them after I had my wisdom teeth out two years ago."

Becca shock her head. "Still. I'm sorry."

Lenz studied her, lines of concern carving his face. "What can I do, Bec?"

She felt herself falling apart, her face crumbling. "I don't know. He promised me he'd tell you." Once again her hands covered her face, and she was crying. She indulged for only a few heartbeats, and then she sniffed and pulled herself back together. "I need to talk to him."

Lenz nodded. "I can be with you, if you want?"

"No. Not right now. But thanks."

He squeezed her arm. "I'm so sorry, Becca. For both of you. Whatever you need, just let me know."

Becca nodded, and then set her sights on Tyler's room.

She knocked. He answered. Pale, sweating, and not willing to look into her eyes. Becca drew herself up, summoning every ounce of courage and resolve she owned.

CHAPTER NINE

(in which all becomes known)

ANGER. DREAD. HUMILIATION. THEY churned together as Tyler listened to the low conversation outside his room.

How could Becca betray him like that?

There was quiet. And then a knock at his door. He didn't want to face her. He didn't want whatever was to come next to happen at all.

Livid was the only way to describe Becca's expression. Her green eyes blazed, and she didn't flinch, even though he knew for certain he looked like an angry bear. She stepped one pace inside his room, shut the door, and glared at him.

"You lied to me. Again."

Yeah, he had. He'd looked straight into the eyes of the woman he loved and had not been straight with her. And he'd hated himself for it. "Becca, I —" He what? What was his excuse now? He didn't have one. He just needed to fix this. "I'll go talk to Lenz. I'll do it now."

"It's too late, Tyler. He already knows. And now you're going to have to deal with the fact that he didn't hear it from you."

"You had no business saying anything."

"No, it wasn't my responsibility. It was yours. But you didn't do it, and you lied about it!"

Everything was falling apart. Tyler forked both hands into his hair and gripped it. What could he do? How could he stop this? He reached for her. "Becca—"

She sidestepped away from him. "No more of this, Tyler."

His heart stalled. "What do you mean?"

She visibly swallowed, and then crossed her arms. "Where were you this morning?"

"I overslept."

Her head shook slowly. "You have more, don't you?"

He looked to his feet.

"When did you get them? Or did you have them and lied about that too?"

"Yesterday. I made a deal yesterday." He'd justified the buy with the paltry excuse that his source had promised the meds had belonged to someone who had recently died. That person didn't need them anymore, and Tyler did, so...

Man, who even was he?

Becca's mouth pressed into a hard line, and she shook her head. "I can't do this." There was a finality in her voice that set off every panic alarm in his heart and mind.

No! Oh God, no! He shot a hand to her arm, catching her as she turned away. "Don't go."

Turning her face back to him, she shook her head. Tears sheened her eyes, but she stubbornly held them back. "I'm so angry, I can't even think straight. Let me go, Tyler."

While his heart sprinted recklessly, he pulled her back around to face him. "I'll flush them."

"You do that."

"Becca—"

She pushed his hand from her arm. "I can't do this right now, Tyler. I'm leaving."

Then she strode out his door. Lenz called her name, but she continued straight on out of the apartment. Moments later, Lenz filled Tyler's doorway. "Man, Ty..."

"Get out."

Lenz shook his head. "She loves you."

Tyler couldn't take the way Lenz looked at him, all accusation and worry. Fighting the urge to beat something—namely Lenz's face—he turned away and marched into his bathroom, slamming the door. The bottle of pills he'd just bought sat on the back of the toilet, right where he'd left it this morning when he'd told himself to get rid of them. He hadn't done it.

But he did right then. Every last one went into the toilet and down the drain. Right before Tyler bloodied his knuckles against the wall.

***

Becca couldn't stop sobbing, so she ignored the knock at the front door.

"Rebecca? It's Lenz. Please let me help."

A hint of relief sagged through her. At least there was someone she could confide in. Someone to help her with this awful weight. Using the cuffs of her sweater, she wiped the pools from beneath her eyes and tugged open the door. Lenz held her with a look that was all compassion, and when he stepped inside to hug her, she wilted against him.

"Man, Becca..." Lenz kept her in a firm, brotherly hold.

A new wave of sobs shook her shoulders. "I don't know what to do."

Lenz simply stood there, his arms around her shoulders, until the fiercest storm of her grief and anger passed. When Becca pulled away, he remained rooted in front of her, a fixed point in the midst of her chaos. With her sleeves gathered in her hands, she wiped her face again.

"What should I do?"

Sadness permeated Lenz's typically easygoing expression, and Becca knew he felt the loss of his friend the same as she was experiencing the loss of her beloved. Tyler had become a different person. The man she and Lenz had known before would never steal from others and certainly hadn't been prone to lie.

"Addiction is powerful, Becca."

She nodded.

"He's still in there though," Lenz said.

"Is he? I see him less and less."

With a hand on her arm, Lenz guided her toward her front room and waited until she sat on her sofa before he lowered himself into a nearby chair. "I've seen this happen once before. My cousin. She and I were pretty close, and then she was in a car accident. Took less than two weeks for her to become addicted to the pain meds her doctor had prescribed, and she became so sneaky. We hardly saw her anymore, and when we did, she was sullen and sickish and, I don't know, just not who she had been."

Painful nausea churned in Becca's gut. "What happened?"

"Her parents figured out what was going on. She went to a place, a recovery center. I can get you the number if you want."

Becca bit her lip. After several moments, she searched his face, his eyes. "Your cousin—is she..."

"She's clean. Three years now."

"And are you close again?"

Lenz gripped his knees, and the squeeze of his fingers seemed telling. "This past summer was better. She and I hung out some, and it was more like old times. Tina would laugh like she used to."

"I feel like there's a giant *but* in there."

"It just takes time, I guess. Tina is really humiliated by what happened, and she still carries the shame, I think. She told me before I came back to school that she feels like she'll always wear the identity of an addict, as well as a fear that she'll fall back. It's a hard place to be—and not who or what she wanted to be."

A fresh trickle of tears seeped over Becca's eyelid, and Lenz reached across the space to take her hand. "Not what you or Ty wanted either."

Sniffing, she shook her head. "I just want him back. To be okay."

"Yeah." Lenz let another quiet break extend between them.

Finally, Becca pulled her hand away to reach for her phone. "You can get that number?"

Lenz nodded. "Seaside Recovery. That's what it's called."

She typed in the name and showed him the search results.

"This one." He tapped the link and handed her phone back. Then he stood.

Becca came to her feet as well and followed him as he wandered to her front door. Lenz turned and gripped her shoulder. "Don't try to do this alone, Rebecca. No matter what Ty says. I'm here, and I know his family. They wouldn't want either of you to go through this alone."

"Thanks." She sounded like a mouse and felt like roadkill.

With a finger beneath her chin, Lenz lifted her face. "Call the center. Promise."

Her lips quivered violently, so Becca could only nod. It was enough to satisfy Lenz. With another quick hug, he left her to it.

Lifting her phone, she looked at the screen. The image of Seaside Recovery was a serene place on the cliffs overlooking the Pacific. She scrolled through the information, and when she came to the section title *Reach Out—We Can Help*, she paused. Her heart squeezed, and her hand shook. But she tapped the number.

It was the hardest call she'd ever made in her life.

***

He'd been set up. Blindsided.

Tyler's emotions thrashed wildly, and all he could do was stare at the woman who had done this. Glare, more accurately. How dare she? The piercing of his heart might as well have been a bloody knife, and the weapon had been from her hands.

And she knew it. Tears threatened to run down Becca's face as she winced before she looked toward the floor. Tyler stepped forward until he towered over her, and then he leaned toward her ear.

"What have you done?" he seethed.

She shrank as she folded her arms around herself.

"That's enough, son." Dad stepped to them and laid a firm grip on Tyler's arm, pulling him backward. "Just sit down."

Come to my place tonight, she'd said. *We need to talk.*

Yeah. Who was the liar now? Since when was Becca deceptive, manipulative? Tyler didn't sit as his father had demanded but turned his attention toward Lenz. "Did you tell her to do this?"

Lenz moved to stand beside Becca, meeting Tyler's angry look with a resolute stare and saying nothing.

"Becca called us here because she loves you and is worried about you."

Tyler jerked his look to the man sitting on a chair next to the sofa. "Who are you?"

"I'm Ben. I'm from Seaside Recovery."

"Well, Ben from Seaside whatever, I've never seen you in my life. You have no part of this."

"Sit. Down." Dad's strong, work-worn hand pressed with crushing force on Tyler's shoulders.

A sniff to his right provided enough of a distraction from Tyler's instinct to shove Dad's hand away that he was able to lower into the chair. Mom.

By the red rimming her blue eyes, Mom had been crying for hours. Probably from the moment Becca had betrayed Tyler's confidence and called them, and every single mile from Sugar Pine to Becca's apartment.

How could she do this? How could she say she loved him and yet betray him so completely?

Rolling his fists, Tyler looked away from Mom, loathing the way her tears sank into him like a gut punch, and saw Lenz guiding Becca to a chair. Heat rushed over his body as rage flared red hot.

"Not missing opportunities, are we?" he spat, spearing Lenz.

Lenz merely shook his head. "You know better than that, buddy."

"Don't call me buddy, you—"

"Tyler." Dad's voice was dead calm and chillingly low. It was all warning with no pity. The way it was when his sons were in deep, deep trouble and they needed to know they'd reached the end of his grace.

Silence rang. Cold and hollow and with something of a finality. His life had shattered. The shards of it had fallen and now lay hopelessly broken at his feet. Tyler found Becca's eyes and saw it there.

The end.

Two words, unspoken. Implied. Seen.

He was gutted. Inside, he thrashed against the wild pain of it.

"Becca called me," Ben-the-unwelcome-stranger said. "Which I know from other experiences was probably that hardest thing she's ever had to do in her life. But she did it because she cares deeply about you, Tyler. As does everyone else gathered in this space. They're here for you."

A chilled numbness took hold, replacing the searing agony that had ripped through his chest. Tyler pressed one hand into the other and squeezed. He stared across the floor, seeing nothing but blurred shapes and muted, lifeless color. He heard the droning of Ben-the-appointed-savior, but few words sank in. Those that did flared momentary spikes of resentment against the increasing relief of detachment.

You need help. He'd needed Becca, not this pompous jerk. She said she'd be with him on this.

You're surrounded by people who love you. Some sort of love. She'd betrayed him. Took his trust and turned it into a blade shoved into his back.

You don't have to live like this. What did this guy know?

There is hope, and we can help you.

"I don't want your help." Tyler ground out every word.

"You don't get a choice on this one, son."

Tyler whipped around to look at his dad. "I'm a grown man."

Dad snorted, as if arguing the point. "You're in a lot of trouble. Stealing narcotics? We can get a court order, if you'd rather go that route. Either way, Seaside Recovery is your next stop."

His dad was threatening him with legal trouble? Who were these people? Love? This was not love. This was...

Bull.

"I didn't steal them," Tyler spat.

Dad shot him a lifted brow and then looked across the room. "Lenz?"

No way. Lenz wouldn't—

Resolution was an immovable force in Lorenzo's folded-armed posture. "I'll press charges if that's what it takes."

Nice. Some friend. Tyler's gaze bounced from his roommate to his fiancée and back again, toxic suspicion steaming through his mind. "This should work nicely for you, huh? Put me in rehab, comfort my girlfriend..."

"Enough." Though laced with exhaustion, Becca's voice held a hard edge. She waited until Tyler's eyes settled on her, and though he could see her lips tremble, she lifted her chin with a look of firm determination. "You can be the biggest jerk sometimes, Tyler Murphy. More so lately than ever. But I still love you."

"This is some way of showing it."

She shook her head. "I'm not marrying you like this."

"We're still talking about marriage, are we?"

"No." At his sarcasm, her expression shifted into something chilled and distant. "Not until you get clean."

"So my dad threatens me with a court order, and you're giving me an ultimatum?"

"Yeah." She continued to hold him with a steely look. "I guess that's about the size of it."

"And this is love?"

"That's exactly what this is." Dad's firm grasp on his shoulders demanded Tyler's attention again. "And right now, this is over. I'm not going to let you sit here any longer saying and doing things you're going to regret. Hurting people who love you. It's time to go."

Bullied and trapped. Without a choice.

As Tyler bitterly complied, what had been the deepest love of his life flipped. The other side of what had been beautiful and good was seething resentment. Those roots took hold with shocking speed.

And he held on to them fiercely.

CHAPTER TEN

(in which the choices are made)

B ECCA'S EYES BURNED. SHE could only hope that the drops she'd put in them that morning had been enough to disguise the fact she'd cried all night. Kevin had gone with Tyler to Seaside, a long drive from the university. Helen had stayed with Becca until yesterday had rolled into today, comforting her as much as she could while the woman struggled in her own grief. Eventually, they parted, Helen to a hotel room ten minutes from campus and Becca to her bed.

"Brace us, Lord." That had been Helen's parting prayer.

Before Becca reached the doorway to her first class, her phone rattled. She checked the text, expecting the message to be from Helen, though she hoped beyond reason that it would be from Ty.

How are you this morning?

Those five concerned words came from neither, but rather from Lenz. A wave of uneasiness moved within her, though she knew it shouldn't have. After last night, after Tyler's clear accusations aimed at his roommate, Becca had felt sick. Not because of anything inappropriate between her and Lenz, but because the thought of Ty really believing that either of them had such thoughts made her desperately sad. He was such a mess.

I can't talk about it right now.

Lenz didn't respond, and she was relieved. Becca had to muster every effort in her mind to pay attention to class. At the end of it, she wasn't sure she'd been successful.

How was Ty doing? Did he truly hate her the way that hard look he'd nailed on her last night had implied? Would he see that she had done this because she loved him?

Would he ever even talk to her again?

The swirl of questions possessed her thoughts as she wandered along the sidewalk. When a tall figure fell into step beside her, she startled. Looking up, she wasn't sure if she should feel relieved or more worried. By the scowl Brandon wore, more worried was the right way to go.

"We need to talk." Brandon's low tone held warning.

Becca shut her eyes but nodded. With a hand to her elbow, Brandon led her toward the side of a building off the beaten path. When he stopped in a shaded spot not readily visible to the average passerby, he released her arm and jabbed forked fingers into his thick dark hair. His expression was angry torture, and Becca leaned back against the cold brick of the building, bracing herself.

After a hard sigh, Brandon shoved both hands into his jeans pockets. "You should have come to me with this."

Blinking, Becca looked up at him. Her heart ached for this younger Murphy, guessing this blow had knocked him off center. Brandon admired Tyler to personal hero levels. Having his brother taken off to rehab had to be a tough pill to swallow.

He stopped shuffling his feet. "Why didn't you tell me first?"

"What would you have done?"

Shoulders stiff, Brandon moved a half step backward. "I don't think going straight to our parents was the right thing to do, Becca. And rehab? Come on—"

"He *stole* narcotics, Brandon."

"I can't believe that."

Crossing her arms, Becca gave way to bitter self-defense. "You think I'd make that up? I love your brother. I. Love. Him. Do you really think I wanted to see the man I'm engaged to taken off to rehab?"

Brandon's jaw moved hard, and he swallowed. "He lost his leg, Becca..."

She shook her head. "Look, I know you and Tyler are tight. This is hard. Trust me, I get it. But Tyler hasn't been right in months, and you know that."

His biceps flexed hard beneath his T-shirt as Brandon crossed his arms. He looked toward the ground. Becca pushed off the wall. "Tell me that's not true."

A hard silence chilled between them. But then his posture sagged, and Brandon blinked. Finally, he dragged his gaze back to her, and she wanted to cry all over again. Tears sheened his eyes. She reached for his elbow and squeezed.

She knew this pain. To the depths of her heart, she knew.

"I just wish I knew, Becca."

Nodding, Becca let her touch fall away. "I wish it wasn't real."

More silence scraped by.

Brandon cleared his throat and tilted his chin into what Becca had come to think of as the Murphy look of sheer will. "He'll get off it. Tyler won't let this beat him."

If only she and Brandon could will that into reality. "I hope you're right."

Brandon held her with a firm look. "Don't doubt it."

And then he walked away.

***

The rhythmic crashing of the surf had initially kept him up at night, allowing Tyler the unwanted space to think. To simmer in his bitterness. But after two weeks, the sound of waves against the rocks below his new quarters became background noise. Maybe even soothing at that, though he'd never admit it.

Against that white noise, Tyler sat against the pillows he'd propped up on the twin bed and stared out the window, across the rolling sea. The moon was a white orb, large and whole and sending a beaming pathway bouncing with the ocean rollers. A year before, he might have sunk against the cushion at his back, relaxed and peaceful, enjoying such a glorious view. Likely even praising God for it.

So much could change in a matter of months. Instead of savoring the enormous beauty outside his room, letting it take him to a place of inspired worship, Tyler maintained a chilled detachment built on a strengthening foundation of anger.

Who was God if He could create such glory and yet not keep Tyler from this wretched place? If God had the power to hold the sun, moon, stars, and the very earth in their right places, could He not have prevented all this? He could have kept Tyler safely on that roof. Or He could have stopped the injury Tyler had sustained from his fall from becoming so traumatic that the surgeon had to take his leg.

God could have stopped all this. And He could have kept Becca from doing what she'd done. Resentment turned white hot as Tyler's thoughts rolled toward the woman he was to marry.

Becca was coming in the morning. He hadn't seen her since the evening of her *intervention*.

Rolling his fists, Tyler clenched his jaw. Just the momentary thought of her betrayal sent fire through his veins. No doubt she'd been encouraged into this—Lenz had left their shared apartment that fateful night when Becca had discovered that Tyler hadn't confessed as he'd implied.

Lenz had always been soft toward Becca. In the two years they'd been housemates, Tyler had always figured that had been because Lenz was just that sort of guy. Easy to get along with. A gentleman to the ladies.

Now... Now Tyler speculated there'd always been more to it than that. Lenz was a sneak. Biding his time, playing his cards right. He could only imagine the scene back at Becca's apartment after Dad had taken him away. Lenz was probably right where he'd hoped to be all along—catching Becca as she fell apart. Holding her. Comforting her.

Stealing her.

Hate was an icy hook sinking into Tyler's heart.

You know it's not like that.

Tyler squeezed his eyes shut, banishing the imaginings that made him furious. Truthfully, he didn't know anything. His mind felt as broken as his heart, and he struggled to separate what was real from what was paranoia. Ben, his assigned counselor, had warned him that this process would be complicated, that healing the body, the mind, and the spirit took time and was likely going to be harder than anything Tyler had ever encountered before.

Even harder than losing his leg.

He would wrestle through withdrawal, and that was enormously difficult, both physically and mentally. The process would mess with his thoughts, ride hard on his emotions. It would be like a squall ripping through him, and it would feel terrifying and impossible.

But he could survive. If he surrendered to the process, Tyler would make it through to the other side.

Tyler had usually shut out whatever Ben said during their required sessions. Usually. Sometimes he couldn't help but hear though, and that part of one of their early talks had stuck.

Ben hadn't been wrong. Tyler felt exactly that—that he was in the middle of the most frightening storm he'd ever experienced in his life. He couldn't separate sky from sea, shoreline from ocean. Reality from imagination. And he wasn't at all certain he would make it through alive.

Becca... She was coming in the morning.

This time, at the thought, he ached for her. Anger gave way to remorse, and all he wished for in that moment was to have her near. He wanted desperately to have her in his arms, to cling to her as if she would anchor him in this chaos, and then he wouldn't feel so terrified. He would swear to her he'd never get so lost again.

He would beg her forgiveness. Plead for her to keep faith in him.

The breakers crashed outside Tyler's window, the high tide strong against the cliffs. He opened his eyes, setting his gaze on the darkness beyond his room. A thick cloud had muted the moon's white light.

There was only darkness now. And the pounding of the waves.

***

Becca paced the empty room, one hand clutching the fabric of her sweatshirt near her heart. The first week Tyler had been gone, she'd called him every day. Some days he'd talk to her. Most, he'd refused. Ben had told her to be patient, to press into the pain, let it push her into prayer, rather than run away from it. And to keep believing that Tyler would reach the other side.

She'd done so, though the second week she'd called only a couple of times. Tyler had been quick to point that out.

"Too busy for your fiancé already?" he'd asked, accusation thick in his voice.

"You didn't take my calls last week, and when you did, you didn't have anything to say. I figured you wanted space, so I'm respecting that."

He'd had nothing for a response.

When she told him she was coming to visit, he'd held a long, chilly silence.

"Unless you'd prefer me to stay away." She'd worked hard to keep her jarred emotions from her voice.

"I'd prefer not to be here at all."

"I know."

"Do you?"

"I didn't want to make the call, Tyler. I didn't feel like there was any other choice."

"Lenz tell you that?"

Wow, Tyler had become so fixated on that. His insinuations were both insulting and brutally hurtful. She hadn't known what to do with the frustration or the pain and didn't think trying to deal with it over the phone was a good idea.

So she'd left it. Changed the subject briefly and then ended the call.

That had been the last time she'd talked to him—the last subject that remained open and raw between them for days. Waiting for Tyler to open the door to the room provided them for visiting, icy panic clawed through her chest.

She didn't know this version of Tyler—the bitter, angry man who barked at her on the phone. He seemed unpredictable and unmerciful in his resentment. She didn't know what to do with him, how to talk to him.

At the rattling of the doorknob behind her, Becca turned. Her heart throbbed, her throat closed, and when those dark-brown eyes clamped on her, she was lost.

Four seasons seemed to pass in his look. Warmth flickered, full of love and longing. Then it cooled and grew distant. A harsh chill settled, as cold and hard as anything that winter could produce. And then a thaw. Slow, timid, and not yet ready to leave the frost behind.

Becca cautiously moved toward him. At her touch, fingertips against his bicep, Tyler stiffened. She read the war in his heart as it played across his face. Uncertain if she should, she lifted to her toes and brushed her lips over his.

His sigh seemed a surrender, and he leaned into her. His fingers curved over her jaw, slipped around her neck in a gentle hold, and his kiss felt both reserved and full of longing.

As she pulled back, she found she was clutching the sleeve of his shirt with a shaking hand. Tyler's fingers fell away, and the tenderness that had been that kiss faded from his eyes. As he studied her, his gaze grew distant and chilled again.

"Ty..." She unclasped her hold on his shirt and curved her hand along his jaw. "How are you?"

He blinked, straightened, and looked away. Mouth pressed flat, he said nothing.

"You're not going to talk to me at all?"

He strode to a window and looked out. The view was of a flower garden, now dormant, waiting for spring's warmth to summon the vibrant colors back to life. "I don't know what to say."

That made two of them. But wouldn't he at least try?

"Why did you do it?" He spun back to look at her.

"Why did I call this place?" She folded her arms as if to shield her heart from the arrows he was sure to fire at her. "Tyler, you know why."

"I asked you not to tell my family. You knew I didn't want them to know."

Nodding, she drew a fortifying breath. She hadn't wanted any of this and hadn't planned to tell his parents. But after her initial phone call to the center and another extended conversation with Ben, it seemed best. People didn't recover from addiction without humility and accountability. Trying to do so in secret, as a solo act, rarely resulted in long-term success. And there was the issue of cost...

The bottom line was Becca couldn't afford this for Tyler. She'd needed help, and it was either call her parents or his. She'd been pretty sure if given that option, he'd not want her dad to know. He'd worked so hard to impress her dad, to win his approval. It'd been the reason Tyler had waited to propose, had insisted they wait to get married until after graduation when she'd wanted to set the date for the end of the summer before they went back for their final year.

It's what your dad would want, Bec. I want to respect his wishes.

But all that felt irrelevant right then. It wouldn't matter what she said— Tyler was going to be mad at her for this.

"Becca?" Tyler's voice bit.

"Yes, I knew you didn't want them to know." She forced her eyes to his and held a steady look on him. "You have to know, Tyler, I didn't want any of this either."

His brows pulled down into a scowl. "Then why did you do it?"

"I think, in your heart, you know why. I think you are putting anger where you don't want to take responsibility."

"Responsibility?" Tyler edged nearer. "I was handling it, Becca. And you promised."

"No. You were not handling it. You were lying. You told me you made things right with Lenz, and you hadn't."

"Lenz. Here we are at the real issue, aren't we?"

Becca pulled back from him, wanting to wilt at his ongoing accusations and yet thoroughly tired of them as well. "This is old, Ty. This delusion you've crafted, it's nothing more than a deflection. A story you've crafted so you can pretend that it's my fault. Or Lenz's fault. Here's the truth, whether you're willing to accept it or not. Lenz is a good friend. To me and to you. He's always been a good friend. Did he encourage me to call Seaside? Yeah, he did, because he's watched someone he

cares about go through this before. And he cares about you."

Tyler rolled his head back and snorted. "Yeah. I'm the one he's worried about."

Frustration erased nearly every scrap of compassion Becca had left. "You know what? I can't do this anymore. You've gone from a logical, kind, reasonable man to someone who can't—or

won't—think straight, let alone take responsibility. I don't know how to deal with that."

Lowering his face back to her, his jaw moved hard, and his eyes became steel. "Then leave."

Though that was exactly what she intended to do, his seething words stung. Becca winced and then nodded.

"I don't want a woman who would so easily betray me anyway."

Her heart came to a hard stop, and her breath caught painfully. She hadn't thought he meant *leave*, as in forever leave. As in they were done.

But as she stared wide eyed and bewildered
at him, an iron mask transformed his face.

He meant exactly that. They were done.

What remained of her heart shredded into a million ribbons as she slid
his ring from her fourth finger. Becca blinked and looked at the diamond
that had been his promise and hers. The symbol of their shared love and
future together. A tear flicked from her eyelash when she looked back up to
him.

Tyler remained unmoving. Stoic. Cold.

Becca had no words. She only felt agony as she set the ring on the
window ledge near Tyler's side and turned to
the door.

He let her go in silence.

***

He couldn't move.

The door shut with a single click, the sound resonating a dark sense of
finality.

Becca was gone.

He'd lost her.

She'd left him.

Which was it? Tyler shut his eyes, tried to sort through the disjointed
thoughts savagely searing through his mind. Stepping backward, he
stopped when his back met the cool wall next to the window and braced
his head against it. The sound of waves lapping the distant shoreline
reached into the chaos of his mind, and he focused on that.

Everything was broken.

He'd broken all of it. Or God had let it all fall apart.

Which was it?

Tyler opened his eyes, waited for the blur of his vision to clear, and
found the simple sparkle of the diamond he'd given to Becca winking at

him from the window ledge. He lifted it between two fingers and then let it slide into his palm. The warmth of her hand still seeped from the white gold of the band, and he clasped his fingers around it.

Fix this.

He wasn't sure if the thought was a prayer—a plea—sent up to heaven, or a desperate command given to himself. Either way, he felt hopeless. If it was a prayer, he doubted his request would find a positive response. After all, God could have prevented all this from the start. He hadn't. And if it was a command...

He couldn't fix it.

Becca was gone, and that ring in his fist told him plainly that she wasn't coming back.

CHAPTER ELEVEN

(in which Becca must pick up the pieces)

BECCA CELEBRATED VALENTINE'S DAY alone, sobbing into her pillow until her emotions finally gave way to sleep. She'd given Tyler's ring back to him only three days before.

Time refused to slide by quickly and was equally as stubborn about that healing-all-wounds adage. Becca was utterly heartbroken, and it seemed she would remain that way for the foreseeable future.

Her birthday in March was spent fake smiling through a dinner with girlfriends and an hour-long phone call with her parents, during which she finally told them everything that had happened between her and Tyler and that the wedding was off.

Why hadn't she said anything to them sooner? Her mom's soft, heart-bled question was legitimate and something Becca had dwelled on for weeks before. She did have reasons. Partly to spare Tyler. At least that had been her initial reason for not sharing her fears and Tyler's looming issues with Mom and Dad when she'd gone home over Christmas break. Later, with the intervention, again, because having her dad know about Tyler's struggle with opioid addiction would be the last thing in the world he would have wanted. Finally, after Ty had ended things and she'd given his ring back, Becca had remained quiet because in her heart of hearts, she'd foolishly hoped he would call her, would tell her it had all been a mistake made in anger and he wanted her back.

Lord knew, she wanted him back.

She'd grieved losing him as if it had been a death, and in many ways, it was. Losing him was the death of their shared love, their hopes and dreams for a life together. Telling her parents seemed like the closing of the coffin. The final burial of the life she and Tyler wouldn't get to experience together.

Why had she chosen to tell them on her birthday? Hard to put into words, but she'd set that day in her mind as the marker—Tyler had until then to reach out, to change trajectory. But on her twenty-second birthday, Becca had determined she would have to face reality. He'd let her go, and that wasn't going to change. She had to begin gathering the broken and scattered pieces of her heart and start stitching a new life together.

One that did not include Tyler Murphy.

Oh, the tears that fell that night, as she exposed her wrecked heart to Mom and Dad. Mom cried with her. Dad...

Dad was angry. At her for withholding the drama that had weighted her life over the past six months. For not being honest with them. And more at Tyler for breaking his baby girl's heart. Becca loved her father for his fierce protection of her, but at times it was too much. Dad was an intense man who held on to high expectations.

The raw part of her had wanted to lash out at her dad, to tell him that in truth, he was partly to blame, both for her not telling them what was going on and for Tyler's unrelenting determination to heal from the loss of his leg and then from his subsequent addiction, without anyone knowing. Yes, that had been Tyler's pride. But it had also been her father's sometimes unreachable standards.

Something Tyler had been all too aware of.

Dad had vetted Ty like he might be a threat to the nation. Then he'd made Ty feel like the ambitions that had come forward in Ty's heart during their freshman year spent at CalTech were insufficient. It had seemed such a waste to Dad that a guy who had been among the few accepted into CalTech's engineering program decided that he really wanted to go back home and work with his own father in construction for the rest of his life. It had seemed unsatisfactory to Dad that Ty wanted a simple life building things—the life he'd loved before he'd tried on the rigorous and competitive academic realm of CalTech. More, Dad couldn't comprehend Tyler's decision to leave the prestigious program.

Especially when Becca had announced she was going to do the same with her own place at CalTech. Something she never would have had the courage to do without Ty's strength at her back.

Like Tyler, Becca had found she didn't love the hard pressure of pursuing an architectural engineering degree at the challenging school. Truthfully, she'd known even before her freshman year that she wouldn't enjoy it. Academically, she could handle it, and she'd gone to the school her Dad had championed for one simple reason: Dad was excessively proud of her for making the cut. But in her heart, she'd known even then what she really enjoyed and could see herself doing daily for years on end was what she practiced in the kitchen. Baking was her jam, and she was pretty good at it. Explaining that to her dad though...

Without Tyler's empowering belief in her and his encouragement to pursue a career that brought her joy rather than frustration, Becca wouldn't have had the courage to tell her dad. To stand up to him. But she had, and it'd been a relief.

For Tyler, though, Becca's breaking free in that small way had added a weight to his shoulders about their relationship. Early on, before the spring of their freshman year while they were still at CalTech, they knew they were in love. They both had been certain they wanted a life together. Tyler never flinched with reserve when the topic of a future together came up. He'd spoken in absolute terms about them being together. Marriage had been assumed. But he'd held out proposing, and Becca knew why.

Dad expected them to graduate college first, and Ty, feeling responsible for the rift of disappointment between Becca and her father, had been determined to honor that.

During that emotional phone call on her birthday, it had been difficult not to lash out about all of that when Dad's voice turned hard. But because in general Becca was a compliant and respectful daughter, she'd swallowed it. It had been Mom who'd intervened.

"Her heart is already broken, Chad," Mom had interjected. "You're not helping."

A pause lengthened over the line, and then, to Becca's surprise, Dad said, "I'm sorry, Becs." A long sigh breezed over the phone. "I really did like him, and I know he made you happy. I just wish that we knew—maybe we could have helped."

Not likely. Not because she didn't believe Dad's sincerity, but because it had become clear that none of them could help Tyler. He'd determined to walk this hard, dark path alone. Without her. Without anyone.

I'm never done with you... A broken promise that festered in her gut.

Becca sniffed, choosing not to address that part. "I'm sorry about the wedding. I know it costs so much..."

"Shhh," Mom said. "Hush that now. We won't even discuss it."

A fresh silence expanded, and Becca had a sense that there were other, related things Dad wanted to discuss. Things like her plans for the future, since everything she'd mapped out before had Tyler directly in the middle. She guessed Mom had given Dad the *look*, though, because Dad didn't pursue it.

Their phone call ended with a weak "Happy birthday, sweetheart."

It had not been at all a happy birthday. But she'd survived it.

***

"I've already done this." Tyler let the weights slam down and glared up at Ben. "PT is a waste of time. All of this is a waste of time. I haven't had a pill in two months—don't you think it's about time to sign off on my release?"

"Wow. Two months? Really, has it been that long? Wow. What have I been thinking? Oh wait... How long did it take for you to become addicted the first round, Ty?"

Tyler pinned his mouth shut and looked away.

"We never did get around to discussing that one, did we?" Ben pushed. "My guess, less than a month."

"Not what we were talking about," Tyler grumbled.

"Sure. Here's the point though: You keep making light of this, and that tells me you're not getting it. By your family's blessing, which I have, I think I'll keep you until you get it."

He got it already, dang it. Hadn't he lost a whole semester of work, and now he wasn't going to graduate on time? Hadn't he lost his parents' respect and trust? And the worst of the worst, hadn't he lost the woman he loved? Yeah, he got it. No need for Ben to keep pushing.

Dropping out was always an option. He could simply leave—he was, after all, a grown man. Yeah, and do what then? Dad had already made it plain that he wasn't working at Murphy Builds until Seaside gave Tyler full release. And would leaving early gain him any ground with Becca?

She's gone, fool.

A fist at his heart squeezed hard, eliciting pain and blocking his breath. *No thinking on Becca.* Back to the present issue, then.

"That still doesn't explain why I'm back in PT for something I've already worked through. I know how to walk. I use the stupid fake leg. Can I just be done with this?"

Ben folded his arms and glanced at Mark, the physical therapist. Mark merely raised an eyebrow. "If you've already done this, then the exercises shouldn't be such a struggle. Do it again."

Not a struggle? Ha. Easy claim to make when a man had two good legs to stand on. Tyler's life was doomed to be an eternal struggle. And now that Becca had left him, he'd lost his reason to pretend otherwise. He wasn't about to play along with the *let's be positive, life can still be amazing* garbage Ben and Mark were pitching at him.

No thinking on her. Stubbornness grabbed hold and gripped hard. Tyler folded his arms, and with a push of his good leg, he spun on the bench away from the weights. "I'm done."

Ben tipped his face toward the ceiling and groaned. Mark nudged him with an elbow. "I've got this. You can go."

Tyler glared at his counselor, who shook his head before he pivoted and strode away.

"You really are some kind of bullheaded man," Mark said. "You do realize that while you're aggravating to those who are trying to help you, the only one you're really hurting is yourself, right?"

"Then let me be."

"I'm paid not to."

Tyler grunted and smirked. "At least you're honest."

Mark straddled the bench beside Tyler's and lowered to sit on it. His phone in hand, he tapped the screen a couple of times and spoke without looking at Tyler. "There's someone I'd like you to meet." When he did look at Tyler, he handed his phone across the space between them.

On the screen was an image of a beautiful woman—rich dark hair, startling blue eyes, gorgeous smile. Eye candy. And a pathetic attempt at motivation. Tyler flung the phone back toward Mark. "Nice try. She's gorgeous, but I've already been shredded by a beautiful woman. I'm not up for another go round just yet."

"Wow. You *are* arrogant, Murphy. You know that?"

"What? Just because I'm not enticed by a beautiful bribe?"

"See there. That's what I'm talking about. If you'd taken just one second to see past your massive ego and out of your incredibly huge sack of self-pity, you would have noticed more than the fact that I showed you a picture of a pretty woman." Mark tucked his phone into his jacket pocket. "Let me be clear, Mr. Big Head. There's no way on this planet I'd try to set you up with my sister. I love her way too much to toss her at a man who is both unstable and incredibly full of himself. Not to mention stupidly stubborn."

A blaze of shame ignited in Tyler's chest and licked all the way up his neck and into his cheeks. "Your..."

"Sister." Mark held him with a death-threat sort of stare. "Punk."

Tyler's mouth went dry. "Why...why would you think I should meet you sister?"

"Because she's a world-class free-climber. That picture you just saw— you know the one where you thought I was just appealing to your base nature as a man?" He stopped there, stabbing Tyler with another silent but oh-so-full-of-threats glare. "It's from *High Adventure* magazine. They ran a feature about Tessa last year."

And now Tyler felt even worse. No, Mark hadn't wanted Tyler to meet a beautiful woman to find a new reason to keep trying. He wanted Tyler to meet a beautiful woman who could do things Tyler would never be capable of doing. Climbing, of all things.

Awesome.

Pressing his lips together, Tyler gripped the bench beneath him and used his good leg to stand. Grabbing his crutch, which he'd rested against the weight contraption, he then hobbled toward the chair where he'd left his prosthetic.

"Why do you keep running?"

Tyler slammed down onto the seat and ripped his fake leg toward him, jamming the socket against his thigh. "You're a jerk, you know that?"

"Only when I have to be."

"How dare you!" He finished attaching the socket and stood, meeting Mark nearly nose to nose. "What kind of jerk tosses something like that into his patient's face?"

"The kind who did his homework." Mark didn't back down. "I know who you were before your accident. I know you loved adventures—

ziplines, skydiving, rappelling. I know you could be found at least twice a week at one of the rock walls near your college campus. I know that the first date you took your fiancée on was a hike—a challenging one. I know —"

"Ex!" Tyler shoved Mark's shoulder back.

"What?"

"Ex-fiancée. Becca left me. And thanks for tossing that up in my face."

"Yeah. I know about that too." The heat in Mark's gaze simmered. "Like I said, I did my homework."

"Then you should have known that this is going nowhere. You're right. I loved all those things. I was Tyler-Tarzan. Now I can't do any of it. I've lost everything, and meeting your beautiful, superstar, adventurous sister isn't going to change that."

Mark's expression morphed into something almost like amusement.

"That's funny to you?" Was this *hate* burning through him?

"What if I told you she's just like you?"

That slow volcanic ooze halted, and Tyler stared. Just like him? How? Stubborn? Likely—only really, really stubborn people acquired the level of expertise Tessa must have in a sport like climbing. Foolish? For certain. It took a special kind of daring fool to free climb. End of similarities.

"She lost her leg when she was sixteen." Mark leaned back against the wall, casual as you please.

Whoa, wait. What? "She's..."

"Just. Like. You." A faint grin covered Mark's face. "Everything you've gone through, that you're going through? Tessa's been there. She pushed through it though. She never gave up."

Tyler blinked, entirely stunned. "She...she free climbs?"

"All the time. She's a sponsored athlete and a spokesperson for Challenged Athletes." Mark withdrew his phone, and after several more taps on the screen, he turned the face back to Tyler. "This was in Tennessee a couple weeks ago."

With nearly black hair pulled back and hanging out beneath a helmet, the tall, slim woman whose left leg was missing from the thigh down dusted her hands for grip, looked back at the camera and grinned, and then began. Climbing. Ascending a wall that most people, including Tyler, could never navigate, whether they had one good leg or two. Tyler watched, captivated, as Tessa took her grip, moved her one foot to stab, stabilized herself, and then made for the next grab. She steadied herself. Took a breath and then reached for the next handhold. Once more, she repositioned her three points of contact, looked up at her next grab and... Missed! She tumbled toward the earth and landed on a crash pad that had been laid beneath her position.

Off camera, a man spoke. "That's all right, babe. That was a good first run. You've got this."

"Who is cheering her on?" Tyler asked.

"Her husband. Happens to be her trainer too."

Tessa shimmied herself up, reset her first holds, and made for another go. Three more times she missed that last lunge grab and hit the crash pad. Each time, her husband encouraged her, but he never stepped in. Never made a move to physically help her. On the fourth effort, Tessa's curled fingers caught the grip she needed, and she pulled herself upward.

"Yeah, Tess! There it is!" the man off screen said.

Two more grabs and she conquered the climb.

"Incredible." Tyler breathed, truly captivated. He turned the phone back to Mark. "Does she always climb without her prosthetic?"

"Depends. She learned to do it without one, so learning to climb with one was kind of a challenge. A good climbing leg is sort of hard to come by. There's a manufacturer in Colorado, though, who sponsors her now, and they've created a specialty prosthetic that she really likes. The foot is shorter and more rigid, so it works for her. She can jam it in holds, and it'll bear her weight in the toe." Mark held up his phone. "There's another video of her climbing with it on here somewhere."

"How long has she been climbing?"

"Almost a decade now. She started when she was eighteen—after she got clean and was released from rehab."

"Rehab?"

"I told you, she's been through everything you're going through. I meant everything. She's the reason I started working with Seaside. When Tessa was released, she felt like she needed something to refocus on—a new challenge and purpose. She'd been a soccer player before, and a good one. She thought about going back, but she'd tried that before, while she was still in high school, and the frustration had been part of the reason she'd landed in drug rehab. She didn't want to risk that again. One day she went to a gym, and there happened to be a climbing wall there. The guy working noticed her. Noticed that she kept glancing up to the top. He asked if she wanted to try."

"Let me guess. She said no." If it had been him, Tyler would have said no. A hard, resounding *no* that would have carried with it all the resentment he had locked inside. He wouldn't have wanted to risk the humiliation of not being able to do it.

Mark chuckled. "It's like you're in her head. Yeah, she declined. This guy though, he didn't let her off that easily. Later he said he just knew she needed to do it. It was like the mountain she needed to summit to see past what she'd lost. To glimpse the possibilities that life still held for her."

"How did he know that?"

Mark shrugged. "Don't know. But he talked her into trying."

"Did she make it to the top?"

"Not until five weeks later."

"Why'd she keep going back?"

"Max got her number. Wouldn't let her quit."

"Max?"

"The guy. He married her three years later."

Tyler laughed. "So his persistence wasn't all about the climbing."

"I can't say for sure on that, but I can say he wanted life to be good for Tessa. And it is."

In the space of a pause that extended between them, Tyler pictured that woman again, only this time imagined her in a crowded gym, removing the dignity and protection of her prosthetic leg, and trying to climb a wall.

Had it been Tyler, he would have quit on the first fall. He'd have left humiliated, angry, and sulking—and in hot pursuit of a pill that would offer him a temporary reprieve. Man, he didn't want to be that guy anymore.

That was the point Ben had been trying to make earlier: Tyler needed to see who he did and didn't want to be. He needed to get a firm grip on that before he left Seaside. Without it, he'd have zero chance of staying clean outside the rehab center's insulated world.

He *didn't* want to be the incredible sulk anymore.

And beyond that? Tyler needed to reimagine his life. Just like Tessa had.

"Can I meet her?"

Mark smiled like a champ. "If you're not a punk while you do your sets today, I'll think about it."

Tyler shook his head as he moved back to the weights he'd abandoned. His first instinct had been right. The beautiful girl in the picture had been a ploy. Just not the way he'd thought. And he had a feeling that meeting Tessa might change everything for him.

For the first time since Becca left, Tyler grabbed on to hope.

CHAPTER TWELVE

(in which light begins to poke holes)

L ATE APRIL BROUGHT MORE sunshine, warmer temps, and the vibrant colors of daffodils and tulips that had been tucked into plant beds throughout the campus. With all that beauty, Becca felt like she should be able to find a genuine smile. She'd grown weary of feeling weary. Tired of crying. And yet the grief within remained stubborn.

It'd been more than two months. Well past time that she let go of the fanciful hope that Ty would suddenly call her. That he'd ask her to come back to Seaside so they could work things out.

He wasn't calling. Wasn't coming back.

Running into Brandon a few days back all but confirmed it. He barely met her soft hello with eye contact, and when she asked how Tyler was, Brandon's jaw clamped hard. After an uncomfortable pause, he shrugged. "Still at Seaside."

"I'm sorry," Becca had choked out. She wasn't surprised though. Ben had said expect at least three months. For lasting results, the more beyond that, the better. Kevin Murphy had been very clear about wanting *better*.

Brandon's chin dipped, and a long exhale sagged through him. "Me too." He'd brushed her upper arm with the back of his knuckles, then walked away.

That was Brandon Murphy's way of saying goodbye. Becca was surprised to discover she still had pieces of her heart left to break. Brandon and Tyler had been best buddies. She and Brandon had also become friends.

So much to let go. Unclenching her hands on all that she'd had before was excruciating. *Why, God?* was a mournful, repetitive refrain surging through her heart.

Graduation was only weeks away, and Becca hadn't made any solid new plans. It was time to work on that. But to do so meant that she needed to make a trip to Sugar Pine, because the owner of the bakery where she'd spent the previous three summers deserved an in-person explanation for Becca's shifted path. After all, it affected Mr. Hadley too. She hated letting him down as much as she was heartsick at the knowledge that she had to put those plans and dreams into the ground.

That scenario—the one of going to Sugar Pine for a face-to-face—was complicated. During those summers when she'd worked for Mr. Hadley, she had shared the apartment above the bakery with two other girls, splitting the rent. Other times she'd gone to Sugar Pine during breaks or holidays, she had stayed with Tyler's family. Neither of those situations felt comfortable now.

She could make the three-hour drive, visit with the bakery owner, and turn around to come back. It'd be a long day...

But it seemed the best option.

Sitting in the shade of a tree off the path that stretched from her apartment to one of the buildings on campus, Becca pulled up the bakery's number, drew in a solidifying breath, and dialed. Within a couple of minutes, she had Mr. Hadley on the line, asked if she could stop in on the upcoming Saturday to talk to him, and then was done.

It was set. She'd just have to be brave, get it done, and then leave Sugar Pine for good.

Why, God?

The refrain had become her sinking anthem, and the hollowness in it consumed her.

***

"I can't say that I blame you." Mr. Hadley sat across the table from Becca, regret etched onto his kind face. "But I must admit that I'm terribly disappointed. I very much wanted to see this place settled in your very capable hands."

Becca blinked against the hot sting in her eyes. It had been such an idyllic plan. After their marriage, she and Tyler would move into the apartment above the bakery. He'd work with his dad and eventually take over Murphy Builds. She would slowly take over the bakery, with the goal of Mr. Hadley retiring in three to five years.

Everything had been discussed. Mapped out perfectly. Or so it had seemed.

"I'm so sorry, Mr. Hadley. I've thought so much about this, but I just can't see around it. I can't live in Sugar Pine..."

Without Ty.

With her thumb, she rubbed the inside of her fourth finger, still missing the cool metal of her engagement ring. She just couldn't fathom being in his hometown without being his wife. Eventually he'd get better. Eventually he'd come home. He and his dad would reconcile. Tyler would be okay.

That was her hope for him, anyway. But even if all of that went as scripted, there didn't seem to be an *eventually* for her.

Blades of regret nicked with stinging persistence. The dark anger Tyler had shown her—she'd been warned about it. A stronger, braver woman would have held on. Wouldn't have let Tyler push her away in the middle of withdrawal. She would have kept the ring, and the faith, and waited out the storm, even if from a distance.

Becca hadn't. She'd given in to hopelessness, to fear. She'd walked away from the man she'd loved when he was in the darkest place of his life. There didn't seem to be a recovery plan for that.

Mr. Hadley covered her hand with his dry, strong fingers. "Do what you must, my dear girl. I do understand."

Becca mustered a nod but no words. She stood, and so did he. With grandfatherly affection, Mr. Hadley pulled her into a hug. "Time does heal."

She doubted it. Or maybe she didn't want it to. Perhaps she'd rather hold on to the sadness, because it was all she had left of Ty.

Such morose thoughts.

Straightening, she managed a thank-you and then wove her way out of the little shop she'd hoped to call her own someday. Once on the sidewalk, Becca pulled in a cool breath of pine-filled air and took in the view. She wanted to lock the image away in her mind. This sweet mountain town with one main street, wide sidewalks, oil lamp–style streetlights, and a backdrop of pine-cloaked hills. The memories would be sweetly haunting.

"Becca?"

At her name on a young woman's voice, Becca turned.

With a hand to her bulging baby bump, Lauren Murphy stepped toward her from the Skyline Grill. "Becca! It is you." Lauren stretched that hand forward, reaching for Becca.

Becca wanted to huddle in an alley and cry. Instead, she cleared her throat. "Lauren. I didn't know you were in town."

"Matt came to help Kevin with—" Lauren cut short, looking toward the ground.

"With a job?" How long would Tyler's oldest brother have to fill in as their father's right-hand man? *Please, not too long, Father. For all of their sakes, speed the healing...*

Eyes sad, Lauren nodded. After a long space, she squeezed Becca's arm. "How are you, hon?"

Miserable. Heartbroken. Lost. "I'm fine."

Lauren settled eyes that held clear doubt about the truth of that on Becca, then shook her head. She took Becca's arm, looped her own through, and guided her up the sidewalk while keeping close to her side. "Not fine, I think." Her head tipped until her brown hair brushed against Becca's shoulder. "Sweet Becca. You don't know how much I've been praying for you. I'm so sorry for everything that's happened. Sorry for Tyler and you both."

Keeping her eyes forward, because she was afraid she'd burst into tears right there in the middle of Tyler's home town, Becca took a moment to steady her emotions. "Thank you, Lauren. You all have been so good to me over the years. I can't believe that..." That she wasn't going to be part of the family after all.

"You'll always be family to me." Lauren spoke with resolve, as if she'd read Becca's mind.

Becca stopped mid-stroll and turned to Lauren. She meant to thank her for her kindness. To say that she hoped they'd always be friends. Instead, she met the deeply compassionate look in Lauren's eyes, and her lips trembled.

Lauren didn't hesitate. She pulled Becca close. "You are our people, Becca. And I know for a fact Helen feels the same way." Stepping back, Lauren gripped Becca's shoulders, the warmth of her hold seeping through the denim of Becca's jacket. "Whatever you need, please tell us."

Still unable to speak, Becca nodded.

As if a sudden realization struck her, Lauren looked back the way they'd just come, pausing her gaze on the sweet shop and then coming back to Becca. "You're here to talk to Hadley, aren't you?"

A nod was all Becca mustered.

"Your agreement with him?"

"I...I backed out." Becca tried to swallow the knot in her throat. "He understands."

"What will you do?"

Becca shrugged. "I haven't figured that out yet. For now, I'll go back home, to my parents'. Something will turn up." It had to. Her heart rate sped up at the thought of not having a plan. No direction and little motivation to find a new dream. Somehow she needed to pick up the pieces, but every time she tried, she would look at what was broken and fall apart all over again.

Please take care of me, Father.

A thoughtful expression passing over her face, Lauren's gaze traveled toward the layered hills beyond the borders of Sugar Pine, in the direction of the mountain pass beyond. Somewhere in the folds of those hills, Matt and Lauren owned a small Christmas tree farm. Almost without thought, her hand slipped from Becca's shoulder to caress the child within her belly.

"This one comes in about a month," Lauren said.

The switch in topics seemed odd, but Becca was grateful for it. A warmth trickled through her, and she smiled. "I know. I hope I'll get to meet her. Or him."

"Let's plan it, not just hope." Lauren's expression brightened. "Will you come to the farm for a visit after the baby comes?"

"I'd love that. Would it bother Matt though?"

The shake of Lauren's head was certain. "Absolutely not. No one among us is mad at you in the least, Becca. This situation with Ty...it's not your fault, hon."

Someone forgot to consult Brandon about that. Locking away the mildly bitter thought, Becca nodded. "Thanks. But still. They're brothers."

"You're my friend—and the sister of my heart. Please come."

She needed no further encouragement. Becca hugged Lauren. "I will."

A small joy. It was nice to have something to look forward to.

Chapter Thirteen

(in which life must go on)

WARM JULY SUNSHINE SPREAD a blanket of cheerful light over everything beyond the large windows. Tall green treetops swayed in the breeze, sure to be salty and cool off the Pacific. At his back, the steady rhythm of the tide spoke of everyday consistency. But this was not every day. This was *the* day.

Tyler stopped in front of the front entry, intentionally taking in the moment. At his side, Ben gripped his arm. "He will be with you, brother."

Inhaling deeply, Tyler let Ben's reminder bleed into the full passage of the Bible that they'd spent the past several weeks gripping. "Isaiah 43:2?"

"Isaiah 43:2." Ben nudged his shoulder, a gentle push into the life that awaited Tyler beyond what had become the refuge of Seaside.

What mystery was that, anyway? The place he'd resented. The very spot he'd not wanted to be. It had become his sanctuary. And Ben—the same man he'd quite possibly (and probably) had hated when the man had been a stranger sitting in Becca's living room, telling Tyler that she'd done this thing, this betrayal, because she loved him—this same man had become a friend. A brother—because clearly six of those were not enough.

An unsure glance backward, nearly giving in to the impulse to cling to the security he'd found there, and then Tyler passed through that door and out into the bath of summer sunshine. Into the world he longed for and feared. As he walked toward the vehicle waiting for him, suitcase in hand and unsteadiness rocking in his heart, he pulled up Isaiah 43:2 from memory.

When you pass through the waters,
I will be with you;

and when you pass through the rivers,
they will not sweep over you.
When you walk through the fire,
you will not be burned;
the flames will not set you ablaze.

"Be with me now, I beg You," he murmured and then caught the eye of the guy sitting in the driver's seat. Not his dad, as he'd expected.

Brandon.

In the months he'd been at Seaside, he hadn't heard from Brandon. Not once. The chilled silence from his brother was like another blade across Tyler's soul. He and Brandon were close. The best of friends since childhood. He realized he'd let his younger brother down. He knew he'd disappointed him.

But the silence was a death. Murderous and lasting. And provoked by his own hand.

Was Tyler now dead to his brother? Brandon gripped the steering wheel, face forward. Unmoving.

Tyler's hand trembled as he pulled the lever to open the hatchback. Brandon glanced at him in the rearview mirror. Their eyes connected in the glass as Tyler settled his bag in the back. Still. Nothing.

Silence.

Be with me in these waters, Lord? They were deep and tumultuous. A storm summoned by Tyler's own fingers, back when he had no idea how ugly and stubborn this curse truly was. A surge of something frightening and powerful, released by the choices he'd made.

A deep breath, another pleading prayer, and Tyler slid into the seat beside Brandon. "Hey."

"Hey." The attempt Brandon made at a smile was futile. An uncertain look held on Tyler, and then, with shoulders sagging, Brandon turned back to the windshield and shifted the vehicle into gear.

The pull away from Seaside was smooth, but the silent storm between brothers swelled on.

Silence became strangling, and Tyler wanted the torture to end. "How are you?"

"Fine."

So far, so good. "How was the end of school."

"It ended. I'm done."

"Done?"

"Yes. Done. I'm not going back."

Tyler sat back at the hard, determined edge in Brandon's tone. "But your degree—"

"Firewood is good money for me. And clearing dead and diseased trees. People are becoming more diligent about maintaining healthy woodlands. I don't need a piece of paper to do that."

This stone-faced young man was a stranger. Brandon had always been bold—they'd tagged him with that very name when this brother had been only four. But rebellious? Not ever.

Was this rebellion?

"Does Dad know?"

"Of course he knows. I don't do things in the dark."

That stab nicked and left a lingering sting. "I see."

"Time shouldn't be wasted. Life can change."

Yes. Tyler knew that quite well, thank you.

"I'm not wasting any more of mine complying with what society tells me I should do."

Well then, there was a sermon for him. Likely, all truth. What was this fire in Brandon's breath though? And why loose it on Tyler?

He resents me. Clearly. *Does he now hate me?*

More than once during the growing years, Mom had pulled Tyler aside to pour wisdom and warning into his thick teenage skull. Certainly she'd done so with all of her boy-men. He didn't know the content of her instruction to his brothers, but for him, most often she would say, *Ty, you lead with your zeal. Even when you don't realize it, you lead. You gain admirers, and Brandon is the chief among them. Lead well, son. Lead well.*

He'd puffed with pride at that, even if done so in secret. *In the dark.*

Pride goes before destruction.

Oh see, now, how the proud had fallen. Tyler gripped the belt keeping him safely strapped to his seat. What should he do with this? He'd let Brandon down. More than he'd realized, he'd disappointed the younger brother who would have been the chief among his followers. Rightly so— for where had Tyler led him?

Into destruction. He'd been Brandon's hero all throughout life. Had reveled in it. And had let him down hard. One more relationship broken by his fall.

Could such a thing be mended? Atoned for? Restored? Tyler squeezed his eyes shut.

These are deep waters, Lord.

"Have you heard from Becca?" Brandon's voice, softer now, as well as that question, jolted Tyler's attention wide open.

Would his pulse always race at the mere mention of her name? Would someday the heat just the thought of her provoked simmer and then die?

No. At least, deep in his heart, he hoped not.

"I haven't." Tyler dropped his hands to his lap and stared at them. Empty. There was pain in that. But at least now, no longer were they clenched in fury, raised and shaking at heaven. "I don't expect to."

A glance at Brandon revealed cold granite.

"Be mad at me, Brandon. None of this is her fault."

He returned that glance, and for a moment, the stone cracked, letting a shaft of painful confusion leak through. Then Brandon regripped the steering wheel, knuckle tight, jaw tighter, and returned his intensity to the road.

Moments scraped by, blades cutting. Was this more injury? Or maybe it was the scalpel applied to something needing to be cut out? Like the dead flesh of his leg that would have killed him if not removed?

Healing was painful. It took so very long and was extraordinarily hard. But he was alive. He still had life.

I'm alive because they removed the death in my leg. Tyler's revelation turned back to prayer, lifted to the greatest of all surgeons.

Remove what is dead here. Let us live.

***

A tender smile eased Becca's face as she cradled the tiny Fiona Elise Murphy in her arms. Five weeks old and absolutely perfect, the little girl who would have been her niece if things had gone as planned nestled into her heart despite the lack of family connection. Warm and smelling of baby lotion and all things new and unspoiled, Fiona stretched her dimpled chin up, mustered a small squeak, and then settled against Becca as if she quite agreed. They were meant to share a connection, Tyler or no.

Becca raised Fiona to her face, inhaled that quality that belonged to such little people alone, and pressed a soft kiss to downy hair. "I am besotted." She looked up, grinning, at Lauren. "You may never get rid of me."

"I can live with that." Lauren passed a soft blanket, the pinks and yellows proclaiming proudly this infant was a beloved daughter, and then ran a motherly hand over Fiona's little head. Then she lowered onto a cushioned chair across from Becca.

Becca could barely peel her eyes from the miracle of life in her arms, but when she did, she found Lauren sleepily gazing out the window toward the rows of Christmas trees marching in orderly fashion on the backside of the property Matt and she had purchased barely into their second year of marriage.

"You look happily exhausted," Becca said.

"That perfectly sums up my current state."

"I would gladly keep this one company." Becca fingered the miniature fist that curled beside a miniature cheek. "You should go for a nap."

"That's a deal. On one condition."

Becca braced herself, knowing what was to come. Matt had come back from his once-a-week prayer and coffee meeting at the nearby filling station with news. The old bread store, just a jaunt down the dirt road from the tree farm, was going up for sale.

Wouldn't it make the perfect cupcake shop?

Her friendship with Lauren Murphy had gone quickly to the deep side after their meetup in Sugar Pine in early May. From that, Lauren had known how deeply Becca hurt to lose so much. Ty, yes. She ached for Tyler Murphy and mourned not being his wife by now. But her dreams, plans for the future, had also slipped from her hands. What was she to do now? For the past months that had been the unanswered question that would not let her gain a full night's sleep.

Why, God? had morphed into *Now what?*, and Lauren knew that question well for herself. Years back, before she'd met Matt, she had asked that question as she'd walked (ran?) from a life in which she'd felt trapped and overlooked.

"God showed Himself good and faithful in the middle of it. I mean, can you imagine any way possible to turn puking on a strange man at an airport from simply horrible to the catalyst that became a gift of grace and blessing?" Lauren had shared the story with Becca the day of her graduation—a day that should have been full of excitement and joy but was bittersweet instead. "Only God, Becca. Only God. Give this to Him. He is an expert with turning ugly into beautiful."

Since that day, Becca struggled to do so. Even to know *how* to do so. Hands clenched, they felt empty and sore. Could she pry her fingers open? And if so, what was there to give? Her palms were empty.

But then there was this reminder—a stinging poke that had unsettled her. She hadn't an answer to *Now what?* other than she'd taken an uninspiring job at a national chain store decorating cakes she didn't bake according to a book of limited options.

Everyone starts somewhere, Her mother had said. And it was true.

You need to keep going. Do the next thing. That next thing for you, Becca, is land a job. Right now, a paycheck is what you require. Dad's nononsense advice. She knew he loved her, and his seemingly cold prod was done out of that love.

But neither her mom's nor dad's nudging had answered that question. *Now what?*

But a building was for sale just down the road from the woman who had become her closest friend and confidante. A woman who leaned into the Bible as if it were breath, and by doing so challenged Becca's spirit in a way that felt necessary. And the woman who was mother to this sweet child twining clear through Becca's heart.

Lauren stood from her curled-up position on the chair and gripped Becca's shoulder. In the middle of thoughts and feelings, something profound landed in Becca's mind.

She still had a heart! It felt deeply and could still love. Still dream. It hadn't been broken into uselessness.

"We'll just go take a peek." The hand on her shoulder squeezed. "How would that be?"

Terrifying. Freeing? Becca tipped her head back and met Lauren's gentle smile. "What if I hate it?"

"Then say so."

The bigger, scarier question bulged on her tongue until it could no longer be kept. "And if I love it?"

CHAPTER FOURTEEN

(in which the way out is upside down)

TYLER'S HEART HAMMERED AS if he were the one hanging by the tips of his fingers and not the woman he'd not yet met in person but had already gained his great admiration. Tessa Drake strained, the muscles in her upper arm flexing with impressive definition. A look of pure determination crossed her face as she narrowed her focus on a hold three feet above and to her right. That grab would require a lunge.

"That's the one, Tess." A man on the ground near a crash pad spoke calmly to her. Her husband Max, likely. "You've got this."

Tessa's muscled shoulders moved with her long exhale, and Tyler found himself holding his own breath. With a solid push on her one leg, she made for the grab, her fingers curling around the minuscule hold with impressive strength. For a moment, she dangled, and the only thing keeping her from gravity's pull were strong curled fingers. Then her foot found the crack she'd already chosen, and her tight body pressed against the boulder.

Tyler exhaled, and a rush of adrenaline flooded his veins. Collectively, the gathering around him had breathed in the same moment, and he had no doubt that everyone watching felt it too.

"One more grab, babe." A smile tinged Max's voice as he shifted his position to gain a better angle of his wife's climb. "Last one and you'll be able to pull yourself up."

Blowing out a breath, Tessa smiled down at her biggest fan, waiting nearly twenty feet below her. "Easy does it?"

Max grinned.

Her chin tipped up again, and Tessa studied the final bit of her assent. From his angle of her climb, Tyler could see her bite her bottom lip. Other spectators must have seen her look of uncertainty as well, as several called out encouragement.

"So close, girl!"

"You're there. Just one more grab!"

"You can do it, Tess!"

A few clapped, but then the noise died away, as if everyone knew she needed to concentrate. Or they themselves were too breathless to cheer more.

Tess looked back to Max. "Left or right?"

"Right looks like an easier hold."

True, Tyler thought, but the leg she stood on was her right. A diagonal lunge would give her more leverage to reach the next grab. Left might be better. He wondered if Max took that into account, or if having two good legs had blinded his suggestion. And if Tessa, the one doing this challenge with only one leg, would take his advice.

She studied the path to her right, eyes trained on that hold Max had seen. And then her body weight shifted. She was going for it—the way Max had told her to go.

A breath. A lunge. A near miss as her vertical motion was short. But her fingers curled, and determination apparently surged. She secured the hold, then moved her foot, jammed her toes, and pushed up again.

Tyler blinked as she scrambled, awe taking him captive. She'd done it. It'd taken four tries—the first three resulting in gravity's victory as she'd dropped onto the crash pad—but Tessa Drake had just proven to Tyler that *impossibly broken* was only something in his head.

Blinking, he watched as she scooted on her backside to sit at the top. Arms lifted high, she first tipped her face heavenward, closing her eyes and smiling, and then looked back at the gathering below. She took a minute to catch her breath, time filled with a hearty round of well-earned applause. And then she waved the group quiet.

"Today was successful, wasn't it?"

The group cheered again.

"Let me tell you though. Every day isn't. Truth is, guys, I fall more often than I succeed. That man down there"—she pointed to Max—"spends hours watching me hit the crash pad and only moments seeing me reach the top."

"It's worth it," Max interjected.

Tessa grinned and then widened her look back to the group. "I've found that life is like this climb. Some crashes—they hit harder than others. Some, well, they can be downright devastating. Like the one I took when I was sixteen. Young, healthy, full of big dreams, I thought that life was wide open. All I needed to do was work hard and stay positive. And then—" She smacked the thigh of her missing leg. "Then everything changed. One night, one car wreck. One lost limb. Guys, I thought my life was over. If you want to know the ugly truth, I was mad that God hadn't just gone ahead and taken my life—because I couldn't see a future like this. What good was I broken? I didn't think it could be any worse. Just to prove me wrong, things got worse. Long story short, I ended up in rehab for opioid addiction."

She chuckled quietly, shaking her head. "This climb you just saw? This was nothing compared to how hard that was. And that's what I want you guys to know before you leave today—we can do hard things. Things that seem impossible. God says that in our weakness, He is proven strong. He also says that for those who love Him, and are called according to His purpose, He works all things together for good. For a while, I stopped believing that. I stopped believing God. But He doesn't quit on us like we quit on Him, you know?"

A few spectators gave Tessa an *amen*.

"Sitting up here, the sunshine warming my shoulders, I'm thinking I have a pretty incredible life. I love what I do. I love that man down there who doesn't let me quit. And I love that I get to meet all kinds of people, offering hope into some real brokenness. The thing that gets me every time I think about all of this is that these things I love right now, they only happened after I lost my leg. *Because* I lost my leg."

The small crowd applauded and then broke away. Tyler stood captivated, watching as Tessa re-rigged her gear so that she could rappel back down to her waiting husband.

"Well?" Mark elbowed him, reminding Tyler he wasn't there alone.

"You were right. She's amazing."

"God is amazing, Ty. Don't lose sight of that." Mark squeezed his shoulder. "But you're right, Tessa is something. Did you want to meet her and Max?"

"I'd like that." Tyler's mind buzzed with questions.

Mark led the way down the winding path that would dump them into the small cove where, after applying rappelling gear to get down, Tessa had landed. Max helped her with her gear. She plopped onto the crash pad, now free of her harness, and was reattaching her prosthetic leg by the time Tyler and Mark reached them.

"Mark!" Tessa beamed at her older brother. "You came." Her eyes shifted to Tyler. "And this must be Ty." She finished with her leg, hopped up to stand, and then strode toward them, her outstretched hand aimed at Tyler.

"It's awesome to meet you." Ty's hand met a strong grip.

"You too." She glanced back at the man coming up behind her. "This is Max. The love of my life."

Tyler reached to shake Max's hand as well. "I've heard quite a bit about both of you. Mark is pretty proud."

"Mark is unrelenting with his patients." Tessa smirked at her brother. "Tell me he isn't a little bit of a pain in the butt."

"Only when I have to be," Mark said.

Couldn't argue that.

"So..." Tessa looked back at Ty. "Let's see it." She bent down and patted her prosthetic leg.

Mark rolled his eyes. "Tess, you don't always have to jump right in with *let's compare*."

"I'm not comparing." She flung a sassy grin at her brother.

"He's wearing jeans."

With a single raised eyebrow, she turned her gaze back to Tyler, glanced up at the hot summer sun, and then looked back at Tyler. "Still keeping it under cover, huh?"

"I almost always wear jeans."

"Did you before?" Tessa reached for the rappelling rope and began coiling it.

"Uhh...usually." Nope. He'd worn cargo shorts—much to his dad's irritation for years. He'd been twenty before Dad had stopped telling him that jeans were the better option for construction. Heat filtered into Tyler's cheeks as he shook his head. "Usually not," he admitted.

"Well, there we go." Tessa had her rope coiled and her prosthetic securely attached, and she stood up. "Let find some food and give thanks, fellas. I think this guy and I have a few things to talk about."

***

She'd done it.

As she scanned the view of Pleasant Valley from the flat rooftop of the building, the heart in Becca's chest trembled with awe and terror. Maybe a touch of excitement? Yes, that too.

The old bread store, a freestanding brick building mere blocks from the local schools, had space in the storefront to serve cupcakes and lemonade, and space in the back for a small office and a decent-sized industrial kitchen, and was now legally in the possession of one Rebecca Colson.

She'd bought it. Using the money her parents had gifted her—funds that had been set aside to pay the balances on things like the caterer and florist and venue for her wedding—and the savings she had stuffed away with hopes and plans for being Mrs. Tyler Murphy, Becca had purchased the old building. Dad had been cautious but not opposed.

The thing that had made that small miracle possible was the living space on the second story. Being in a small remote community made property costs low, and with the living space included in her mortgage for the building, this purchase actually made her monthly expenses less than if she'd found a place to rent in the city where her parents lived.

If she could make her business plan succeed, she'd be just fine.

Could she make it work?

There was definitely more anxiety than excitement zipping through her limbs. Who was she to attempt such a thing? Without the exhilarating gust of daring courage that had been Tyler Murphy at her back, she was merely Becca Colson, small and timid. And fearful.

A long rumble rolled through the heavy cloak of dark clouds as the summer storm continued its journey east. The sky above her had finished its weeping, leaving the early morning with a taste of rain, a scent of newness. Becca inhaled, hoping to find a breath of courage in the washing.

"Today it begins." Lauren's soft, smiling voice drew Becca's attention from the skyline and the hoped-for sunrise that lay hidden behind the clouds.

Commanding a smile to her mouth, Becca felt her lips twitch and knew Lauren would see the truth. And she did. Tipping her head, she reached for Becca's hand.

"Courage, dear heart." Lauren quoted C. S. Lewis. "And remember you are not alone."

"This was a crazy thing to do."

"It was a brave thing to do." The hand holding hers squeezed. "And don't forget—you have your parents' support, and Matt and me are right here with you. For you. In fact, my husband is waiting downstairs with the contractor Dad Murphy recommended." She grinned and winked. "Let the work begin!"

Becca drew in a shaky breath. "I don't think I can do this." A ridiculous thing to say. It was too late—she was in it. Money paid, papers signed. No turning back.

"Aw, Bec..."

Sudden tears wetted her cheeks. "What was I thinking, Lauren. I'm not Ty. I'm not...brave."

In a breath, Lauren had her folded in close. "My sweet friend, you are no wispy girl. And even if you were, God does not frown upon the small and humble. Remember, He told the prophet in Zechariah, 'Do not despise these small beginnings. For the Lord rejoices to see the work begin!'"

Becca breathed a teary chuckle. Of course Lauren would have a verse to press into her heart. "I'm not attempting to rebuild the temple here." She pulled back from her friend's embrace. "But I do appreciate the encouragement."

Lauren set a rather reprimanding look on her. "You don't think God delights to see you do this?"

Hmmm... Becca hadn't thought much about that at all.

"Becca, I think what you need are battle cards."

"What are battle cards?"

"I'll work on some and give them to you tonight. You'll come for supper, right?" Lauren's tone held all expectation and little room for rejection.

And why would she? She felt small and alone in this big undertaking. She was not about to turn away a friendly invitation. "I'll be there."

"Good. For now then, do me a favor as you go over plans with the contractor and begin this new work."

"What's that?"

"Trust in the Lord with all your heart." Lauren reached for Becca's hand and squeezed it one more time, then turned to walk across the roof to go back down into the mess that would hopefully transform into her very own cupcake business, Just Eat It.

Becca was once again alone. *Trust in the Lord...* It'd been a while since she'd thought to try. A cool, rain-soaked breeze stirred from the east, and Becca turned to let it wash her face. Shut her eyes and breathed deep.

Do You delight in this small beginning? In me?

The question—the prayer—felt so utterly daring. And yet... Becca opened her eyes. Above the dark lip of that moving storm, golden radiance gleamed strong, conquering the darkness. Infusing the world with brilliance.

Becca lifted her head. And smiled.

***

Two weeks after meeting Tessa and Max, Tyler had his own harness on. Drenched in sweat and tempted to swim in the familiar frustration of defeat, he blew out a long breath. His arms were noodles, muscles quaking. Hand stiff from gripping. Leg tired and oh-so-sore.

"Enough for today, Ty." Max stepped from the sidelines of the climbing wall.

Tyler looked across the wall that had been his defeat toward the path Tessa had nearly completed.

"Don't do that."

Swiveling his head, Tyler looked at Max. The older man came closer, lowering his voice. "You can't spend your life comparing. It will be an endless game that you will never win."

Tyler tipped his chin, letting his gaze travel back up the wall he'd just attempted and failed at several times. "I thought today was the day."

"So you should every day. But you're done for now." Max smacked his back. "And it wasn't a defeat. You showed up, after all. Put on the gear.

Revealed your weakness to everyone here who cared to see. And proved that hard work takes guts. There is no failure in any part of that."

Swallowing, Tyler let Max's words sink in deeper, and in the space of silence between them, he thought back to the words of that woman—the one in the book that Tess had given him after their second meeting.

We're not adrift in chaos. We're held in the everlasting arms.

He'd found it odd that Tessa wanted him to read from and about a woman who had died a few years back. Whose life and ministry seemed better suited to women than to himself. However, he'd accepted the book by Elisabeth Elliot, thinking that he'd likely pass it on to his mom, who would more appreciate whatever this kind-faced old lady had to say.

He had not expected to be thoroughly wrung out, captivated, and inspired by Ms. Elliot's words. Her story, so full of hard things, of deep heartaches, was somehow rich with goodness. How could that be?

Pain was the ultimate leveling place. The common ground on which one stood not as a man or a woman, black or white, free or slave. But as one who suffered and must find a way through, else they writhe into forlorn nothingness. And into that place, hard and unyielding, Ms. Elliot spoke profoundly.

Your suffering is never for nothing.

God, is that so? What is it for then?

Tyler's fall from the roof—a crash he felt all the way into the marrow of his spirit as a splintering fall from grace—what was it for? If not that it had been a fall from God's good favor, then what?

Why?

Why?

For over a year now, that had been the resounding question. The one steeped in the darkness of bitterness and anger. The one he couldn't silence, though he'd tried to ignore. It had been the question without an answer and the hollow spot he'd sought to numb.

Why this suffering? Why let him fall? Why take his leg? Why take his future? Why take it all?

Leg wobbling beneath him, tired from a day of trying what he'd once thought impossible, Tyler looked back at Tessa. Did she ask this empty question? Did she have an answer to offer?

"Home, Ty." Max nudged his back. "Hot shower, sustenance. Whatever it is that is plaguing your mind right now, you won't find answers here. Go home and pray."

Tyler followed Max's advice, and two hours later, hunger satisfied, body cleansed, muscles unwinding, he sprawled on his bed, Bible at hand, and the book Tessa had given him spread open. He read as if his starving soul had found life-giving nectar, stopping often to look up the Scriptures Elliot referenced.

She had found something profound in her suffering, and she was offering it to him. Straight to *him*.

Could she be right though? Her instruction seemed so...upside down. But as he looked up the verses she'd quoted, reread them again and again, his spirit yielded. Cracked painfully but with relief. For the bitterness seeped out.

And this secret?

Shall we accept good from God, and not trouble? What did Job mean? Tyler's mind baulked at this, but a small voice in his heart whispered, *Listen! Here is the mystery!*

He continued to read what Elisabeth Elliot said about such—and the woman knew of which she spoke. Life had been a series of heartaches for her.

And what of Tessa? She lived this mystery, didn't she?

Sidetracked, Tyler did some research, some digging into others who had done so as well. Joni Eareckson Tada. Nick Vujicic. Lives that seemed devastating. And yet...

And yet they did as Elisabeth had done. They lived with...

Gratitude.

With his finger skimming the tiny black print, Tyler reread the last verse he'd looked up, 1 Thessalonian 5. "Rejoice always, pray continually, give thanks in all circumstances; for this is God's will for you in Christ Jesus."

Give thanks. Gratitude.

The word was a lead weight dropping straight through Tyler's misery. Shattering his self-pity. The breakage was both painful and freeing. He felt light shine through the bondage of his pathetic darkness and knew with everything in him: this was the way. Broken though it might be, this was the way to a life of joy.

CHAPTER FIFTEEN

(in which battle cards are drawn)

MORNING COFFEE IN HAND, Becca had climbed to the rooftop of her building to witness another Pleasant Valley sunrise. Tucked under her arm was her Bible—not nearly as worn as Lauren Murphy's—and a small baggie of three-by-five cards. She settled on the used patio chair that Matt had given her, one of a set of four he'd spotted outside a shop near the lodge in Lake Tahoe where he was still working until his brother Connor settled in to take over.

"Thought of this rooftop view you have, Becca," he'd said. "Figured you needed a seat from which you could savor it."

Thank God for Matt and Lauren.

As she did exactly that, her thoughts turned to another Murphy, and a weariness sank into her spirit.

Becca hadn't expected Kevin Murphy's recommended contractor to be one of his sons. Particularly when that son had a different job on a regular basis. Hadn't Matt said that Brandon was dropping out of school to work his timber-removal-firewood gig full time? Pretty sure he had—she remembered the whole topic seeming a little like a resignation on Kevin's part for Brandon. Then again, maybe that had just been Matt's interpretation of the situation. Either way, Brandon didn't typically work as a contractor.

But he'd been the young man waiting for her to go over the renovation plans.

If Becca didn't know better, she'd suspect that Kevin had arranged this situation intentionally. In fact, she didn't know better—she was pretty sure that was exactly what this was. And she wasn't sure what to do with it. She couldn't confide in Lauren about how awkward that was. As much as she shared her heart with her best friend, she'd left Brandon's hardness toward her out of the Tyler-Becca saga. Matt and Lauren, as well as the rest of the Murphy family, had already endured much with Tyler's fall and resulting issues. They didn't need to concern themselves with Brandon's cold attitude.

So then maybe this wasn't a sort of setup for reconciliation after all? If Matt and Lauren didn't know about the iceberg between her and Brandon, was it likely their parents knew?

Becca reached for the small stack of cards, freeing them from the plastic. The pile had grown a little bit every day, ever since that evening Lauren had supplied her with the first one.

Battle cards. The perfect way to shift her mind from things that wound anxiety in her heart toward the peace that passeth all understanding. It'd been a week since Lauren had passed her the first few cards. On them, in black ink, Lauren had scrawled out a verse. One card, one verse.

Zechariah 4:10: "Do not despise these small beginnings, for the Lord rejoices to see the work begin."

Isaiah 50:7: "Because the Sovereign Lord helps me, I will not be disgraced."

Genesis 50:20: :You intended to harm me, but God intended it for good to accomplish what is now being done, the saving of many lives."

Jeremiah 29:11–14: "'For I know the plans I have for you,' declares the Lord, 'plans to prosper you and not to harm you, plans to give you hope and a future. Then you will call on me and come and pray to me, and I will listen to you. You will seek me and find me when you seek me with all your heart. I will be found by you,' declares the Lord, 'and will bring you back from captivity.'"

Luke 12:6–7: "Are not five sparrows sold for two pennies? Yet not one of them is forgotten by God. Indeed, the very hairs of your head are all numbered. Don't be afraid; you are worth more than many sparrows."

Becca stopped there, though the stack contained at least a dozen more. Battle cards. This was how Lauren became the warrior of God that she was. Strength not in flesh but in the spirit. Courage not of herself but firmly fixed on God.

Maybe Brandon's working on her bakery renovation hadn't been set up by the patriarch Murphy. But it had been ordained by God. If He knew the number of hairs on her head, surely He knew how difficult her relationship with Tyler's younger, starry-eyed brother had become. But He'd sent him anyway.

Don't be afraid; you are worth more than many sparrows.

Okay. And so was Brandon then, right?

This reunion had purpose, and Lord willing (and lend her courage), she'd make the most of it.

The sun peeked over the wavy mountaintops, pink and yellow-orange declarations of hope renewed, day reborn. Becca filled her lungs with courage drawn from truth implanted. Let the new day begin.

Thirty minutes later, in worn jeans, tennis shoes, and a well-worn sweatshirt, she met Brandon in the cleared space that was to become her industrial kitchen. His dark eyes serious, and not a trace of the charming Murphy smile almost all seven brothers owned, Brandon grunted a good morning and whipped out his tape measure. He measured the length of wall that would be stainless-steel countertop. Then the side that would host her massive double sink and industrial-grade dishwasher. He checked his numbers against the clipboard hanging on a nail in the brick wall, nodding.

All things he'd already double checked.

"The plumbing is done, right?" An inane question, as she already knew the answer, but Becca needed to break the chilly silence.

Brandon didn't spare her a glance. "It's done."

"Shelving and counters next?"

"Flooring."

"Ah. Well then, tell me what to do."

"You're paying me to do the work." His sharp glance left her no doubt —he didn't want her there.

Becca folded her arms. "It's my kitchen."

"My job."

Sighing, Becca uncrossed her arms and watched while Brandon concentrated deeply on little things that had already been done. She summoned a verse that she hadn't looked over that morning but had been lingering over for a couple of days.

Love must be sincere. Hate what is evil; cling to what is good. Be devoted to one another in love. Honor one another above yourselves.

"Romans 12:9," she whispered.

"What?"

"Oh. Nothing."

Brandon scowled.

"Actually, not nothing." *Courage.* "Brandon?"

His back to her, his shoulders moved with a hard breath. "What?"

"We used to be friends."

Brandon froze, his posture stiff. Slowly, his chin came around, and then he turned to face her.

She met his eyes, though the fire in them made her quiver. "I'm sorry we're not anymore."

The blaze flickered and then dimmed, and then Brandon looked to the floor. His fists rolled closed, and then he stretched his fingers open again. "Why didn't you warn me about Ty? I'm his brother, Becca. You should have told me."

Biting her lip, Becca fought away the rise of self-defense. "I know, Brandon. I'm sorry that I didn't. I'm sorry that it blindsided you."

"I would have tried to help." When his face lifted and she could see his eyes again, she found misery there rather than anger.

Had the anger he'd held ever really been about her? Intuition told her *no*. Goodness, but people were complicated.

"I know you would have." Becca blinked, the thought of Tyler a piercing stab in her chest. Imagining Brandon's loss, not only of his brother but of his close friend and hero, made that pain worse. Would having Brandon know have made a difference? Could Brandon have done something, said something, that would have turned Tyler's deepening addiction away? Altered the trajectory that had crushed them all?

Brandon rubbed the back of his neck, his attention wandering back to the floor. Then he nodded slowly. "I'm sorry you were in it alone. And that Ty—" He cut short, swallowing. After an extended pause, he emptied his lungs slowly and looked back at her. "He's out now. Did you know?"

"I didn't." She'd asked Lauren not to give her updates. Cowardly. "Is he okay?"

A silent nod. Then, "You won't call him?"

Should she? Tyler had the past six months to call her. His silence had told her, even more painfully than his ugly declaration back at Seaside, that he didn't want her. Couldn't forgive her for what he'd seen as betrayal. Becca rubbed her fourth finger, the one that no longer wore Tyler's ring. Did she do that often? The emptiness whispered *alone*.

In the silence, Brandon stepped toward her, his lips pinned to a flat line. He stopped in front of her, studied her with a furrowed brow, and then sighed. Suddenly, his arms were around her shoulders. *Not alone. Matt. Lauren. Mom. Dad. And...Brandon.* They all knew the pain. Shouldered the burden.

And God? Did He feel this great sadness? Another battle card floated to memory: *Close to the brokenhearted and saves those who are crushed in spirit...*

That closeness, she longed for it. *Be near me, oh God!* Hadn't that been the cry of the shepherd-king? More than anything else—Tyler, or courage, or new direction—God's nearness was what Becca craved, though she didn't know it until this moment.

Brandon tightened his hold. "It's not your fault, Becca." And then he stepped away.

The nearness, however, stayed.

***

Tyler tipped his head back, focusing his attention on the bell at the top of the blue run—a 5.7-rated climb. That was the goal. Maybe today would be the day.

A new day. The sun rising, warm and bright. Phone call from Dad—a job I can do with him. Friends who challenge me to be better. Learning to climb again.

Learning gratitude.

Tyler lifted up his mental list and gave thanks.

"One grab at a time, eh?" Tessa came and stood beside him, a smile in her voice. "Today's the day. I can feel it."

Did Tessa do this daily exercise of giving thanks too? Tyler suspected yes.

"I hope so." His arms ached, and he had more bruises on his back and butt than he'd ever accumulated in his life. But he wasn't about to complain. *Sore muscles.* They meant life was still flowing in him. *Still work to be done.* He sent those up in gratitude as well.

"One of these days you and I will get to race to the top."

Tyler looked down, catching the woman's smile pointed up at him. *Tessa Drake.*

"Why on earth did you even try that first time?" He'd been wondering that since he'd first had the opportunity to meet this fiery, inspiring woman. Especially after he first gazed at this very wall the day after Mark had introduced him to Tessa and Max. Man, it had been intimidating to stand on the ground in front of a climbing wall knowing he had two arms

—both needing bulked up—and only one good leg to get up those holds on that vertical challenge. Even now, after trying and failing for weeks since that first effort, Tyler had to silence the persistent voice in his head telling him that it was impossible. To give up and walk away. And to bury his losses and failures in something that would numb his mind and body.

I'm not gonna be that guy anymore. Tyler looked back at the wall. *Please help me not to be that man, Lord.*

Then he switched. *Lifted from darkness to new life. Failure doesn't have to be the end.*

Gratitude. The mystery of joy.

At his side, Tessa laughed quietly. "You want the truth? I tried that first day because a super-hot guy working the ropes asked me to. And I kept coming back because his smile kind of made me weak in the knees. Knee."

"Weak, huh?"

"I was smitten."

Max walked over from the equipment desk and stopped behind his wife. "What are you smitten with?"

"You." Tessa turned and winked at her husband.

A man of few words, Max merely grinned and planted a kiss on Tessa's nose. "Good."

"Love at first sight?" Tyler asked.

"For me?" Tessa began slipping on her harness. "Yep. Max?"

The look Max held on his wife read quite clearly *man gone and not sorry*. But even as he grinned in a way that told Tyler the truth, Max shrugged. "You were nineteen."

Tessa tossed her head back and laughed, then patted her husband's whisker-shadowed cheek. "Cradle robber. Is that why it took you three years to propose?"

"I'm almost a decade older than you." Max shifted his look from Tessa to Tyler, his expression serious. "I thought her dad was gonna take me to the back shed and hand me a shovel. Not kidding."

"You're kind of cute when you act all scared of my dad." Tessa pecked Max on the cheek and then stepped to the climbing wall—her chosen route a 5.12, a much more technical climb than the one Tyler would attempt. She sat down and detached her prosthetic, then reached for her fist hold. "Climbing!"

The guy at the equipment counter responded, "Climb on!"

Tessa scrambled up the first grabs as if she were a monkey and this was her playground. About the truth of it. Max kept watch on her with a calm but steady eye—and a look that was all protective and smitten.

Love that sees hope and refuses to quit. That joy was bittersweet.

"Seriously, I thought her dad would kill me," Max muttered in a low tone. "Not to mention Mark."

It was sort of amusing. Not simply the boy-in-love face Max unconsciously wore but also thinking of him being intimidated by anyone. The man was an iconic specimen of muscle tone and athletic prowess. Tall, powerfully built, and with the kind of looks that had, without a doubt, drawn plenty of female attention.

"Mark?" Ty snugged the belt on his harness. *Relentlessness, for good.*

"I met him before I ever asked Tessa for a real date. He came to the gym with her one day. Eyed me with a death glare and said if any part of my body breached propriety with his sister at any point in time, he would personally remove it with a rusty knife."

A burst of laughter erupted from Tyler's chest. "That. Is. Epic." *Brothers.*

Max planted a stern, none-too-amused scowl on him. "Laugh it up. Just wait until you meet the one, buddy."

Tyler sobered immediately, shifting his attention back to the climb he was about to attempt. A slow ache cut down his chest, and he couldn't help but picture Becca on the day he'd proposed. Tearful smile making her beautiful eyes shimmer as she lovingly gazed at him. Warm lips welcoming his kiss.

Becca. That one was sacrifice. Tyler lifted it anyway. *She rescued me, even though I despised her for it. I'm not dead, not in prison, not somewhere on the streets, because she loved hard.*

Someday, maybe he could tell her. *Someday?*

"Uh-oh," Max said, his tone apologetic. "I hit something, didn't I?"

"Actions and consequences." Tyler cleared his throat and gripped the rope that would connect to his harness. "That's what my dad would say."

"Any shot at reconciliation?"

With a long, painful breath, Tyler considered it. Thought, for the millionth time, about seeking Becca out, apologizing. Begging her for another chance. But he couldn't do that—not yet. Not when he didn't think he could brace himself for her rejection without tumbling back into the deep pit that had torn them apart in the first place. He couldn't do that to his family. Mostly, he couldn't do that to her.

"Ty?"

He shook his head. "I broke her heart, and it was ugly. I can't risk that again. Especially when my brother tells me she's starting to rebuild her life." *Matt and Lauren.* He clipped the rope into place, secured the carabiner, and tugged on the auto belay so that it'd activate. Then he lowered to the ground and removed the leg that would only get in his way and set it aside. *Options.* Every motion was a silent *topic closed*, and Max read it loud and clear.

"Climbing!" Ty called. *Adversity.*

"Climb on!" the gym worker responded—though he wasn't actually belaying.

Three grabs into the climb and Tyler had to narrow his thoughts onto what he was doing—which was a relief. There was only enough room to think about the next grab, the next foot placement, securing three-point contact, rebalancing, and maintaining the fingertip holds. He couldn't leave space to dwell on how much he missed Becca, on how lonely life had become without her. He couldn't dwell on regrets.

Climbing demanded his absolute, undivided attention. And he was thankful for it.

Chapter Sixteen

(in which time has gone by)

"**H**ERE'S TO ANOTHER LANDMARK moment, son." Dad held up a glass of sparkling cider as a toast, and the friends and family gathered in the Murphy family home.

Three years.

Tyler looked around the room, intentionally taking in the faces of the people who surrounded him for this celebration. Friends and family, all with proud smiles. Expressions of hope, energy buzzing with positivity. *More time. More grace.*

Three years before, he'd entered Seaside an angry, upside-down man. Six months later, Ben had taken his hand in a strong grip, then pulled him into a firm hug. "There will still be hard days, Ty. But I wouldn't have signed off for you if I didn't believe you could handle them."

Stubbornness aimed for good.

For all the animosity and trouble Tyler had tossed at the man, Ben had persevered. More than that, he'd become a good friend. A reliable, honest friend who, in the last twenty-four months, had consistently been a rock when Tyler needed one. Tyler was glad Ben had made the trip to his family's home for this day. A day he'd chosen to celebrate, rather than the anniversary of his release, because he could remember more clearly who he was now, and who he never wanted to be again.

"Proud of you, buddy!" *Restoration.* Lenz had come too. Hadn't even hesitated when Tyler had invited him, which wasn't surprising. That was just Lenz—easygoing. Not one to hold a grudge. He'd been the first person Tyler had sought out after he'd left Seaside, after the first stumbling steps of reconciliation with Brandon. Lenz didn't even need to hear Tyler's full apology—first for stealing from him, second for being such a suspicious jerk about Lenz's motivation in helping Becca.

Becca... She should have been the first of the wounded he'd gone to. He hadn't been able to do it.

Lenz had held a hand up in the midst of Tyler's apology and then wrapped a bear hug around him. "It's good to have you back, bruh." From there, their friendship picked up where it had dropped, and even now, two years post-reconciliation, Tyler was in awe of the grace Lenz possessed.

Tyler had been handed grace all around. Mom, Dad, his brothers. He'd been given love, forgiveness, acceptance, and a new start. Celebrating that, even more so than his two-year mark of staying clean, was a deeply moving heart experience.

Every face here, and a few who aren't.

"Will you share this celebration in your next presentation?" Tessa asked. The young woman, who had become the sister Tyler never had, beamed at him.

Behind her, Max rubbed her shoulder. "You have way too much energy, Tess. Some of us just want to stay in the moment, you know?"

Tessa batted the air. "No harm in thinking forward. Next week will be the largest group Ty's addressed to date. Perfect timing too, right after we do that Big Bend bouldering film over in Moab." She stepped forward to hug Ty. "Good things happening, right?"

Borrowed energy. Enthusiasm on lend.

"Good things." Tyler squeezed her shoulders as soul-deep gratitude reached through him. Climbing with Max and Tessa had been an epic challenge and solid direction for his post-addict life. At some point, though, he needed to shift back to the life he and Dad had arranged before everything had gone sideways. Tyler knew it in his gut this season of climbing and speaking was drawing to a close even if Dad had never once insinuated so. Mostly he knew, because he truly wanted to come back.

Solid relationship with Dad. Again.

One thing continued to put him off that redirect though. Rather, one person. She was the one missing in that celebratory gathering. The one he'd injured the most, regretted the most. Missed the most. The one he still lifted up in gratitude, though it stung each time.

The one he still hadn't mustered the courage to face.

Why? Why could he still not go to her? It was as if there was an invisible hand, an inaudible whisper saying *not yet.*

Or he was making up excuses. Deep down, he knew why.

While Tessa moved away, Max at her side, both chatting easily with Brayden, who would graduate from high school in a few weeks, Tyler scanned the familiar faces he loved, until he found Matt. Almost three years old, sweet little Fiona sat on her daddy's lap, hands petting Matt's dark beard. *Pudgy cheeks and little-girl grins.* Matt turned suddenly to nibble her fingers, and the adorable mini-Lauren squealed in delight.

Midplay, Matt glanced up from his daughter and met Tyler's gaze. A silent question passed between the brothers. One Tyler had yet to verbalize and one that had placed an unvoiced but much-felt breach between Matt and himself.

How was Becca? Was she happy? Did she ever ask about Ty?

Matt and Lauren had become protective of Tyler's ex-fiancée, particularly when Becca moved to the valley where their tree farm was located, opening her own small bakery near the farm shortly after little Fiona had been born. That had been no accident. Lauren had adored Becca from the first time Tyler had brought his then-girlfriend home to meet the family. Nearly three years before, while Tyler was still in rehab, what had been a week-long visit for Becca to meet baby Fiona turned into Becca's new direction in life. Becca had set her old dreams for a specialty cake shop into motion—only not in Sugar Pine, as they'd originally planned.

Beautiful life for her. He hoped it as much as he was thankful for it.

All this Tyler knew from Mom. The one time, about a year before, when Tyler had even come close to asking about the woman who still made his heart ache, Matt had leveled him with a hard look. "She's figuring it out, Ty."

That had been it, though the layers beneath that simple statement were many and hard. Honestly, Tyler was glad Becca had Matt and Lauren, and he was grateful for their protection of her. Even if it did mean shutting Tyler out about it.

Keeping her safe from all the harm he'd done.

Actions and consequences. That was the reality of life. Because while Tyler was deeply moved and appreciated the grace all these people had offered him, the reality was he'd messed up big time. He'd inflicted wounds, caused mistrust. All of that didn't simply wipe away so easily.

Even if he wished desperately that it would.

CHAPTER SEVENTEEN

(in which paths cross again)

B ECCA PULLED OUT THE cooled cake layers from the refrigerator and laid them in order on her work counter. This concoction was to be five layers—her favorite size—of butter pecan yumminess, and as she finger-checked the center of each cake for firmness, a familiar buzz of energy zipped through her. This was the part of her bakery business she loved most. While cupcakes were her best sellers, and much easier to produce, decorating a cake with a unique design summoned the artistry in her in a way nothing else matched, and she thrilled at the clean canvas she was about to make amazing.

With a sharp knife, she leveled each layer, then rechecked the thicknesses for consistency. A few years of experience had made this little section of building a cake easily navigated, but Becca could easily recall the frustration she'd hit when she'd started doing layered cakes her first year in college. Getting them level and consistent in thickness had not been as easy as the professionals made it appear. But with all things worth doing, practice made...easier.

Perfect, in this case.

Satisfied the layers were equal, Becca reached for her phone, tapped until she found her playlist, and put on a little wiggle when the big-band stylings of Harry Connick Jr. filled her kitchen. As his smooth voice sang through variations of jazz, ballads, and more big-band music, Becca slathered caramel-vanilla buttercream on one layer after another, building her newest creation into a solid, mouthwatering stack. After double-checking that the build was plumb and straight, she transferred the cake to her turntable and then smoothed icing over the final layer and around the dessert tower until it was a seamless, smooth thing of mouthwatering beauty.

Flawlessness. Careful to keep it level, she slid the cake board off her turntable and carried the hefty stack back to the cooler, sliding it in next to a boxed chocolate creation scheduled for pickup before closing. Becca blew a playful kiss toward the cake-in-progress and shut the refrigerator door.

"And that's how it's done." With a playful smack of her hands, she turned back to the single layer that remained on the counter—her insurance cake in case something had gone wrong. It hadn't, and she could use the extra layer to build something for Fiona. Well, for Matt and Lauren too.

She could turn it into cake pops. Decent sellers with the mom-of-littles crowd. But...

Becca chuckled. She'd make this one hot pink and swirl green in decorative patterns all over. Whenever Becca delivered a *surplus* to Matt and Lauren, they all knew whose smile she was really aiming for.

They loved her anyway.

A quick flick of her wrist gave her a sufficient glance at her watch. Three twenty. Gave her about ten minutes to get started, and she dug in, mixing color into a reserved tub of buttercream. Her free minutes slid by quickly, and the tinkling bell from the storefront let her know school was out—time to serve up some sweetness.

A half dozen junior high kids filtered through her front door, chatting excitedly. She knew them by name and was fairly certain what each would order. Amie would go for a fudge dream. Leah would want a peanut butter explosion. Tate was a bit of a wild card, but if she had to guess, he'd likely go for a lemon-blueberry twist. Ashlynn, Brett, and Bailey would go for the Mississippi mud.

Meeting each kid with eye contact, Becca served them with a smile. Tate threw her off—and surprisingly, so did Ashlynn—when they both opted for a cookies and cream. Becca suspected one was trying to impress the other—which seemed silly considering these were cupcakes—but they were thirteen. There was no logic in thirteen-year-olds.

A pair of high schoolers strolled through the front door next, Luke and Kerrigan, Just Eat It regulars who were apparently dating now.

"Whatever you want." Luke draped his arm around Kerrigan's shoulders and stared at her like a lovesick pup.

Becca suppressed a quiet laugh. She was ending her second year in business in Pleasant Valley, and she'd learned quick during her first season when major dances were coming up based on how the kids entered her bakery and ordered. Prom was happening in three weeks.

Becca enjoyed the simple interactions with the students fresh out of school. The thirty to forty minutes after school let out was her busiest time of the day—and those minutes put Just Eat It in the black. Matt had been right. The location of this old bread store turned Just Eat It had been perfect. But more than a financial boon, Becca liked seeing the kids, liked knowing them by name, and liked being a small part of their lives.

The rush ended, and Becca wiped down the five tables in her small dining area and then swiped her washcloth over the display case and counter. Her back was to the front door when the bell chimed again, but she smiled.

"Hey, Nathan. I'll get that lemonade in just a second." She kept her rag moving, not glancing over her shoulder. "Did you know Luke and Kerrigan were a thing now? They're in your fourth hour, right?" She rounded the counter, tossed the rag into the small sink at the back wall, and turned.

And her heart screeched to a halt.

The man who stood on the other side of her counter was familiar, but not Nathan.

"Ty..." His name was a breath barely exhaled, and she stared at the man who had, not so long ago, possessed her whole heart.

The heart that maybe wasn't working at the moment.

He held her with an unflinching gaze, those brown eyes warm and searching. Was there a smile in them? Did he hold back hurt and bitterness as he traced her face in that silent look?

"Hi, Becca."

A shiver traced down her back at the low rumble of his voice.

Needing to brace herself, Becca reached for the counter. The coolness meeting her palm lent her a sense of reality. This was her shop, the one she'd scraped together with Matt and Lauren's help as she'd rebuilt a new life. The man in front of her was...

Oh man. He was handsome. Every bit as handsome as she'd remembered in those dreams that had become less and less consistent these days—an answer to her heartbroken prayers.

Becca cleared her throat. "You surprised me. I didn't know you were in Pleasant Valley."

A touch of color brushed his cheekbones as Tyler glanced to the floor. "I know. I'm here..." He looked at her. "I'm here to help Matt. They're adding on to that little house. You knew that though, right?"

That Matt and Lauren were adding on? Yes, she'd known that. Lauren had shown her the floor plans, and together they'd perused paint samples. The new space would be their new family room, and off that, a new master bedroom. The old family room would become office space, and the old room that served as a tiny mimic of a master bedroom would become the nursery for baby Murphy number two.

"I knew there was an addition planned. I thought that Brandon was coming to work with Matt though."

Tyler's inhaled breath sounded shallow, and his shoulders tensed. "Yeah. That had been the plan, but something came up. Brandon's not available and won't be for at least three months." He looked down again. "Since the baby's due soon, I'm here instead."

"I see."

The way Tyler barely lifted his head to peek at her caused a warm ache to ooze in her heart.

"Is that okay?"

"Of course." Yikes, that came out super high pitched. Becca cleared her throat and tried again. "Of course it's okay. Matt's your brother, after all." She swallowed, commanding herself to say what she should. "It's good to see you."

His brow lifted, and something like hope flashed over his expression. Or maybe it was a question?

"How are you?" she asked.

"Clean."

Becca flinched. She hadn't meant to provoke something ugly in him. And maybe she hadn't—his voice hadn't turned hard. But his answer made her feel bad nonetheless. She nodded, not knowing what to say.

"Becca."

She found herself staring at the three remaining Mississippi mud cupcakes in the case. How long had she been avoiding eye contact? Becca forced her gaze back to him.

"It's good to see you again."

The way he looked at her...

The bell chimed, startling Becca and breaking whatever spell had held her captive in his gaze.

"Hey, pretty cupcake la—" Nathan's greeting cut short.

With a plastic smile, Becca swiveled her attention to the man she'd expected to see when Tyler had come through her door. "Hi, Nathan." Her voice sounded high again—way too perky for normal. But she turned up her smile, focused it on the guy she'd gone out with a handful of times over the past several weeks, and walked his way. "Looking for your daily lemonade fix?"

Nathan's grin faded, and he glanced in Tyler's direction before settling his look back on her. Shoving his hands into his pockets, he strolled closer.

"Among other things." Nathan leaned over the cupcake display and reached a hand to capture her cheek. Becca held him with a wide-eyed look as Nathan proceeded to plant a kiss on her temple.

He'd never done that before. They'd barely reached the kiss-her-good-night stage in this awkward-but-maybe-worth-a-try relationship that had budded between them. Or maybe it had been grafted? Heat flooded Becca's face, and she spun around to mix Nathan's lemonade, thankful she had to give both men her back to do so.

"I don't think we've met," Nathan said, his tone neutral to friendly.

"Tyler Murphy."

Becca couldn't read Ty's tone, and that made her sad. He was a stranger now. The man she had been ready to marry had become a stranger.

"Murphy?"

"Yeah. Matt's my brother. I'm guessing you know him?"

"Sure. The valley is small and pretty tight. Everyone knows everyone here—and we take care of each other."

"That's good." A subtle edge infused Tyler's tone—one Becca did know. Ty was an easygoing, likable guy. But when it came to a challenge, he wasn't one to back down. And Nathan had just dropped a challenge.

Disquiet wove through Becca, and an irritation with it. At both men. Nathan really didn't have any business acting like an alpha dog protecting his territory. They were barely dating. She was *not* his territory. And Tyler...

He'd clearly assumed that people around here knew about him. By the cold edge in his voice, he wasn't happy about it.

Which made her mad. What had happened between her and Tyler had stayed between her and Tyler. Outside of his family—and that had been a matter of necessity, a situation in which she'd told the truth but left out the details—she'd not spoken about their breakup. Not to anyone in Pleasant Valley, and certainly not to Nathan.

Lemonade ready, Becca turned and passed it to Nathan.

"Thanks."

She nodded.

"Three fifty, right?" Nathan pulled cash from his pocket and moved toward the register at the end of the counter.

"On the house today." *Please, just go...*

He held a confused look on her, maybe waiting for her to smile? Probably she should, but she wasn't feeling it and had lost the inspiration to act.

Nathan cocked his head to one side. "See you tonight?"

Becca wanted to growl, knowing what that would sound like to Tyler. And actually, it sort of was what it sounded like. She was going to the baseball game. So was most of the town, including Nathan. But he would be there as the coach—and also with the hope that Becca would stick around after the game, as she had done before, and he could take her out for pizza.

Feeling Tyler's eyes on her, Becca nodded. "Yes. I'll be at the game."

Nathan held a questioning look on her, then flicked it back toward Tyler. But he said nothing more as he left.

***

Matt had given him a heads-up about Becca seeing someone. Had said it was a recent development and Becca was proceeding with caution. That should have been enough warning for Tyler so that he'd handle this scenario better. But hearing that the love of his life had moved on, and actually witnessing it happen before his eyes, were not the same thing. If he'd thought the news had stung as it came from Matt's lips, seeing another man caress and kiss the woman Tyler had intended to marry was like being caught in a swarm of wasps.

No, he was not at all prepared for that sort of pain. *Gratitude...* Surely he'd find something here to be thankful for?

By the look of it, Becca wasn't ready for the awkwardness of having two men circling each other like pack dogs in her bakery. Her mouth pressed with concern, her brows folded inward with discomfort, and the spark in her eyes boldly proclaimed irritation. As he watched Nathan push through the door, Tyler glanced at Becca's reaction to the other man's departure and felt a touch of smugness that her annoyance wasn't solely aimed at himself.

Unless he misread Becca, Nathan was in trouble.

No, that was not the thing for which to lift up praise.

The upward tip of Tyler's mouth fell the moment Becca turned that fiery look toward him. She arched a brow and held him for a silent heartbeat before she spun around to clean up the lemonade counter.

"Matt says your lemonade is killer," he said.

"Does he?"

Yeah, Nathan wasn't the only one in trouble. "Yeah."

She mixed and poured and capped a cup and then held it out to him. "Three fifty."

She might as well have slapped him across the face. Maybe he deserved it.

His fingers closed around the cold cup, hers slipping away without contact, and he dug into his pocket for cash. His hunt produced a bill, and he passed it across the counter without looking at it. Becca swiped it up and started to count his change.

"Keep it."

With a handful of bills, she looked up at him. "This is a Ben Franklin, Tyler."

Man, he missed those expressive eyes. Mossy green, full of soft humility with a touch of spunk. He missed the way he could watch her process life through her unique gift of empathy, and the way she would warm to a challenge, never wanting fear to rule her decisions. He missed the way love would warm her gaze when she held him in it.

That wasn't what filled those green eyes in that moment. There was lingering anger. And sadness. A whole heap of sadness—and he'd put it there.

Why had he waited so long to seek her out? He knew why, and it only added to his mound of regret.

Tyler reached across the counter and closed her fingers over the money. "Keep it. It's the least I can do."

Mentally he scoffed. Ninety-six dollars and fifty cents? Pathetic. As if any amount of money could ever begin to make up for what he'd put her through.

I can't find the gift in this, Lord.

Heart heavy, Tyler moved for the door, one clear thought stamping into his mind.

Even if Becca couldn't forgive him—and he couldn't blame her for that —he'd love her until the day he died.

Was that the thing for which to give thanks?

***

"So..." Coach Nathan Gallop held on to the end of that simple word, a hanging intro to nothing good, if ever there was one.

Becca pulled in a long breath, knowing exactly where this was headed. She picked a pepperoni off her pizza slice and set it to the side—Nathan would grab it, as he had before. This time, though, she doubted he'd tease her about leaving off the best part. "So what?"

"Tyler Murphy."

"Yeah, Tyler Murphy." She scanned the ball field beyond the shade of the tree. An hour ago, the Cats had claimed their eighth victory of the season. In his third year as head coach, Nathan was making a strong charge toward the state tournament, impressing everyone in Pleasant Valley as he went.

"Obviously you know him. Could almost taste the tension between you at the bakery today. Something like bad wine—dry and super bitter."

That was an interesting description, and not something she expected from the high school gym teacher-slash-baseball-coach. "Yes. I know him. At least, I did."

"Dated him, right?"

Becca sighed. "We were engaged."

Nathan's brows shot up. "Whoa. More than I'd guessed. He ended it?"

"No."

"Hmm."

"What does that mean?"

"Just not what it looked like. He seemed a little more, uh, relaxed than you did."

Hiding under the bill of her Valley Cats ball cap, Becca set her pizza down and sipped her lemonade. Not because she was thirsty but to douse the rising heat and to swallow back the anger she felt pushing toward her mouth. "Thanks for that eval, coach. I ended things—and it's complicated."

Sort of. The series of moments that led up to her handing back his ring and walking away were crystal clear in her mind. He'd said he didn't want her, but Tyler had been out of his head. Withdrawal would do that, and she'd known it. She'd promised him she'd never give up on him. And then did. Had she done the right thing?

"Complicated, meaning none of my business?"

Exactly.

She sucked down another swallow rather than spitting that word out. Did she have any business being this touchy about Nathan's questions? After all, wasn't it natural to want to know a person's history if you were dating them?

Probably. If that relationship was serious. This one wasn't. Becca's flare of irritation died there. Maybe Nathan was hoping they'd go from causal pizzas to late-night, moonlit strolls. From saying an awkward good night with a peck on the cheek to long, sweet kisses and whispers of love. But despite what the ladies at church and her best friend had hoped, Nathan and Becca weren't gonna make it. Not when one simple encounter with Tyler Murphy caused so much unsettling to Becca's peace.

Nathan reached from his place beside her, picking up that pepperoni just as she'd guessed he would. "I see."

Misery replaced the flames she'd just battled back. "Nathan..."

"I get it, Becca. He was the one, right?"

She bit her lip, unable to look at him.

A long, super-uncomfortable moment stretched. Goodness, it was warm for April, wasn't it? Becca blew out a slow breath, hoping to find calmness.

"It's okay." Nathan nudged her arm with his elbow. "Better we get this cleared up now, right?"

She wished he'd say something not so nice. Then maybe she wouldn't feel quite so awful. "I'm sorry, Nathan."

He didn't answer. Instead he stood from the picnic table they'd been sharing, gathered his plate and napkin, and started away. He paused behind her, just long enough to lay a hand on her shoulder and give it a gentle squeeze. "Thanks for giving me a shot."

And then he walked away.

CHAPTER EIGHTEEN

(in which Tyler is a celebrity)

"JUST DO IT." MAX'S voice came as a command over the phone.

Tyler arched his back, tipping his face toward the happy blue sky. The warm sunshine on his face didn't sway his mood. "What are you, a shoe commercial?" *Yellow light, warm on my skin.* Still, a little grumpy.

"Look, you're there anyway. What will it hurt? I don't understand why this is an issue. You love speaking to students. Just do it."

The opportunity to help shape an upward perspective. This tension of annoyance should be loosening at this point. But...

Who had told Pleasant Valley High who Tyler was and that he was in town, anyway? It wasn't like he was a *real* celebrity, someone easily recognized. The climbing world was small, and he'd only become a name in it over the past year. That had been all Max and Tessa's doing—and Tyler suspected they were hoping to pass the baton, so to speak. He couldn't blame them. Tessa wanted kids. She wanted a more settled life. Max, as usual, wanted Tess to be happy. And they genuinely believed in Tyler and wanted him to excel in life.

And he was. Climbing had opened a whole new world to Tyler, and with it a fresh gust of purpose, even though he knew in his gut that particular purpose was seasonal. In the long run, he wanted to go back and work with Dad.

But for now, exhibition climbing and speaking was his calling. With the stubborn support of his new friends and of his family, and a new determination to live in gratitude every single day, Tyler had forged a new path. One that included not only climbing as a sponsored athlete, but as a speaker who often addressed the high school and college crowd. It was like the best of what was inside him got to come forward in this new life. If he hadn't had the accident that had cost him his leg, he never would have experienced this new adventure. Tyler's joy in adventure and challenge and his high-energy personality flourished in a climb. And his genuine love for those who would follow him met with great satisfaction when he spoke to young adults.

Which was likely why Max was currently confused about Tyler's unwillingness to answer a request from the Pleasant Valley FCA group about coming to address a gathering that first week in May.

"Ty? What's really going on, buddy?"

Tyler sighed, lowering himself onto a bench at the end of a row of Frasier Fir trees. He rubbed his neck and then dropped his hand to his knee. "Becca lives here." With Max, he could be raw. It was sort of expected.

Max waited, allowing Tyler the opportunity to unjumble his thoughts. No wonder it'd been a greater challenge to pull out simple, everyday blessings and return them to heaven with praise. He couldn't think straight.

He hadn't seen Becca up close and in person in a couple weeks because he made a point not to. But having her right down the road from his brother's tree farm had made not *thinking* about her impossible.

"She's dating the high school gym teacher, who is also the baseball coach." A truth he kept reminding himself about every time the longing to catch a glimpse of her smile, to hear the sound of her voice, pushed into his impulsive thoughts. "She's moved on, and I'm glad for her. I just don't want it to appear that I'm trying to...I don't know..."

"Impress her?"

"Maybe. Yeah."

"Would you being a guest speaker at FCA impress her?"

That was possible. She'd liked volunteering at the youth center with him every bit as much as he had.

Immediately Tyler's mind went to their second date. He'd taken her to a youth rec center where he'd volunteered as a sponsor. That particular day, there had been a basketball tournament, and he was a coach. Honestly, he'd taken her as sort of a test. She'd already passed the first—the one where he'd led her on a challenging hike, and she'd met it with smiles and fun. Looking back on those first couple of dates, Tyler sort of wondered if he'd been a selfish jerk, putting Becca up to these secret little challenges to see how she handled both adventure and kids. Maybe he had been— hadn't been thinking much about what she would want but rather had in view the life of never-stop adventure, along with the quiverful of kids that he'd wanted in his future. So yeah, pretty selfish. Then again, that was dating for you, wasn't it? At least the early stages?

He'd done it to other girls too. One would embrace adventure but dislike the time poured into stinky, mouthy kids. Or she'd buckle at the first switchback of that hike—freaking out because of the ledge eighteen inches away and the steepness. It had seemed a good filtering system. He wanted a girl who could match him adventure for adventure and enjoy kids at the same time.

Becca had been that girl. She was everything he'd ever wanted, and that hadn't changed. And secretly, yeah, he hoped in his selfish heart that Becca would be impressed with him if he spoke to that FCA group.

And that was the issue. When it came to Becca Colson, he couldn't trust himself, because he'd proven to be selfish. Not just once.

"She's settled here, you know? Max, I really blew it with her, and I don't want to interfere with what she has going now."

"How do you know you'd be messing with anything?" Max's voice took on the elder tone, the one that had a way of setting Tyler straight when he needed it. "Look, if she's really settled and happy, she'll stay that way. You showing up to encourage some high school kids shouldn't be a tidal wave to a stable life."

Yeah, but what if it was?

"And if it is..."

Sheesh, it was like Max had been through this stuff before. How did he possess the wisdom he had?

"Then her life isn't as stable as you think. Maybe it needs shaking up."

"What does that mean?"

"It means if seeing you is an undoing to her, then there are things not finished between you. That's not good for either of you."

Tyler leaned back against the bench. He couldn't think of a rebuttal, but he still didn't want to agree to this opportunity.

"Maybe you're the one being shaken up?"

And that right there... Max was, as usual, on point.

"I saw her the other day. Face to face."

"And?"

"And it shook me."

"Ah. Is this a challenge to be met or one you truly do need to walk away from?"

"I don't know for sure."

"I get it." Max cleared his throat. "In that case, I really can't tell you what to do. But I think that you should pray about it. Tessa and I will pray with you."

That was how Tyler had become certain God had sent Max and Tessa to him by design. For all of the things there were to admire about them—and that was a long list—they lived and loved by faith. Over the past eighteen months of reinventing his life with them as his guides, their commitment to live fully and joyfully before God was the single characteristic Tyler had come to admire most about them.

It was what he wanted more than anything to rebuild into his own life.

***

Becca stuck to the back wall, in the shadows, hoping not to be noticed. She wondered why she had come to the event at all, but only for half a second. She'd come to see Ty speak. Or just to see him.

Every day for the past couple of weeks, she'd become a bundle of jittery nerves and hopes that she couldn't quite bat down every time she'd heard the bell above her bakery door ring. Would he be the one entering her store?

It was telling how much she hoped for it. Equally telling, the fact that he hadn't darkened her door since he'd left her a ninety-six-dollar tip.

She had no hopeful reason to be there tonight, except to catch a glimpse at who he had become. As she watched the man up on stage finish his demonstration of the different types of prosthetic legs he used, the pinch in her heart tightened. And then he switched topics. He replaced his "everyday leg" and walked back to the table and stool at center stage.

"Some things need to be part of our everyday routine. I'd like to share with you what my can't live withouts are." He patted his leg and then lifted a Bible from the table. "I can't do life without these. But I had to go through some hard things before I understood this." He laid the Bible back down.

"There's a verse in Proverbs that says, 'Though the righteous fall seven times, they rise again, but the wicked stumble when calamity strikes.' I've spent the last eighteen months carrying that here." Tyler patted his chest as he scanned the gathering of kids, carefully making eye contact as he captivated his audience.

Becca sat spellbound. He stood up there among several different prosthetic legs, five blown-up images of him climbing—three of them without a prothesis at all. Who Tyler had become really wasn't that different from whom he'd been before his accident. That was the man she'd known—full of life and energy and an unquenchable love for a good challenge.

And yet the Tyler who addressed this gathering of near a hundred students was...more. He was settled, even with his high energy. Self-possessed, yet humble.

"I've had to study the words," Tyler continued, "trying to understand the meaning, the big idea. Why would a righteous man stumble seven times, you know? Seems like that would disqualify him from the title *righteous*. And what about that wicked one? What sort of calamity are we talking about with that guy?"

Tyler switched the mic to his right hand, snagged the stool, and rubbed the thigh of his residual leg. Becca knew that move—he did it when he was sore. Did he still suffer from pain?

That provoked a quiet alarm. Pain led to painkillers...

"I came to a desperate place where I needed to *know* who this godly man was who would get back up. Because, friends, I was knocked down hard. You're sitting there seeing me stand in front of these blown-up images of climbs I've done and hearing how I was able to learn how to do them even without my leg. But I left some things out. Parts of my story that are dark and hard. Parts that even now, I don't love to talk about.

"See, the thing is, right after my accident, I fell. I fell hard, but I didn't want anyone to know. The life I had going for me before I lost my leg had been good. I'd actually say it had been perfect. I was engaged to this beautiful woman who loved me, and we had a plan for our future. I was one year from graduating college and moving on to what I really wanted to do. I had life planned out and under control." Tyler slid his hand down and detached his leg. "And then this happened. I didn't want to deal with it. It may not make sense, but I wanted to pretend that it had never happened, and in doing so, I took shortcuts on my PT, which caused damage to what I had left of my leg. I didn't allow for my mind and body to heal and get past the bizarre phantom pain that plagued me and sent me searching for easy solutions. Know where I found them?"

He propped his leg next to the stool and reached into his pocket.

Becca held her breath as Tyler withdrew a prescription bottle.

"I thought these were the solution. Easy fix—take a pill, keep on going. If you want to know the truth, I was addicted long before I realized it, and by the time I was willing to confront all the things that had me facedown in the mud, I'd lost everything. I'd turned into an unkind liar and a thief. Honestly, I should have ended up in prison.

"The trust of close friends and family—I destroyed them. My hopes for the future I had planned—gone. And my fiancée—" Tyler's voice caught, and he lifted his gaze until it landed on her. Could he see her, out there in the cloak of shadows at the back of the room? "I pushed her out of my life." He paused, swallowing, and looked down at his prosthetic leg. Slowly, using the stool to brace himself, Tyler moved from the chair and lowered onto the floor.

"The godly man will fall, but he will get back up. There is nothing more demoralizing than realizing that your life is out of control. That you are flat on your face and can't get back up. Guys, I needed desperately to know what qualified as a godly man, because I wanted with everything in me to get back up. And I couldn't do it—not in my own resolve or strength. The harder I had fought to keep the perfect life I had, the deeper into the mud I sank. The more I lost. So I needed answers, you know?" He scanned the room, his personal desperation palpable to everyone.

"I met some new people at the end of my stint in rehab—yeah. Rehab. As in drug rehab, because I became a statistic. Side note—do you know that close to thirty percent of people who have been prescribed opioids misuse them? That means if I have ten of you stand up here, only seven of you get to sit back down without having to pass through the exceedingly difficult process of breaking free from addiction. Three of you get to do rehab—if you're lucky enough to have people intervene to get you there. If not? Well, there's a high probability that you'll graduate to heroin. Awesome, right? Okay, back on the main road again: rehab. That's where I'd landed. And even then, it took me *months* to really recognize how deep in I was.

"Eventually, my eyes opened. As I shared with these new people in my life about how hopeless I felt, we talked about that verse in Proverbs, and I asked the question that had been plaguing me. Who is that godly man who gets back up? My friend Tessa—you saw her climbing with me in that boulder video—showed me Romans 1:17. It says that *the* righteous will live by faith. The godly man will live by faith.

"Faith, guys. Not just any kind of faith—like *I believe in myself, so I have faith I'll get through this.* Nah. That sort of thing had already failed me big time. When the Bible talks about faith, it's talking about faith that saves—faith in God that He'll save us. Buy us back from our sin. That's called redemption.

"So maybe that verse in Proverbs could read that 'the redeemed man may trip seven times, but he'll get back up.'" Tyler set the mic on the floor next to him, reached for the leg he'd set aside, and reattached it. Then with the mic in hand again, he pushed up to stand. It was such a normal, everyday thing, but a wave of applause crashed through the room.

With the spotlight on him, Tyler's chin fell toward his chest, and Becca could see a small tremble roll through his shoulders. After a long moment, he brushed the corner of one eye and looked back up. "Guys, here's what I want you to remember from tonight—not that I lost my leg or that I ended up addicted to painkillers. I don't care if you remember that I learned how to climb without one of my legs. You don't even have to remember that video I showed you of me trying, and falling time after time when I first attempted a basic-level rock-wall ascent."

He stepped to the edge of the stage. "Take one thing away from meeting me tonight: The power that raised Jesus from the dead and declared our sin paid in full is the same power that can lift a redeemed man up after he falls. That promise is not just for me, not just for the opioid addicts out there, not just for those who have nothing but desperation left. The power of Christ in me is what lifts me back up, wipes the mud off my face, and whispers, 'My son, walk on.'" Tyler moved back to the small table next to the stool, lifted his Bible, and opened it. "In Second Corinthians, Paul wrote about his own weakness—something that caused him suffering, something that he'd asked God to take away. God said no. Here's how Paul handled that. He writes, 'And He has said to me, *My grace is sufficient for you, for my power is perfected in weakness.* Most gladly, therefore, I will rather boast about my weaknesses, so that the power of Christ may dwell in me. God's grace is sufficient for me, and His power moves into my weakest places. I promise you, guys, no matter what you face, what you go through, His grace will be sufficient for you too."

Becca felt a single tear run down the side of her nose. Her mind settled on a verse from one of her battle cards, Psalm 32:1–2:

Blessed is the one
whose transgressions are forgiven,
whose sins are covered.
Blessed is the one
whose sin the Lord does not count against them
and in whose spirit is no deceit.

Tyler stood as testimony to that psalm, a redeemed man held safely in the hands of God's grace. Such a thing to behold.

Quietly, Tyler closed the evening in a prayer that resonated with heartfelt sincerity for every person in that room as he echoed the prayer Paul had penned for the believers in Ephesus, that each one would be "rooted and established in love," that they would "have power, together with all the Lord's holy people, to grasp how wide and long and high and deep is the love of Christ," and that they would "know this love that surpasses knowledge"—that each would be filled to the measure of all the fullness of God.

Becca felt her heart near to bursting with a range of emotions. There was so much joy in her, so much thanksgiving as she saw the work of God in the man who had been drenched with anger, saturated by bitterness. She knew perfect amazement as she beheld this miracle who was Tyler Murphy.

And she knew deep, aching sorrow—like the grief of losing him all over again.

Tyler had become a stable, godly man. He had indeed been lifted back up, set on his feet to walk on into a new and unexpected life.

Without her.

CHAPTER NINETEEN

(in which Fiona loves cupcakes)

S HE'D COME TO HEAR him speak.

He'd caught sight of her when she'd slipped in late and nestled against the wall at the back of the room. That had been days before, and he hadn't seen her since.

Instability rocked Tyler to his core as he thought about that for the hundredth time.

She came... Could he list that as a gift for which to offer praise? Should he? *Give thanks in all things...* Even the hard ones. The ones that shook his peace. The ones he longed for and yet was fearful of?

With his forearm, Tyler rubbed his brow and then reached for his level. Though on solid ground, he really needed to discipline his thoughts. Construction was an endeavor riddled with possible mistakes—some that could be catastrophic. To build or body.

He glanced down to his cargo shorts and caught sight of his everyday leg. Yeah, some mistakes could literally change life as he knew it. Mistakes that could have been avoided by just paying attention.

But I've become a better man without my leg. Mistakes made grace. All glory to God.

Still, his spirit rode waves that rocked.

He pulled in a deep breath—one full of cool mountain air, the crispness of the creek that ran nearby, and the deep fragrance of fir trees. He shut his eyes and trained his mind away from Becca Colson, aiming instead for the One who made all moments a gift.

Lord, You have been our dwelling place throughout all generations. Before the mountains were born or You brought forth the earth and the world, from everlasting to everlasting You are God. He transferred the recitation from Psalm 90 to prayer. *Lord, You have seen me through the pit of despair. Before I destroyed my life and You rebuilt it, You are God. Help me to entrust my heart to You.*

And then... *This moment, this day, is a gift. I'll take it.*

His grip on the level tightened, and he waited. A breeze rustled through the valley, and across the creek a bird trilled. The shaking of Tyler's universe calmed, replaced by the familiar and needed grounding he found in God's Word and in prayer. In thanksgiving. Opening his eyes, he stepped back and examined the work that had been done.

He and Matt had finished the framing for the addition. Matt needed to help Lauren with something out in the tree rows that morning, leaving Tyler to double-check for soundness—that everything was squared, leveled, and plumb, and nothing had settled off since they'd finished framing. Then they would begin drying-in the new rooms. If Tyler would stop letting his mind drift, he could get a jump start on laying out the sheeting and determining which pieces they'd need to cut.

Right. He pressed the level in his hand against the doorframe and paused long enough for the bulb to settle. So far, dead on. He moved toward the corner on his left, and from there continued his way around the room, checking every eight feet.

"Unca Ty?"

Tyler kept the level on spot and turned his head to catch sight of little Fiona skipping into the construction. *This cherub face.*

"Hey, sprout. Whatcha up to?"

She came straight to him and wrapped her arms around his prosthetic, clearly not caring one bit if it was his real leg or not. "Daddy say to me make sure you not working too hard."

"He said that, did he?"

Fiona tipped her angelic little face up with a smile that could melt an iceberg. "He say it."

Ty slipped his tape measure onto his belt and leaned the level next to a stud before he bent to lift his nearly three-year-old niece. Once settled in his arms, she framed his face in her pudgy hands and squeezed his cheeks. He sucked them in to make fish lips and smothered her chubby cheeks with kisses.

"Unca Ty, you whiskers tickle me like Daddy's!"

High-pitched laughter. Her squeal of delight provoked his chuckle, and he leaned back to look at her delight. "Well, my Fi-Fi girl. If I'm not supposed to work too hard, what do you think we should do instead?"

Fiona wrinkled her nose and twisted her mouth, as if in serious thought. And then...oh, that smile. This little girl could gain a kingdom with a grin like that.

"Know what I like?"

"I can't guess."

She leaned in, brushing her nose to his. "I like cupcakes!"

Tyler shook with laughter. "It's ten in the morning, kid."

"Becca say anytime is a good time for cupcakes."

At the mere mention of her name, Tyler's heart went into a mild skid. "That sounds like something Becca would say."

Fiona's brow scrunched in confused surprise. "You know my Becca?"

She once was mine, kid. Tyler swallowed. "Yes. I know Becca."

Arms flailed out, Fiona leaned back, entirely certain Ty would keep hold of her. Which he did. She came back up right. "She my best friend."

He tried not to be jealous. "That's a good match, Fi."

"Know what else?" Fiona's pencil eyebrows bounced with mischief, giving Tyler the distinct impression he had been set up in grand Fiona fashion.

"What's that?"

"Becca make *gooooood* cupcakes!"

Despite the tender spot of ache in his chest, he chuckled. Yep. Fiona had set him up perfectly for the win. He lowered her to the ground. "Let me call your mom and make sure it's okay."

With a flash of baby teeth pointed at him, Fiona twirled, making her pink-and-green-striped sundress fan out like she was a flower.

"Ty." Lauren's voice filled his phone. "Is Fi being a pest? I told Matt he shouldn't—"

"My little Fi-Fi? Never. However, she's spun a plan that likely needs your approval."

"Of course she has," Lauren said dryly, clearly neither surprised nor irritated. Fiona possessed all of Matt's charming personality, along with Lauren's take-it-as-it-comes tendency. The blessed child. "Let's hear it."

"She likes cupcakes, I'm told. I'm also told that Becca is her best friend, and Becca also makes *goooood* cupcakes."

A pause rested on the line, pinching Tyler with a touch of apprehension. If it hadn't been for Lauren's uncharacteristic frown when she'd found out that Tyler had visited Becca's shop his first week in town, Ty would have supposed her distinct hesitation was about the fact that cupcakes were not breakfast food.

But that was not the case.

"Umm..."

"I can tell her no." Tyler knew there was no disguising the disappointment in his voice—it sounded exactly like Fiona's slumped little body looked the moment the little girl heard him.

"No. I mean, there's no reason..."

"Lauren?" Tyler turned and paced several feet away from Fiona, lowering his voice.

"Yeah, Ty?"

"I won't do anything to hurt your friendship. I promise."

"Becca's my best friend. You don't have the power to damage that, my brawny brother-in-law." Lauren's return to an upbeat tone, as well as her gusto commonly used on all her brothers by marriage, set him at ease again. For a second. And then her voice became heavy and full of warning again.

"Here's the thing though, if you want the blunt truth of it. If you hurt her again, you and I might not be okay."

Whew. That was serving it up real. But he got it, and he respected it. *Becca has someone.* "Understood, Lauren. Just cupcakes for my niece."

"Cupcake. Singular, Ty." Her smiley voice returned.

"Got it."

"Tyler?"

"Yeah?"

"Thanks. For indulging Fiona."

He laughed. "Hanging out with my niece is no trouble at all." Having an excuse to see Becca again? Much as it should not be, that was icing on the proverbial cupcake. And he was thankful for it, even as the waves rolled on.

***

Becca pulled the pan of cookies and cream cupcakes out of the oven and slid it onto the counter to cool. The Mississippi muds were in the cooler and should be about ready to come out for frosting. The batch of red velvets would go in next...

The bell out front drew her away from her process. While her storefront was open from nine to five, it was a little out of the ordinary to have someone stop in at ten. Mornings tended not to be prime time for cupcakes, giving her space to bake up fresh batches for the afternoon. But sometimes there were special orders or the wild-hair cravings...

Becca pushed through the door between her kitchen and the storefront and halted.

...Or there was Tyler Murphy. That happened...never. Well, once before, but not at 10:00 a.m. and several weeks back. She'd all but given up hope.

Her heart leapt in a wild kick that had her pulling in a sharp breath. "Ty..."

Brown eyes held on her, his look warm, deep, and...

Stop it. She was not some swoony female who got lost in a man's stare. Even if it was Tyler Murphy's. Not anymore. Luckily, the little girl holding Ty's hand, who had been unnoticed by Becca until she commanded herself to behave like a grown-up woman, skipped forward, tugging the man with her.

"Hi, my Becca!"

"Fiona!" As she rounded the counter and moved into the dining area, Becca trained all her energy and attention on the Murphy in the room who did *not* make her head spin. "Whatcha doing, flower face?"

Fiona framed her chubby cheeks with wiggly fingers, pretending to be a sunflower, as Becca had shown her last fall. "Nana say I a good sunflower."

"I bet she loves that."

"Yep! Nana loves flowers, Becca!" Fiona hopped into a chair at the table where Becca stood and then grinned wide enough to show off all her baby teeth. "Know what I love?"

"Puppies?" Becca answered.

"Oooh!" she squealed. "Puppies!"

"Nice." Tyler's deep voice sent a thrill down Becca's spine even before she looked up at his laughing eyes. "Lauren's already not impressed with me for taking her to get cupcakes for a late breakfast."

The lilt of joy in his voice made her think of sunny afternoons. Of easy, happy times spent laughing, talking, or just being together. For some reason, those memories didn't sting in that moment the way they had in recent days. Becca pulled out a chair and slid onto it, grinning up at him. "Better you in trouble than me."

"From what I gather, I don't think it's possible for you to be in trouble. I'm guessing that has to do with a steady stream of cupcakes. Payoff." Tyler lifted Fiona up, tossed her playfully in the air—making her squeal and giggle—caught her, and lowered onto the chair with his niece on his lap. Nary a sign of any hitch in his leg.

Healed. Restored. Could she doubt it still, even after hearing him speak?

Becca filed the thoughts to examine them later. "Gathering intel, are we?"

He lifted his brows and gave her a *wouldn't you like to know* look.

Was he flirting with her? Oh goodness, but she wanted that to be Tyler flirting with her. *Grown. Up. Remember?* Yes, exactly. She was no longer the starry-eyed college girl who thought Tyler Murphy could do no wrong and their future together would be charmed. He'd proven he absolutely could do wrong—and they didn't have a future together anymore.

His life had changed so much.

And there was the sting that had been absent moments before. Becca knew her smile faded, and she did little to mask that. Instead, she refocused on Fiona. "What brings my little flower face to the bakery today?"

"Cupcakes!"

"Of course. Pink?"

"Eeee!" Fiona squeezed her hands together and shook with joy.

Becca moved opened her front cooler to retrieve Fiona's favorite strawberry-slam cupcake. "I dipped strawberries in green candy coat this morning because I was thinking of you, little girl."

"I love green! Green and pink are the bestest ones!"

A Fiona fact Becca already knew. The girl loved flowers, ladybugs, swings, and cookies too. All favorites.

"Know what else?" Fiona asked.

Becca plated Fiona's snack and then plated a half dozen chocolate-dipped strawberries as well. "What else what?"

"What else is the bestest, silly."

"Oh. Of course. What else?"

"Unca Ty aannnndddd..." She held that out for an unbelievable length. Then finished her thought with a finger pointed straight at Becca. "...*you!*"

A wave of warmth filled her face as she sat back down, catching Tyler's gaze. She smiled in spite of it, raising an eyebrow. "You've made the list,

Unca Ty."

"I've always been on the list, right, Fi?"

Fiona was too busy stuffing strawberry-slam cupcake into her mouth to answer that. In the absence of little-girl chatter, the bakery fell into a quiet that Becca couldn't define. Not awkward really. But not settled either.

"The strawberries are for you, if you want them," she said.

"Thanks." Tyler pinched one between his meaty fingers, as she suspected he would. Tyler had never met a treat he'd turned down.

"I didn't think to ask you. Do want a cupcake too?"

Tyler leaned to look at his niece. "Think I should try one, sprout?"

"Mmm-hmm!" She poked a finger into her mouth to lick the frosting.

"Strawberry-slam, caramel apple, or lemon dream?" Glad to have something to do again, Becca named the selection she'd prepared the night before while she walked back to the cooler.

"Tough choices…"

"I'll bring all three." Might as well. She'd plated one of each while she'd finished naming them.

"That's not—"

Too late—she already delivered the bounty to the table. "Don't tell me you can't put them down, Murphy. I know better."

He held her gaze for a lingering moment, a smile shared between them in the beat of silence. Fiona licked her little fingers, making a smacking noise as she went, and then hopped off Tyler's lap and headed for the short easel chalkboard Becca kept in the corner for her smaller customers. More specifically, for her little buddy named Fiona Murphy. Leaning her chin in her hand and her elbow on her table, Becca watched the girl wander away. Untamed wheat-colored curls bounced carelessly as Fiona moved, and a smile seemed to emanate from her little frame.

"You came the other night." Tyler's quiet interruption nearly caused Becca to startle.

She brought her gaze back to him. "To hear you speak? Yes. I was there. You did well. I—" She slipped her hands to her lap and fixated on the pair of cupcakes and two strawberries left on the plates. "I was proud of you. I am proud of you, I mean." Forcing herself to look at him, she found his expression solemn. "You found your way out, Ty. I'm proud of you for it."

He didn't flinch or fidget. "I didn't do it alone."

That sting grew into a mighty, throbbing pain. No, he hadn't done it alone—he'd been clear about that the other night in his presentation. But he'd done it without her.

A flame consumed her face, and she swallowed against the building lump in her throat. A nod was all she could muster.

"Unca Ty! Lookie!"

Saved by the innocent charm of a child. Becca turned to see what Fiona wanted to show Ty. A rainbow, jagged and thin but still recognizable.

"Beautiful, Fi."

Fiona grinned her triumphant smile, set her fistful of chalks back into the bucket of colors, and dusted her hands on her dress. "Time to find Daddy again!" She punched her fist onto her little hips.

"Right." Tyler snagged a napkin from the table and dusted first his fingers and then his mouth with it.

Becca retrieved a small to-go box from beneath her cash register. Tyler followed her, both plates in hand.

"I really don't need all this," he said.

"If you don't take it, I'll have to throw it away. It's been served."

"Can't have that." He slid the plate toward her, and she boxed up the remaining cupcake and strawberries. "How much?"

She snorted. "You overpaid by ninety-six dollars last time. I think I still owe you."

He took the box from her, but his hand covered hers more than the carrier. And squeezed. Becca felt his stare long before she looked up to see it pinned on her.

He leaned and then spoke low. "You don't owe me anything, Becca."

Heaven help her, as he walked out that door with Fiona's hand in his, Becca's heart went right along with him.

CHAPTER TWENTY

(in which brothers have a talk)

"S O..." MATT DRAGGED OUT that loaded intro and then grunted as he hefted a sheet of plywood into place.

Tyler knew what was coming. A big-brother speech. He'd had plenty of them in his life, being Murphy boy number five. Usually the big brother talks came from Connor, but Matt ran a close second. Come to think of it, though, he'd had a few little-brother talks from Brandon too. Those had been not so fun, even if they'd been necessary.

And things were so much better now, with Brandon and him.

Brothers. The kind who stick close and don't give up. With the nail gun, he tacked the plywood into place, telling himself to lower the wall of self-defense he felt rising. "So what?"

Matt stepped back after the sheet was secure, looked over the nearly enclosed frame, and then over his shoulder—his glance directed toward Becca's shop across and down the road from the tree farm. Brows slightly peaked, Matt's attention found Tyler again. "So cupcakes for breakfast?"

Tyler chuckled, pretending it wasn't a nervous, self-conscious sound. "Surely Fiona had breakfast before ten, right? The girl gets up early."

"Huh." Matt kept his raised brow look on Ty.

Shrugging, Tyler continued nailing in the rest of the sheeting they'd tacked into place. "Second breakfast, then. I asked Lauren."

"Yeah, she brought it up."

Tyler lowered the nailer and turned back to Matt. "Let's stop doing this dance, eh? If you want to say something to me, then just say it."

"Give me some slack here, little brother. Right now I'm caught between the wife I adore and my little brother, who I also kind of like."

Adjusting his ball cap, Tyler enjoyed a moment of cool mountain breeze against his sweaty scalp. "I get it, Matt. And I wasn't—"

"The thing is, Ty, Becca was pretty torn up after—"

"I know. I said I get it, and I really do." He wondered if his plunge into self-destruction was going to stain him forever. In some things—such as the girl he'd loved wildly—that answer was yes. Likely, who he'd become as an opioid addict was going to leave it's mark forever. And that hurt. "I promised Lauren that I wouldn't do anything to hurt her."

"See, this is what has Lauren worried. Maybe too much. I mean, she is nearly nine months pregnant, and everything seems bigger than maybe it is. But she might have a point."

"What point? I haven't done anything."

"Maybe the problem?"

"What?" Tyler's lingering shame twisted into frustration. He dug deep to see the gift. *People who look out for Becca.* "You guys aren't making any sense."

"She was dating a guy from church we kind of set her up with. A teacher."

"I know. The baseball coach. I met him. And I won't interfere. I promise."

"*Was*, Ty."

Tyler felt the weight of his brother's meaningful look. "Was?"

Matt lowered onto the raw-wood step that would lead to the sliding door off the new master suite. "She and Nathan broke up."

"I swear, Matt. I didn't do anything." Tyler tried to punch down the involuntary bubble of glee that swelled in him. This shouldn't make his list. Instead of that effort being successful, his mind went straight for *she's available!*

Matt cocked an eyebrow. "The same day you waltzed into her bakery."

Tyler looked away—happened to be right toward that cute little bakery. A sudden urge to break into a run, his path set on that direction, and burst into Just Eat It took on nearly undefeatable strength.

"Tyler."

That sound—Matt's authoritative, commanding, big-brother inflection —flared a hot flash of annoyance. "I didn't do anything, Matt. I went to see her because I figured if I was going to be here on this project for a while, we'd bump into each other at some point, small town that this is. I didn't want it to be random, and I didn't want it to look like I was hiding from her. I certainly didn't think that I was going to walk back into her life and suddenly we'd pick up where everything went wrong."

He hadn't. Had he?

Hmmm.

Maybe he might have entertained that fantasy a few times. Even going so far as digging that ring box out of the old shoebox of stuff he'd packed when he'd been released from Seaside. The diamond had still been securely tucked into the black velvet. Still sparkled in the light. But just as quickly as he'd found it, he'd closed the lid and put it back into that shoebox he kept in a closet at Mom and Dad's.

It was still there. Out of sight. Out of reach. He understood reality, even if he wished with all of his heart he could change it. "What am I supposed to do here, Matt? Fiona adores Becca, and she loves cupcakes. Lauren and Becca are close friends. Did you expect me to hole up and pretend I'm not here? That *she's* not here?"

Rubbing his neck, Matt sighed. "No. And I think Lauren knew that you and Becca would meet again."

"I didn't think Lauren hated me." It was hard not to allow resentment to settle as the feeling of being small and exposed scraped through him.

"She doesn't. In fact, Lauren likes you. And I think that if things worked out between you and Becca, she'd be thrilled—for both your sakes. It's just this murky middle part where she can't predict the outcome that has her a little wound up." He pressed both hands to his thighs and then stood. "She loves her friend, and she witnessed Becca go through a pretty rough patch. That's all this is." With one hand he squeezed Tyler's shoulders. "Don't hold it against her, okay?"

Tyler was fairly certain it would be impossible to hold anything against his sister-in-law for long. Lauren was a good-humored person, a woman who loved God and loved every part of the rambunctious and enormous Murphy family, and a woman who occasionally forgot that she couldn't schedule everything according to a precise plan. Everyone had their faults.

Nodding, Ty looked back up at Matt. "You know I won't. I hope you also know that the last thing on this planet that I would want to do is hurt Becca more than I already have. I still care about her." So, so much. At the thought, a deep ache spread through his chest. Cared wasn't quite the right word.

"I know. And Lauren knows." Matt cleared his throat. "My wife suspects strongly that Becca still very much cares about you. Part of the reason she's concerned. Nathan was the first guy Becca's even sort of dated since...well, you know. And even that, if I'm being honest, was a stretch."

Love is a gift. But he'd broken it. Did God want that too? What would He do with broken love? Tyler glanced down at his leg. "They weren't serious then?"

Matt snorted. "No. Not even in the same neighborhood as serious."

Hope kept on rising. Fast. The image of that diamond ring made an intrusive and uninvited appearance in his mind.

Easy, Tarzan. Don't prove all of Lauren's worries true.

Oh man though. Becca was right there. Just right down the road. Still kind. Still laughing easily. Still being all brave, going after her dreams. Still beautiful. Still single.

And still in possession of his heart.

CHAPTER TWENTY-ONE

(in which Fiona makes a cake)

LAUREN HADN'T BEEN FEELING the best the past few days. Several days in a row, Becca had seen her friend's tired eyes and slow waddle when they met in the early mornings for coffee to read over battle cards and pray, and concern had been gnawing at her. Baby Murphy number two wasn't due for four more weeks, and the local hospital wasn't equipped for preemie babies. When Becca expressed her concern for that yesterday, Lauren had waved her off.

"A few weeks isn't that much premature. Besides, I'm not in labor. No need to worry, Becs."

Even so, Becca formed a quick plan, hoping to help her friend. "How about Fi spends tomorrow morning with me?"

Lauren laughed. "Don't you have cupcakes to make and a business to run?"

"Sure, but I can make my batches tonight." Becca's mind set on the idea. "I'll just work late. And then Fiona can hang out with me. We can decorate a mini-cake together. She'll love it."

Eyeing her with doubt, Lauren didn't answer right away.

Becca was not going to take no for an answer. "It's settled. I'll pick up Fi at eight. I'll text Matt so he knows. You sleep in."

"Matt can watch her..."

"Matt and Tyler are plowing hard and fast on that addition. It'd be a shame to set them back now. At the pace they're going, it'll be done next week, and you'll be able to bring this baby home to a house not under construction. That was the goal, right?"

With just a bit more persuading, Lauren agreed, and gratefully so, although she insisted Matt could bring Fiona to Becca's shop. She'd left the bakery as the sun came up with a hug for Becca and a thank-you that seemed heavily laced with relief.

Becca had missed their daily morning coffee, but as she waited for Matt to drop off his daughter, she squeezed her hands and tucked them under her chin with a buzz of anticipation. She might have had a slightly selfish angle on her offer. Unca Ty had quickly gained Fiona's adoration, and Becca was not about to be supplanted just because the man had whiskers Fiona loved to pat and could toss the girl into the air, making her squeal with sheer delight. No way was Tyler pushing ahead of Becca's place—after all, Becca had cupcakes. Fiona loooved cupcakes.

Rolling her eyes and shaking her head, Becca laughed. She wasn't really engaging in a charm-the-kid competition with Tyler. But she sure was looking forward to making a sweet frosting mess with her favorite little girl.

And...well, maybe secretly hoping Tyler would find his way to the bakery to pick up his niece.

Fanciful. That was what that was. And ridiculous. Why would she think he would do that? Matt was there and completely capable. And actually, much more likely, Lauren would come find them, because the woman wasn't much of a be-still sort of girl. Even so, Becca had to admit that small hope of seeing Tyler again. He'd kept away over the past several days, ever since he and Fiona had come for cupcake breakfast. His withdrawal had bothered her. Could it even be called withdrawal? He hadn't shown up in Pleasant Valley looking for her in the first place, had he?

He hadn't come looking for her at all in the three years since she'd given him back his ring. That should be a loud and clear message to her: he's moved on.

Deflated, Becca's shoulders sagged, and she sighed. But then a knock rapped softly on the back door to her kitchen, and she recovered. Today was about having fun with Fiona, and she fully intended to do exactly that.

Matt smiled at her as he passed his daughter from his arms to Becca's. "Thanks for this. Lauren would never admit it, but she really could use a break."

Aha. Becca had been right. "I'm glad to. Haven't seen as much of my little flower face since Unca Ty came and stole the show." She winked and then kissed Fiona's soft hair. She smelled of baby soap and warm sleep, and Becca pressed her cheek against her curls.

Matt studied Becca for a moment, something curious about his look. But then he smiled, ran a large hand over his daughter's hair, and passed a bag that he'd hung over his shoulder to Becca. "I'm just down the road if you need anything."

"We won't, will we, flower face?"

Thumb in her mouth, Fiona looked up at Becca and shook her head and then rested against Becca's shoulder again.

"Thanks, Bec." Matt squeezed her shoulder and left.

Becca set the bag on the floor beneath her coat hooks and carried Fiona across the room toward her small office space set up in the corner. She lowered onto her desk chair and resettled her little charge comfortably on her lap. Fiona was content to snuggle, her thumb tucked securely in her mouth. Lauren had told Becca that she worried about that—Fi's thumb-sucking. Said she shouldn't have allowed it in the first place, but at this point, she was too tired to fight the habit. *Maybe after the baby comes*, Lauren had said.

Becca closed her eyes and rested her cheek on top of Fiona's head, breathing in that lovely scent of sweet little girl. Thumb-sucking seemed such a small worry as she held her. These things would pass, and Fiona was a healthy, happy, well-cared-for child.

Unexpected emotion swelled through Becca as she savored this unusual moment. Tyler had wanted a big family. He loved kids and had loved growing up with so many siblings. By now, if they had stayed together, they would have been married for nearly three years. Would they have had their own little Murphy to hold and cherish and to worry over trivial things?

A swell of loss and regret pushed through her, and Becca swallowed back a sudden cry.

"Becca?" Fi spoke around her thumb.

"Yes, sweet girl?"

"You my best friend."

Now she might not be able to stop the tears—but oh! How sweet this moment was. "I love that, Fi."

The girl sat up, forcing Becca to lean back, and then slipping her thumb from her mouth, she smiled. "Unca Ty my best friend too."

And why wouldn't he be? Unca Ty was all fun and laughter and energy and excitement. Becca had loved him too.

Had. Did?

She ignored that and leaned to brush her nose over Fi's. "You have good taste."

Fiona beamed with delight. "And I like cake."

That earned her a full belly laugh. "This I know, kiddo. This I know. But we're not having that for breakfast today. I leave that bit with Unca Ty. You and I are having scrambled eggs and orange juice, and then we have work to do."

"Work? I gotta go to work?"

Becca winked. "You know it, sister. You're helping me decorate a cake!"

"Eeeee!" Fiona clapped her hands and then wiggled her way to the floor. "Let's do it!"

Snuggle time was over, then. No matter. The day was shaping up to be all sorts of wonderful. Becca wanted to clap and squeal too.

***

When the phone in his shirt pocket vibrated, Tyler paused from punching finishing nails into trim. The air compressor hissed as he lay the trim gun down, and he guessed it would be about a minute before the motor would kick in to rebuild pressure.

With practiced moves, he turned from his backside and made it to a standing position. The everyday leg gave him the ability to work on his knees, but he found doing so for too long was hard on his thigh, so for this job, he'd taken a seat on the floor. Worked just as well.

As his cell vibrated again, he stepped toward the door that would lead him outside. Fresh air would be a good break anyway. Moving with a slight limp because the past few days of working furiously had provoked a small ache in his thigh and in his lower back. *But work!* He could still do the work. On the heels of that noted gift, Tyler sent a prayer heavenward.

Please protect Lauren and the baby. Give her doctor wisdom to know what to do...

Matt had taken Lauren to see her doctor a little more than an hour before, an unscheduled visit. While the plan had been for Lauren to rest throughout the morning—at Becca's insisting, and bless her for that—Lauren came out to find Matt at about 8:30. Something just didn't feel right. She was sure it was just Braxton Hicks, but maybe...

That *but maybe* turned into *let's go* when Lauren went wide eyed and said she thought her water broke. Matt didn't waste a moment, and Tyler couldn't imagine how his brother must have felt. For his own part, his pulse had raced recklessly.

A breath of mountain-fresh air filled his lungs as he stepped out of the house and into the late-morning sun. He walked toward the rows of two-foot-tall fir trees and pulled his phone from his pocket. Sure enough, it was Matt.

Doc's sending Lauren down the mountain. Her water did break. This baby is coming sooner rather than later. I'll text Becca a rundown in a bit.

Can you take care of Fi this afternoon though? Lauren is upset to think that Fi will be in the way during Becca's busy hours.

Stopping beside the first tree in a long row, Tyler looked from his phone toward the little bakery down the road. A green-and-pink-striped awning ruffled in the calm breeze. A smile teased his lips—he loved that Fi's favorite colors happened to be Becca's too. He also loved that despite him messing things up for them, and ruining Becca's plans in Sugar Pine, she'd found a way to pursue her dreams anyway.

Don't think about it. I've got Fi covered. I'll go talk to Becca now.

Tyler didn't wait for Matt's response. He simply pushed his stride toward that green-and-pink awning—to the two girls who could make his heart turn to mush with only a smile sent his way. Heaven, but he couldn't help himself.

***

Becca tugged open the back door, ready to tell Matt to get back to work—she wasn't ready to let Fi go just yet.

That Murphy man was not who stood on the other side.

"Unca Ty!" Fiona scrambled down from the stool she'd been standing on near Becca's worktable. Hands and a good part of her face smeared with hot-pink frosting, she barreled toward the back door, where Becca stood in front of Tyler. "You come to eat cake?"

Tyler caught his niece and flung her upward. Before he could dodge the sugary mess on her little fingers, Fiona smeared bright pink over his almost black beard. Becca couldn't help but giggle.

"No cake for me yet, sprout." He nipped at Fi's fingers. "I came to talk to your friend Becca. Who is laughing at me."

His scowl pointed toward Becca looked anything but upset. The heart in Becca's chest skipped at the impression that Tyler was flirting with her. She leaned back against the opened door. "I never would have guessed that pink is your color."

"Huh. Real men wear pink, right?" He lowered Fiona to the ground. "But I'm gonna need a towel anyway, I think."

Becca nodded toward the sink across the room and then walked that way, grabbing Fi's hand as she went.

Tyler followed. "You girls are sure making that cake look good."

As she passed it, Becca glanced at the pink tower of little-girl effort. The birthday cake's flavored layers were plastered with bright pink, and the top held a thick layer of green and purple sprinkles. It had every mark of a three-year-old's effort, and Becca loved it. Not that she wanted to eat it. Talk about a sugar rush.

Reaching the sink, she pulled a clean towel from an open shelf above and handed it to Tyler. He wiped his face, leaving long streaks of frosting on her white towel, until he thought he'd got it all.

He hadn't. One pink glob hung conspicuously on the dark beard covering his jaw near his right ear. Becca told herself to ignore it. "What brings you away from all that work you're supposed to be doing?"

"Huh. Nice to see you too." He winked, but then his face switched to all seriousness. "I just got a text from Matt. They're heading down the mountain."

"I thought Matt was working with you?"

Tyler's lips rolled together. "Lauren came out this morning saying she felt off. Then she thought her water broke."

"You're kidding." She knew it. Becca had known Lauren needed to take it easier. She should have offered to help with Fi sooner.

"Matt took her to the clinic a while ago. Just now he texted and said they're going to a hospital down the hill. The baby is coming."

A happy squeal cut through the solemness of the conversation as Fiona bounced between them. "My baby is coming!"

"It's too early," Becca whispered.

Tyler held her with a long look, not quite concern as much as it was... something warm. "It'll be okay, Becca." His low-spoken words held a hint of something just between them, an admiration and a bond. One sealed by the touch of his hand on her elbow. "God hears our prayers, and He sees what's happening. His eye is on the sparrow, and He watches you and me. Matt and Lauren too."

His steadiness recentered her thoughts. It also plunged a new level of appreciation for the man. He'd always been compassionate, but not this deeply rooted. In fact, his wild personality had often led him to react in the opposite way. This version of Tyler, still the man she'd known but tempered with a more firmly anchored faith, plunged into her heart and left her breathless.

She was staring. Heat bloomed on her face as she jolted into awareness. Either she had stepped closer, or he had. She wasn't sure which, only knowing that the gap between them had shrunk.

Fiona stood at the side of their legs, gazing up. "Unca Ty?"

Tyler's brows jumped, as if he felt caught too, and then he quickly moved back and looked down. "What's up, sprout?"

"You still have pink on you face!" Fiona covered her mouth with both hands and giggled.

"Think that's funny, huh?" He bent and poked her little belly, provoking another round of high-pitched giggles. Then he stood and wiped his face with the towel again. "Clean now?" He directed his query to Becca.

Smirking, she shook her head. "Still missed. Here." Covering his hand, she directed the towel to the glob of frosting by his ear.

Those dark-brown eyes held on her face again, and a current of electricity traveled from the hand that touched him through her arm. While her heart hammered, she pasted on a smile she hoped wouldn't betray the real state of herself, and dropped her touch. "Got it."

He visibly swallowed. In the silence, things were spoken...things Becca had dreamed of, things she hoped for.

We're not done.

Or maybe that was all in her head. Becca cleared her throat and turned to the sink. After flipping on the faucet, she reached for Fiona and lifted her so she could plunge those frosted fingers into the running water.

"I can watch Fi for the rest of the day." Becca hoped the color sure to have painted her face as bright as Fiona's cake would diffuse before she had to face Tyler again.

"Lauren would be upset if you did that. She doesn't want your business to suffer—"

"It's no problem." Fiona finished washing before Becca was certain the flames in her cheeks had been doused. Even so, she had no excuse not to return her look to Ty.

He shook his head. "Fi and I will hang out this afternoon."

"But—"

"I promised." His response was final. After a beat throbbed between them, he looked down to his niece. "We'll find things to do, right, sprout?"

"We'll eat cake!"

Tyler glanced back at Becca, his look mildly trapped.

Yikes. If he tore into that pink tower of frosting, he might go into a sugar coma.

"How about if I bring over some supper after I close up tonight?" Becca looked down at Fiona. "*Then* you can have a little bit of that pink creation. Okay?"

One small bottom lip poked out. With her index finger, Becca tucked it back in. "How about you take Unca Ty to the park with the twisty slide you love?"

"Yes! And then we go to libby. We read the princess hiking book." Fiona grinned triumphantly.

"The *library*?"

Fiona nodded at her uncle.

"I'm in." Tyler tapped Fiona's nose and then addressed Becca. "Can she stay until noon?"

Becca quelled the impulse to tell him he could stay too. Or that she'd close shop and join them on their afternoon together.

She didn't have the luxury to just close up shop and take the afternoon off. And, more importantly, she obviously needed the time to discipline her heart.

"Just like we planned."

Chapter Twenty-Two

(in which walls are painted)

NERVES JITTERED THROUGH TYLER as if he were getting ready for his first date, not awaiting a pizza dinner with an old friend.

Becca is not just any old friend.

A fact that neither required a reminder nor proved helpful. Tyler ran his fingers through his wet hair and then over his heavily bearded face. He'd never grown out his dark whiskers back in college. Not like this. What did Becca think of it? Scratching at the thick hair, he considered shaving it off.

Nonsense. He'd worn a beard for the better part of a year now. A pizza dinner with an old friend was hardly a reason to change it. Not to mention, he hadn't brought a razor in his travel bag anyway—just the electric groomer he employed once or twice a week.

Settled then. He leaned closer to the mirror to inspect his face.

"What's you doin', Unca Ty?" Fiona skipped into the bathroom and climbed onto the closed toilet, then onto the bathroom sink counter.

"Gonna brush my teeth, sprout."

She wrinkled her nose. "We not eat yet."

Fair point. He reached for his toothbrush anyway.

"Unca Ty?"

"Yeah?" He applied paste and shoved the brush into his mouth.

"You smell pretty."

Chuckling, he started in on the job. "Thanks."

"Unca Ty?"

"Yeah."

"I pretty?"

He smiled and spoke around the toothbrush. "The prettiest almost-three-year-old I know."

She rewarded him with a show-all-her-baby-teeth grin. "Know who else pretty?"

"Who?"

"Mama."

"Yep." He leaned to spit, placing a hand around Fi so she wouldn't slip off the counter as he crowded the small space.

Fiona leaned in to whisper straight into his ear. "And Becca."

Tyler choked. What was his precocious niece up to? The little matchmaker. Did three-year-olds even know what a setup was? Tyler spat again, ran some water to rinse out his mouth, and then stood up.

Fiona tipped her head back, following his movements. "I say Becca pretty, Unca Ty. Right?"

He turned to snag a towel. "She is pretty, Fi."

"She my best friend."

"I've heard that." With both arms, he scooped her up and carried her out to the kitchen. He couldn't figure where Fiona was going with all of this—likely it was just innocent chatter from a toddler—but he was pretty sure Becca would be mortified if his niece continued on this track when Becca arrived with their food. "Pizza sounds good, doesn't it?"

Fiona leaned back in his arms and patted her belly. "Mmmm-Hmm!"

And the distraction worked. Just in time, because a knock sounded at the door. Fiona wiggled, and once he set her feet on the floor, she raced to answer the door. He trailed her, still wondering what the girl had been thinking.

"Hi, Becca!" Fi flung the door open wide.

"Hi, flower face. You hungry?"

"Yes. Cuz Unca Ty forgot my snack."

He had not. They'd had snacks every fifteen minutes, it seemed like. He was pretty sure Lauren would not have approved of either the frequency or choices of said snacks. Privileges of being the uncle—and the one currently competing for Fiona's top affections with a beautiful woman who had the advantage of living down the road and owning the cupcake shop.

"Huh. That doesn't sound like Unca Ty." Becca tossed a grin his way. "He was the snack king."

"I just kidding." Fiona laughed like she was hilarious. Watch out, Unca Jackson. Their niece was gonna chase his funny-bone ways. She sure had Jackson's mischievous bent.

Becca walked into the house like she'd been there many times before. Certainly she had, being such close friends with Lauren. Not to mention Fiona's *best* friend. She slid the box of pizza onto the table and then turned. "Your cake is out in the car. I'll be right back."

"I come too!" Fiona gripped Becca's hand and nearly dragged her out of the house.

Tyler followed them to the door, bracing himself on the frame with a raised hand as he watched his favorite girls in the world walk to Becca's car. Fiona chatted like she'd been saving all her words for Becca—blatantly untrue, as Tyler had heard an endless stream of *guess what, Unca Tys* and *how 'bout we* all afternoon. As Becca carefully pulled a cakebox out of her car, Fiona said something that made the woman stop, toss her head back, and laugh.

Yep. Unca Jackson better watch his career. Fiona Murphy was bound to steal the stage.

The pair came back to the house, and once inside, Becca stopped near Ty. His heart skidded in the most delightful way as she leaned in near, her nose aimed at his neck. She inhaled dramatically and then exhaled, and the warmth of her breath fanned over his skin, making him ridiculously lightheaded. He looked down, hoping she'd be waiting for his gaze, and forgetting all but that Becca Colson was close enough for him to wrap in his arms and that her breath had just scattered a million warm thrills across his neck.

The nearness of a beautiful woman...

She did not meet his gaze, nor did she stay put. Instead, she laughed and moved with Fiona toward the table. "You're right, Fi. He smells pretty."

The fog in his brain took a second to clear, and he required another beat to catch up to what she'd said. He felt hot crimson crawl up his cheek. Good grief. And also, should he leave that mental note on his gratitude list?

Oh, he was gonna.

"He say I pretty. An' he say Mama pretty. Annndddd..." Fiona twirled around, gave him a wiggly-eyebrow look, and then gripped Becca's hand, tugging her down until Becca stooped. "...he say *you* is pretty."

Becca's look lifted back to him. "Did he?"

The warm green gaze of that same beautiful woman. His stomach clenched, and he held his breath as the amusement faded from Becca's expression, replaced with something serious but not unpleasant. Tyler felt the pull between them as sure as gravity kept his feet firmly planted on the earth. By the slight parting of her lips and light dusting of color across her cheekbones, he was fairly certain she felt it too.

A buzz worked its way into his chest. A buzz? Was that an actual physical buzz? What could have caused that? It vibrated again. What the —Oh! As if shaken from a stupor, he patted his shirt pocket—the usual place for his phone. Sure enough, it had been his phone and not some bizarre visceral reaction to Becca's captivating look held on him. Someone had texted him.

Murphy clan, welcome Helene Alice Murphy, born at 6:58 p.m. 4lbs 10oz. My wife and daughter are both doing well. Helene is tiny but tough. We'll be in the hospital a little longer because she's so small, but all seems good.

A picture of a tiny, pink-faced baby girl followed. From her miniature nose, closed eyes, perfectly adorable chin, and the closed fist she held against her cheek, Helene was perfection. Tyler grinned. *The perfect miracle of new life.*

"What is it?" Becca asked.

He felt his smile grow as he turned his phone so she could see. Pure love washed over Becca's expression as she studied the picture, and as he watched her, a rush of warmth surged in Tyler's chest.

Becca hadn't changed. She was still the warm, loving woman he'd wanted for his wife.

"I see?" Fiona tugged on Ty's pant leg.

Without looking from Helene's picture, Becca knelt beside the little girl and wrapped an arm around her. "This, my sweet friend, is your new baby sister."

Fiona's mouth gaped, and she leaned in close to the screen. "She small!"

"Very small. Her name is Helene."

For what seemed like the first time all day, Fiona was speechless. She simply looked at the baby, wonder in her eyes. Then her face snapped up to Becca. "I hold her!"

"Yes, I'm sure you will, when Mommy and Daddy bring her home."

Fiona wiggled out of Becca's wrapped arm and darted to Ty, snagging his hand. "We go."

"Hold up, sprout." He tugged her back and then lifted her up. "We can't go see her right now."

Her bottom lip poked out. "She my baby."

"I know, but the hospital is a long way away, and your mama is very tired."

And then there were tears. "I miss Mommy! I want Daddy!"

A quiet chuckle moved through Tyler's chest, though he muffled it as he cuddled Fiona close.

Becca came near, rubbing Fiona's back. "Poor sweet girl. Stuck here with us."

Over Fiona's fair curls, Tyler met Becca's eyes and they shared a smile. "Surely we can't be that bad. I let her eat cheese puffs all afternoon, and you made her a pink cake." He winked and lowered his voice. "But I don't think she likes pink cakes, Becca. I think you and I are going to have to eat it for her."

Quick as anything, that little head came off his chest, and Fiona scowled up at him. "I love pink cakes, Unca Ty!"

"You're kidding me."

Becca smirked. "You're confused, Unca Ty. Fiona loves my cakes. It's pizza she doesn't like."

Fiona whipped around to look at Becca. "I love pizza!"

"No way!" Becca said.

"Way!"

Tyler shifted Fiona to one arm and started toward the table. As Becca turned to go that way too, he rested his free hand on her back. It felt natural and right to touch her with such subtle possessiveness.

Becca didn't react in any sort of way that would tell him how she felt about his hand on her back. For the rest of the evening, they ate, laughed at Fiona's expressive antics, and admired the pictures Matt continued to send to Tyler so that he could show Fiona more of her new baby sister.

It was all so laid back and easy. Like they were supposed to be this way. Together.

By the time the evening ended, Fiona tucked into her toddler bed and Becca saying good night, Tyler was utterly convinced that was exactly the truth. He and Becca were supposed to be that way.

Together.

Broken love mended. That might be premature. But he would give thanks for it anyway.

***

They had three days.

Becca gave herself a quick mental pep talk as she opened the back door to Tyler. Three days, and they'd better make the most of it. Which meant that she didn't waste a moment. As soon as Tyler crossed the threshold, Fiona snuggled in his arms, Becca turned to address him.

"We have work to do, Murphy."

"Excuse me?"

"Matt and Lauren can't come home to a half-done project. Not with a little girl waiting for them and a new baby."

A slight scowl lined his forehead. "I'm putting up trim today, Miss Taskmaster. I promise to work fast."

"The flooring is scheduled, right?"

"Day after tomorrow."

Becca reached to take Fiona from Tyler's arms. "Good. Tomorrow is painting day, then."

"Uhh...I'm not sure that's a great plan."

"Why not?"

"I don't do interior design."

Having Fiona settled against her shoulder, she swatted the air at him. "The paint is already ordered, and I know what goes where."

"You do?"

"Of course I do. Lauren had it picked out since the day the blueprints were finalized."

"Oh."

"So tomorrow. Bring your brushes and your best paint game. It's on."

"Don't you have to sell cupcakes tomorrow?"

"I'll close the shop." Even if she still didn't necessarily have that luxury. She was doing it.

At that, his scowl returned tenfold. "Lauren will not like that."

"Lauren's not here to say."

"I'm here to say."

"You're not the boss of me."

His eyes widened with a hint of shock and a splash of amusement. "Is that so? You think you're the boss of me?"

"Watch."

"What will you do if I say no?"

"You won't."

"How do you know?"

With her brows raised, she simply held a challenging stare on him. After a moment, he crossed his arms.

"I dare you." She stepped nearer.

His throat bobbed in a swallow, and she saw his cocky smirk slip. "You dare me what?"

Had his voice just cracked? She edged closer still. "I dare you to tell me no."

The intensity of his eyes shifted from laughter to something else altogether, and for a moment Becca lost herself in that look.

Last night it had been easy to play house with Ty as they took care of Fiona, especially when he touched her as if he had a right to. A small corner of her mind had whispered a warning that she was tugging on a string that could cause her to unravel, but she'd hushed it. Pizza and laughter were harmless. A few shared smiles, a couple of touches she savored more than she was going to admit. They didn't amount to much.

As she stood there, her heart throbbing into the silence, warmth suffusing her body as Tyler hovered near her in an unnervingly attractive way, she knew that was an outright lie. What it had amounted to was her heart sliding toward a man who had moved on.

Except for when he stared at her that way.

Becca cleared her throat. "Can't do it?" she squeaked out the words, and they didn't sound nearly as playful as she'd intended.

"That wasn't a fair dare."

She tipped her chin, clawing her way back to light and sassy. "Why?"

One dark brow arched into his forehead, and he leaned near to press a kiss onto Fiona's curls. Before he stood back, he moved just enough to whisper near Becca's ear. "You know why." Then he stood, turned, and walked out the way he'd come.

Becca stayed rooted to the spot, staring at the door even after he was long gone. Her heart pulsed with aching delight.

***

Tyler's right arm throbbed, but as he leaned against the doorframe to Matt and Lauren's almost completed new master bedroom, he sighed with a smile. Across the floor that would proudly boast carpet tomorrow, Becca ran her brush skillfully along the window trim, dragging a faint robin's-egg blue onto the lightly textured wall. They'd spent the day doing this—she, with her steady, artistic hand, had done the trim work, and he'd followed with a pan of paint and a loaded roller.

The new front room was done, and he had to say the buttercup yellow Lauren and Becca had selected was perfect for that space. From there, they'd moved on to the en suite bathroom, in which a silvery white was now drying. After that job had been done, they'd stopped work for supper, for a short video with Fiona, followed by three books (she could have gone for double that), and then tucked her into bed.

This pretend-this-is-real-life game Tyler had been silently playing, casting Becca into a role that they'd once been certain she'd play in truth, would come to an end in a matter of days. The house project would be done. Tyler would pack his things to head back to Sugar Pine, still uncertain as to what his future should look like. And most pertinent to the moment, he would say goodbye to Becca Colson.

That sat about as well as plunking down on a spread of cactus. He gazed at her back, appreciating her figure as she moved, and prayed for a way to change course. She had seemed open to possibilities over the past few days, hadn't she? Spending time with him. Never shrinking from his touch. Returning his smiles. Flirting.

No. They weren't done. They had never been done. And he wasn't ready to walk away now that he had her back in his life.

The song that had been playing on her phone, which sat against the window, stopped, and Becca paused her work to change the playlist. When the music started, he could see the joy on her profile, and it pulled him out of his serious line of thought. He grinned as the music worked its way into her being, first producing a small wiggle. Then a couple of steps—quick, quick, slow. Not even fifteen seconds into the song, her whole body was into the salsa-inspired tune. Brush in hand, Becca danced with abandon.

And Tyler watched, mesmerized. Delighted.

On a turn, her eyes caught his. When he thought she'd freeze, maybe glance away shyly, she grinned, with a challenging glint flashed straight at him—the same sort that she'd showed him when she'd dared him to tell her no about the painting. A dare he'd told her was unfair—and she knew why.

Tyler was putty in Becca's hands. Always had been.

So when she waved him into the room, he pushed off the doorframe and strode her way. He was no dancer—didn't have Becca's natural rhythm, not to mention the background in dance she had from her years on a squad in middle and high school—but he had no objection to moving with her. Or relishing the way she clearly enjoyed herself as she danced.

The song stopped before she was ready, and her solution was to race to the window where she'd propped her phone and hit repeat. She laughed as she made her way back to him.

"You know, Murphy, for a man with only one leg, you can move."

Tyler snorted. "Was that your version of a compliment?"

She shrugged, still dancing, and then grabbed a fistful of his shirtfront. "Let's see what you've got."

Laughing, Tyler let her tug him into her salsa. "You know I was never very good at this."

"Just move." She raised her arms and tapped out a rhythmic turn.

When she turned back to him, he let his hands drift over her back, onto her waist, down to her hips. She lost herself in the music. He lost himself in her. One song bled into two, then three. All high energy, nothing slow. At the end of the third song, her eyes were bright with delight, cheeks colored in the loveliest of energetic pinks, and she was breathless.

Tyler wasn't sure he was breathing at all. Especially when her feet stilled and she pinned her look on him. Another song started, but this time the music was lost on them both. Grin fading, Becca licked her lips, drawing his glance and making his gut clench. But he stood motionless, one hand resting on her hip.

Her hands raised to his chest, and then she was gripping the fabric of his shirt front. Tyler felt her pull—he wasn't sure if she'd done so physically or if he was simply captive to the gravity she exerted over him.

Warm, sweet breath fanned over his chin. Hers. His fingers curled into the fabric of her shirt.

"I keep trying to forget you." He told himself to move away. None of this was helping him to forget anything. Instead, as she moved closer, he leaned down. His claim wasn't true, anyway. Hadn't he prematurely listed *broken love mended*?

When her warm lips caught the edge of his bottom lip, Tyler caught a groan at the back of his throat. Was this happening?

"Becca..." Forget her? Never.

He dipped into her, finding her mouth still there, sweet and warm and willing. That was all it took to convince him. Sliding his hand from her hip and up her back, he greedily took her in, taking her upturned mouth with his. Every kiss became longer, more breathless. Each one erasing the hesitancy between them that had been created by time and distance, hurt and disappointment, until there was only the certainty of her with him, as they had been before. As they should always be.

Tyler turned until Becca's back was against the wall and then moved his hands to frame her face. Her hands slid over his shoulders and found their way into the hair at the nape of his neck. His skin tingled as she trailed her fingers from there, along his jawline and into his beard.

Head spinning, heart pounding, Tyler leaned a hand against the wall. Something cool and wet met his palm, and reality crept into his euphoria. Breathless, he pulled his mouth from hers and looked above her head at the spot he'd braced against. He pulled his hand from the wall, a faint crackle sounding as he did so.

Robin's-egg blue covered his palm.

"Oh no." He tugged Becca away and looked down her back to examine the damage. Her left shoulder and the left side of her dark, swept-up hair were smeared with paint. Chuckling, he tipped her chin with the crook of his finger. "I might have made a mistake."

He thought she'd laugh. It was just paint, after all, and a little funny. Instead, she shrank away from him, hugging herself. "Yeah." She bit her bottom lip and looked away.

Tyler closed the space she'd pried between them. "It's not a big deal. Pretty sure it'll wash."

Two breaths passed and still she wouldn't look at him. This couldn't be about wet paint. "Becca, I—" He reached out to cradle her face again.

"I'm gonna go." She dodged his touch and scurried away.

"Wait."

She shook her head, quickening her steps.

"Becca."

She didn't even glance his way. Just barreled out the room, through the front of the house, and out the door.

For the rest of the night, Tyler replayed every bit of that scene. The dancing. The laughing. Those long-yearned-for kisses. Granted, they'd been pretty passionate, but he didn't think they'd done anything wrong. And he hadn't been the one to start it.

He couldn't say he was sorry for any of it. Apparently Becca was. He stayed up the rest of the night painting. And trying to understand.

CHAPTER TWENTY-THREE

(in which Tyler admits the truth)

BECCA DIDN'T EVEN CRAWL into her bed to attempt sleep. She'd raced home, climbed into a hot shower, making a long effort to remove the paint from her hair, and then slipped into some sweats. At that point it'd been close to eleven, and her mind still whirled, her body still abuzz with the electrifying memory of Tyler's touch. The sound of his rough voice breaking on her name as if she were somehow holy to him. His passionate kisses.

Kisses she'd initiated.

What had she been thinking? Not just with that, but over the past few days, what under heaven had she been thinking? She'd flirted and reveled in the way he responded with smiles aimed only at her. She'd basked in the fanciful thought that those thrilling moments could be more than a passing thing. But that wasn't reality—it couldn't be reality.

Could it?

Needing something to do with her hands as she mentally worked through the tangles of her heart, Becca padded down the steps from her apartment and into her work kitchen. Moving on autopilot, she prepped the stand mixer and measured ingredients.

She had built a life in Pleasant Valley. It'd been hard work, and it was good. And Tyler... The life available to Tyler now was not at all what she'd imagined—what either of them had imagined. In the process of his recovery, he'd found something so much more. He'd become something so much more. How could he ever go back to the small hopes they'd once shared for a simple life? The one she lived and loved now?

The batter smoothed to perfection, and Becca shut off the mixer. She'd already prepped her largest pan with paper cup liners. Using her favorite scoop, she filled each cup to the right measure, her movements more muscle memory than thought. Which allowed her mind to linger over the man who had once again claimed possession of her heart. Or, more exactly, who had always possessed her heart.

She relived the kiss they'd shared. The way he'd taken her into his arms as if she'd always belonged there. As if nothing had ever changed between them.

But it had. While she'd stayed the course of their life's ambitions—just doing so without him—his path had altered. More, *Tyler* had changed.

Truth be known, Tyler's wild personality was well suited to a bigger, more out-loud kind of life—the sort that this climbing platform had opened for him. All the best of who Tyler was came out in both the sport of climbing and in his speaking opportunities. His unquenchable thirst for adventure and his unequalled determination, combined with the opportunity to speak, to inspire and encourage others with his story, made for the perfect presentation of who Tyler Murphy truly was. Compassionate. Fervent. Compelling. *That* was Tyler, and Becca thrilled to see him owning it all.

When she really looked back and considered, he wasn't nearly as well matched to what they'd planned before his accident compared to what he had in front of him now. And what he had now didn't really include her. Becca was small, quiet. She wasn't adventurous, and she certainly didn't shine in public. Her dreams were simple and existed right there in Pleasant Valley.

Her breath stalled as a pain clutched in her chest. She had to set down the scoop and grip the edge of the counter as a sob shuddered through her. Tyler had outgrown her, and she felt certain she would never find a place in the life he led now.

Letting Tyler Murphy go three years ago had broken her heart. She'd instigated the intervention because she didn't want to be the reason he never got better. Because she had loved him. Now, she didn't want to be the one to hold him back.

Becca slid the hefty pan of cupcakes into the hot oven, then wiped the tears from her face.

She still loved him. But their lives had changed. They were no longer going the same direction.

***

Wow. That was *a lot* of cupcakes. Tyler stepped into Becca's kitchen, scanning the long stainless-steel worktable as well as the countertops running the length of two walls. Every inch was filled with cupcakes, half of them frosted.

It was only six in the morning.

He looked back, taking in the shadows beneath Becca's eyes, the slump of her shoulders. She hadn't slept last night. Made two of them. If it hadn't been for the little girl snuggled against his shoulder right then, he'd have caved to the desire to come seek Becca out after she'd fled last night. They could have talked this out, and perhaps both of them would have found some rest.

Or he'd have defaulted to kissing her again. That had been much easier. And oh, sweet heaven, had it felt good to have Becca Colson in his arms again.

Didn't do either of you a whole lot of good, by the looks of it.

Fiona sighed, her little body pressing against his. With a glance, he saw her long dark lashes fanned against her baby-soft cheeks, her thumb sagging out of her partially parted lips. Asleep. A pang of guilt ricocheted through him. He should have left her in her toddler bed instead of wrapping her in a blanket and bringing her to Just Eat It. He should have waited...

But he had things to say, and he was gonna run out of time to say them. Or courage. Maybe both. And besides, he couldn't get Becca out of his head. He couldn't make the questions about her stop, and it seemed reasonable to simply go to her and ask. Up until his accident, they had always talked things out. That seemed like a good place to begin again now.

Tyler focused on the woman who had owned him. "Do you have somewhere I can lay Fi? We need to talk."

Looking distinctly uncomfortable—or perhaps miserable was closer to the truth—Becca rolled her lips together, scanned her industrial kitchen, and then sighed quietly. "Upstairs. She can sleep in my bed."

"You live above your shop?"

"Yes. It's how I can afford it."

A hollow yearning expanded in his gut. They had planned on living together above her bakery—only that plan had existed in Sugar Pine. It was like she'd gone on ahead with their life dreams without him.

Your fault, Ty. Not hers.

Becca fingered Fiona's hair. "I bunked with this sweet flower face while the apartment was being fixed up my first six months here." But then she removed that tender touch and moved away, avoiding all eye contact with him.

As quietly as possible, Tyler followed Becca up the back steps and into her apartment. It was small—a love seat and a rocker, a doorway that led to a small bathroom, and a bedroom with space for a bed. She'd covered the mattress with a mint-green spread, onto which Tyler lowered his niece. Fiona moaned and wiggled and then sucked her thumb before dropping back into a hard sleep. If she kept with her usual routine, Tyler would have about an hour before she was up for the day. Time not to be wasted.

He turned and found Becca at the doorway, looking like a mouse with her back in a corner. Like she would bolt or burst into tears any second. Suddenly she scurried to her front room, and it occurred to Tyler that she might feel weird about him standing in her bedroom. He followed her, heat creeping up his neck.

"It's pretty early." Becca turned, her expression schooled and raising her brows in question.

"Yeah. Like I said, we should talk. I couldn't sleep last night."

"Hmm." She looked toward the floor.

"Kind of looks like you didn't get much rest either."

A shrug was all she offered.

Why did this have to be so...awkward? It wasn't like they'd never kissed before. Tyler scratched his arm and searched for the best way to dive in. "The family will be descending soon."

Yeah. That was the best way to get to what they needed to discuss. Tyler wanted to smack his forehead. Had he always had this yellow streak hiding beneath a veneer of adventure-loving fun?

Becca's expression was mild surprise. "All of them?"

"Well, no. Not all at once anyway. But Mom and Dad will be bringing Gertrude this way and staying for a week or two. They'll get here a couple days after Matt and Lauren bring little Helene home. And I'm pretty sure Connor and Sadie will come over the pass to meet our new niece ASAP."

Becca looked at him like he was a geometry problem. "Gertrude?"

"Oh. Right. That happened after..." Tyler rubbed his neck and cleared his throat. "Gert is Jacob and Kate's old skoolie. They sold her to Mom and Dad this past winter after they found out Kate is pregnant."

Becca blinked. "Nothing you just said made sense. What the heck is a skoolie?"

"It's a school bus converted into an RV."

"Jacob and Kate *owned* a school bus?"

Tyler chuckled at her astonishment. It was understandable—no one within the Murphy clan would have predicted the sharp turn Jacob and Kate's life had taken a couple years back. "It's a little more shocking than that. Jacob and Kate *lived* in a skoolie for a little more than two years. They traveled all over. Jacob picked up seasonal jobs, and Kate blogged about their life as boondockers. It's quite a story. But they sold Gert—their skoolie —to Mom and Dad before Christmas and moved into a little house on Main in Sugar Pine. This is their third or fourth pregnancy, and Kate's seven months along—a real answer to prayer."

Lips parted, Becca stared at him as if he'd made up some kind of fantastic tale that couldn't be true.

Broken love mended. That was a reality for Jacob and Kate, and Tyler rejoiced in it.

"God works, you know? He still does miracles." He wanted to reach out and touch her, to trail his fingers along her jawline. He wanted to tell her how much God had worked in his own life too—and that maybe He was working with them, right then and there, so generously restoring what had been lost. If only they'd cooperate.

If she wanted it...

As if sensing how close he was to doing all those things, Becca shrank away, her gaze drifting toward the window across the room. Maybe she didn't want him after all. "I'm glad things worked out for them. I'm thrilled to hear their expecting a little miracle of their own," she whispered. "And it's good that your parents will be here to help Matt and Lauren."

A soft snore sounded from the bedroom at his back. Fiona would wake in earnest soon. Time was running out.

Enough sidetracking. "None of that is what I really came to talk with you about."

Becca visibly swallowed.

He inched nearer. "Last night—"

"Was a mistake." Inhaling deeply, she pushed her gaze back to him. There was a wild pleading in her look and a scared vulnerability that nearly made Tyler change his mind about pushing into the matter.

He could simply go back to life in Sugar Pine, taking climbing gigs and speaking opportunities when they came. And back to trying to forget how much he loved her. Other than the consistent ache in his heart where she'd permanently imprinted herself, it hadn't been a bad life. *Love is a gift. Even the broken parts.*

He could still be thankful for having once been loved by her. For the joy of what they'd shared. After all, he still wouldn't trade it. He could be thankful and walk away...

But then he remembered the hunger in her kisses. And the other things Matt had told him about her not dating. Tyler wasn't the only one of the two of them who hadn't forgotten. Who didn't want to forget. Good reasons to push forward, even if she wasn't comfortable with it.

"You kissed me." He held a steady gaze, not allowing her the escape of looking away as he stepped closer still.

"That was just—" The pulse in her neck leapt, and she swallowed again. "It was...nostalgia. Please, Ty. Let's forget it."

As if that were possible. "Only after you tell me why you didn't sleep last night."

Becca stepped back, bumping into the sofa behind her. She gripped the edge of it and closed her eyes.

Tyler narrowed the gap between them. "Or you can tell me why you haven't dated much in the past three years. And why the one guy you were dating, you broke up with about two minutes after our reunion."

Splotches of red mottled her neck. "Who told you that?"

"Matt. Is it true?"

"Matt had no—" Becca pursed her lips and scowled. "How about you? Have you dated?"

He shook his head once. "I told you...I haven't been able to forget you."

"It's been three years, Tyler. Three. Years."

"I know. Three very long years." Long, good years of growing though pain, becoming a better man, of seeing God's goodness in the easy and the hard, and still missing this woman.

"Don't lie." Fire flared in her green gaze, and she stood straight, crossing her arms. "Don't try to charm me. In three *very long* years, you've never once reached out. Never once tried to contact me. It's not like you didn't know where I've been. It's not like you couldn't figure out how to reach me."

All true. He hadn't wanted to disrupt her life. No, that wasn't all. Tyler squeezed his eyes shut, reaching deep for hard honesty. "I...I was awful."

At that her bottom lip trembled, and she looked away.

Tyler's heart crumbled. "Becca." Unable to fight against the need to touch her any longer, he reached to cup her jawline. "Rebecca, look at me."

She wouldn't. Couldn't. This was what he hadn't wanted to face, because the shame of seeing the depth of the wound he'd inflicted was too much. "I was too ashamed to face you." His voice broke. "I am ashamed of it still."

Shoulders quivering, Becca gasped on a sob. "I thought you resented me." A tear edged down her face as she forced her gaze back to him. "For all of it—telling your parents and them sending you to rehab. For giving you back your ring because I wasn't brave enough to be what you needed me to be."

All this time, she'd thought *he'd* resented *her*? Lord, he'd been a fool. Why hadn't he listened to Brandon when his little brother had told him to talk to her? Why had he let so much time go by in silence? He'd gone to Lenz, faced him with an apology. Why had he been too cowardly to face Becca, when she more than anyone deserved his repentance?

Tyler shook his head. "You did what you needed to do. I didn't leave you a lot of choice in it."

It was too much. He pulled her close, bundling her tight against his heart.

"But three years, Ty." Tears strained her voice, and she pulled stiffly away from him, a deep scowl creasing her brow.

Earned anger. Even so, it still nicked. Tyler swallowed, still fumbling for the strength to speak the truth. "I thought you wouldn't want to see me, and I didn't want to upend your life all over again."

Mostly true. Not all. Becca had always been brave with him. She had followed him into so many of his adrenaline-spiking adventures, even when she'd been terrified. He'd never truly appreciated how brave that really was until this moment.

This raw, terrifying moment.

The least he could do was employ some courage of his own. "I was too afraid to face your rejection to come tell you how sorry I was—I am. And how much I miss you." He stepped back enough to frame her face, his thumbs wiping the damp streaks on her cheeks, and waited for her eyes to connect with his. "I miss you, Becca. I know I broke your trust, your heart. Us. I know I don't deserve another chance, but there's never been anyone else. I'll always miss you."

Her eyes closed again, but she didn't pull away. Instead, her hands found his waist, and then she fisted the material of his shirt. "There's a lot of time and life in three years, Ty," she whispered. "Things change."

That was true. Things did change. He had changed. But that didn't mean that his love for her had. "I can't fix the past, even though I wish I could. With everything in me, I wish I could go back and not break your heart." He bent closer, his voice becoming a mere whisper. "But maybe we can change the direction we're going now. I want to try again. I think you do too."

Becca rolled her lips together. The empty space of silence between them felt like that moment when he would begin to rappel from a climb on an auto-belay, and the drop would be a freefall before the catch would kick in. Usually, he thrilled at that. Right now, however, it was all fear and not much else.

"Ty..."

The moment he had been too afraid to face. His heart slammed to a stop. *Will you give thanks in this moment too?*

What would he choose to do with it? Was God God, or was He not?

You know the beginning from the end... Gratitude was sometimes sacrifice. Hard and painful. Even so. *You are God.*

Becca pulled in a breath and then looked at him. One hand released his shirt, and then her fingers grazed his bearded cheek. "I can't jump back into where we were before. Our lives are different now."

He couldn't deny the truth of that. But the difference? It was a good thing. At least for him. He'd been changed for the better, and he was desperate for her to see that. He lowered his forehead to hers. "Becca, I'm not the same man who said those horrible things to you at Seaside."

"I know that." Her hand turned to cup his neck. "Truth is, you were never that man—not really. That was pain and anger and withdrawal." That warm touch, so gentle, so wonderfully tempting, slipped away, and she gently nudged him back.

Confusion swirled within him, and his hands slipped to his sides. If she knew that, then why was she rejecting him?

"I think we both need to think this through."

"I've missed you for three years. I'm not sure how much longer I need to think."

"There was always attraction between us, Ty. Obviously I can't deny that's still true. But we're not a couple of starry-eyed college kids anymore. There's more here than our feelings, and it would be irresponsible not to think things through."

"Okay..."

"You have a very different life than what either of us thought possible."

"Are you worried about my leg?" Since when had his amputation ever bothered her? Of the two of them, she had been the one to first embrace the belief that his life would go on perfectly well after he'd lost his leg.

"No." She sighed and leaned back against the sofa. "You know me better than that. I'm talking about this amazing platform you have in front of you. I saw you speak, Ty. And I've pulled up some videos of you on YouTube, both of you climbing and you speaking. You're gifted. More than that, I think you know the pleasure of God when you get up in front of people and share His goodness with them."

The very thing he'd been wrestling with over the past few months. Would he continue climbing, pursue more speaking? Or was he to be at home, where he was more comfortable, working alongside his dad as he'd always thought? "You're right—and I have some things to pray through with that and with how that may figure into me working with my dad. But I'm not seeing how that prevents you and me from trying again."

"My life is here." Becca bit her lip and looked away. "I'm scared."

At last they'd come to the truth of it. Tyler couldn't blame her. And for once he wasn't going to simply squeeze her shoulder and tell her to trust him, that it'd all be fine.

"Okay." He fingered a length of her dark-auburn hair, noting a small streak of light-blue paint still there. "If you think we need time, then I respect that. Tell me what that looks like. Do I leave you alone?"

Her face whipped back up to him. "No. That's not what I want." Then her eyes widened as if she'd said something she hadn't intended. "I mean... I don't know..."

"Then we take it slow?"

Rolling her lips together, she didn't answer. Tyler could feel her slipping away. He reached for her, tracing her jawline with the pad of his thumb. "Becca, look at me."

Shaking her head, she sniffed. "You're making this really hard."

He cupped both hands to frame her face. "I'm not meaning to."

When she finally turned her eyes up to his, he found a dull helplessness in them. His heart pinched. "Sweetheart, help me to understand. Are you afraid I'll regress?"

"No." She winced and then drew a staying breath. "I don't fit into your life. You've outgrown me."

At that he gathered her into his arms, tucking her against his shoulder. "You fit." He pressed a kiss to her hair, then brushed the strands away from her forehead and kissed her there. "You fit perfectly. Right here."

Her arms snaked around his waist, and for a long, fortifying moment, she clung to him. But then, yet again, she nudged him away. With her fingers, she swiped away her tears and sniffed. Finally she tipped her chin to look him in the eye. "I'm not saying that's not what I want. But I have a life here. A good one. I just...we'll see."

"We'll see?" Was she afraid he didn't have room in his life for her, or that his world would swallow hers if she let him?

He'd been that way before, hadn't he?

Swallowing, she nodded, tentatively reaching to clasp his fingers. "Slow."

He exhaled a controlled breath, firming the tentative grip she'd initiated. "So we'll try?"

She bit her lip and then nodded again. A whimper sounded from the room behind him, and Tyler knew their time was up. Fiona wouldn't know where she was, and he'd better not dally in getting her back home. Even so, he couldn't resist one last touch.

He caught Becca's cheek with the back of his knuckles and bent to press a gentle kiss to her mouth. "Slow then."

Fiona's whimper became an earnest cry. Tyler moved to rescue his niece. After calming her and gathering her against his chest, he strode from Becca's room toward the stairs that would lead him down and out of her shop. He stole one last lingering look before he went.

She'd held his gaze, and there might have been a ghost of a smile on her lips. He hoped.

And there was hope. Tyler still wasn't clear what *slow* looked like. But she hadn't rejected him, and that was a relief. He'd do this blind and scared if that was what it took. And pray that in the end, they would both get beyond their regrets and fears about a future that no longer seemed as clearly defined as it had once before.

Broken love mended.

More selfishly, he had every intention of begging God for Becca to fall in love with him once again. For that item of gratitude to ring true. He wasn't sure what that made him exactly—besides desperately in love with her—but he planned on doing so anyway.

CHAPTER TWENTY-FOUR

(in which Becca knows the truth)

"I FEEL TOO SMALL, too unremarkable." Becca barely peeked at Lauren as she stroked the fine baby hairs of little Helene Murphy. Lauren had been blunt in her questions about the situation between Becca and Ty, telling Becca that she had spent so much time in prayer for them both because they mattered so much to her and Matt.

Across the nursery, her friend rocked back against the glider, and Becca could feel Lauren's slightly amused stare. "Unremarkable?" The word came out as an astonished chuckle. "He has never once thought of another. I can promise you that. How could that make you unremarkable?"

Becca felt her brow wrinkle. "I am the girl he loved back in college. That's all."

"That's all? Yes. You are the girl he loved. Loves. To my knowledge, and let's not forget that I'm your best friend, you haven't changed."

"He has." Drawing a breath, Becca forced herself to cast more than a peek at Lauren. "Tyler has changed—his life is so very different. You can't deny that."

Lauren studied Becca with a soft smile. "His life is different, that's true. He travels now, speaks publicly. Climbs rocks with only his good leg. Inspires people to overcome and to believe that goodness can and does spring from bad things." Gripping the arms of her glider, Lauren leaned forward. "But, Becca, *he* is still *Tyler*. Maybe a slightly better version than the young man you were engaged to—stronger in his faith and steadier in his convictions—but not very much different. Not in the way I think you imagine. He isn't self-important, not demanding."

"I didn't imagine that. But—" Becca sighed. "But this public life he's accumulated. It isn't for me. I feel like...like I'd be lost in it."

"I would say a public life isn't necessarily for Ty either. He doesn't crave it. He doesn't even seek it out. The speaking engagements he's done have been by request. The climbing videos also by request. Neither are things he chases after. Matt says he struggles with how long he'll continue as a sponsored athlete. That Tyler and Kevin have talked often of some things being seasonal opportunities but not necessarily permanent."

Becca pulled back at that. Didn't sound like Kevin Murphy to discourage his sons. She wondered if Tyler's climbing was an issue between him and his dad. That wasn't what she and Lauren were talking about right then though. She mentally jogged back to Tyler climbing and speaking by request—that was the rub with her right then. "But that's just it, Lauren. He's sought after. And why wouldn't he be? He's very good at both."

Did she sound jealous? Was she?

Lauren's gaze narrowed with thoughtfulness as she once again studied Becca. She pressed back against the chair at the same moment little miss Helene cut into the uneasy silence with a squeaky cry. Becca lifted the tiny babe to press a kiss to her warm forehead and then walked her over to lower her into the arms of her mother. Becca wandered to the window that looked toward the folds of the rising hills, now blue against the gathering of day's end. She felt the sunset as much as she could see it—time was slipping away.

That morning Kevin and Helen Murphy had arrived in Gertrude, the adorably quirky green skoolie. The three Murphy men present in Pleasant Valley had spent the day moving furniture according to Lauren's instructions. Right now, Helen was happily making the rearranged beds, having shooed Lauren and Becca out with a gracious, loving smile. All was coming to completion with Matt and Lauren's renovation project.

Tyler's role was finished, and he would leave in the morning. Kevin had left a job half-done in a town south of Sugar Pine. Tyler was to go see it completed. And, she noted silently, there had seemed nothing amiss whatsoever between Ty and his dad. They were as they had been before Tyler's accident, as thick as thieves.

"Have you talked about your worries with Tyler?" Lauren asked.

Becca glanced over her shoulder and then turned back toward the western hills beyond the window. "A little."

"Becca, talk to him. Be honest. You might be surprised by what he has to say about it."

Wrapping her arms around herself, Becca leaned against the windowsill. "I have a good life, Lauren. You know? Just Eat It is a dream come true, thanks in great part to you and Matt." A dream she hadn't dared to chase before she'd met Tyler Murphy. He had been her courage back then... Becca clenched her jaw, tamping down the emotion that welled hard. Life changed. There was no going back. "And here, I have you and your sweet girls. I'm happy."

She was happy. Had been settled, right up until Tyler had walked into her shop a few weeks back.

"You're content." Lauren let that hang for a moment.

"That's not a bad thing."

Lauren shook her head. "But I've seen you with Fi. And I just watched your face as you held Helene. More than that, I've seen you with Tyler. Then and now. Contentment is a good thing when life isn't ready to change. But maybe now you're calling something contentment when it's actually fear because change is right in front of you. For both you and Tyler. Perhaps even a redeeming."

Becca's heart tugged as she heard the men's chatter in the other room. Kevin was updating his sons on how Brandon fared with whatever his odd arrangement was with a family somewhere north. At some point in Kevin's telling, there was a drawn silence that seemed serious. Then laughter. She could pick out Ty's without trying. It was deep and melodic, rich with good nature and fun.

It stirred her heart with a tender ache.

"Think he'll stick it out?" Tyler had asked.

Becca had no idea what he was talking about, nor did she hear the answer Mr. Murphy gave. While she cared about whatever Brandon was doing, the reaction of her heart had more to do with the man in the other room than with what was going on with any of his brothers.

He was leaving in the morning. She shut her eyes.

From the beginning, dating Tyler had always been a little bit scary—in an exhilarating way. He was all flying energy to her steady calm. He was the dare to her meticulous plans and compliant obedience. With his unquenchable love for adventure, he'd always challenged her to be braver than she was, and though she'd done a lot of things scared, she hadn't regretted them. Rock walls and ziplines and breathtaking hikes, those were one thing. But this different sort of life Tyler had found, it felt like something entirely different.

Sort of like it had felt when she'd told her parents she didn't want a degree in architectural engineering. That she found delight in baking, and Tyler thought she could make a happy career of it. Yeah, that had been scary. But she'd had Tyler at her back then.

Now?

Becca liked the stability of the life she'd carved out. The one she and Tyler had talked about and planned together, the one into which Tyler had breathed belief. Without that she wouldn't have tried. Now that she had and was succeeding, it felt safe. Comfortable. And she could keep it that way. That could be as far as she would go with her courage.

But that might mean losing Tyler all over again. Had she already reattached herself so securely that the very thought of severing from him should painfully steal her breath? The moisture in her eyes said yes. How had this happened? A few meetings, some lingering looks. A passionate kiss.

His declaration of...missing her. Wanting to try again.

Stubborn love.

That was what had happened. Rooted deep in her heart was an immovable attachment to Tyler Murphy. It didn't matter how comfortable the life she'd carved out was, nor did it matter how *uncomfortable* his life seemed. Didn't matter that he would forever push her boundaries.

She loved him. Still. And that felt tremendously scary.

***

Tyler dared to take her hand. Just as he'd dared to ask to see her home.

Of all the intimidating things he'd done in his life, this seemed like the most challenging. Because the thing was, his body would mend. Wounds would heal, becoming scars. He'd lived through physical trauma and knew it to be so. His heart?

Well, likely it would mend too. But he so much preferred that it wouldn't break again. More, he rather that hers not ache all over either.

Broken love mended. This had become the plea of his heart—one he was already, tenuously, perhaps presumptuously, raising as a line of gratitude.

Becca's hand softened, and then her fingers burrowed between his. His heart leapt, and he glanced down to see her look up at him. Timidly. Determinedly. He knew that look. She was deciding to be brave.

He didn't want her feeling like being with him required courage though. He'd done that to her more than enough. *Father in heaven, give me wisdom to know what to say. What to do. I want to be with her, but I want what You want for her more.*

At the end of the long driveway from Matt and Lauren's tree farm, they paused in unison. Tyler looked at her. "Would you be willing to take the long way around?"

"Sure." She sounded hesitant, but a small smile lifted her lips.

He tugged on her hand, pointing down the road toward the rising hills, away from her shop and apartment. Their strides scuffed against the gravel on the dirt road, and as they walked, the quiet between them became incrementally more comfortable. Tyler lamented that this was his last evening in Pleasant Valley. Why had he waited all these weeks to ask her for a walk? To take her hand? To tell her...

Slowly. You promised.

"I heard you talking about Brandon earlier."

Becca's implied question caught him off guard. Here his thoughts had been solely focused on the two of them. Why was Becca thinking of his younger brother?

"Yeah. Dad said Brandon had made a quick trip home, and it seems things are...uh, complicated."

"Things? What things?"

Good that they were taking the long way around on this walk, because Tyler didn't know where to begin with Brandon's *things*. "Brandon's on an interesting..." What on earth should he call it? "Assignment."

"Assignment?" Becca shot a wrinkled-nose look at him. "What does Brandon do now?"

Tyler found himself caught off. He'd never asked, but it surprised him to discover that Brandon and Becca hadn't kept in touch—even a little bit. They'd been decent pals during their days in college. He'd known that Brandon had heartily approved of Becca. Considering how greatly disappointed in Tyler Brandon had been, he'd sort have figured his younger brother would have commiserated with Becca. Especially since Brandon had so firmly insisted that Tyler take time to see Becca when he came to help with Matt's project. Hadn't that indicated a residual relationship between them?

Apparently not. Strange that the subject had never come up between Tyler and Brandon, now that he thought on it. Some books were still closed when it came to the way he'd failed everyone. How long would that be so?

"Brandon works with Dad when needed and runs his own business. Firewood. He fells dead trees on private property and turns it into firewood. It's actually a lucrative business for him. But that's not really what he's doing *right now.*"

Becca's brows shot up.

"About five months ago Mom got a letter from an old friend. I don't know this woman—she and her husband moved from Sugar Pine when I was little—but apparently the Murphys left a lasting impression with her. Anyway, she wrote to Mom saying that her daughter was in some kind of trouble, and the thing she thought would remove the danger was for Megan to be...uh, engaged."

"Engaged?"

"Yeah. Crazy, right?"

"Your brother's *assignment* is to be engaged to some girl he doesn't know?"

"Exactly. Sort of." Tyler shrugged, not envying Brandon's situation, particularly after hearing how bizarre the whole deal sounded coming from Becca's lips.

"An arranged marriage..." She shot a furrowed brow up to him again. "That is very strange."

"Not necessarily a marriage."

Her expression shifted as her mouth drew into a long *oooo.* "A fake engagement. What kind of trouble was this girl in?"

Was it a fake engagement? Tyler had no real grasp on what Brandon was doing, let alone why he'd agreed to it. "I don't know exactly. Just something that her mother thought would be fixed by being engaged to a Murphy."

"Why a Murphy?"

"Like I said, she and Mom were friends back when the older among us were younger. Mrs. Alexander had apparently been impressed with the sons Mom and Dad were raising, and she thought that they'd be upstanding, godly young men. She even went so far as to research Matt and Connor to see that it was so."

"Just Matt and Connor?"

He chuckled. "Yes. Good thing she didn't dig into the middle of us— particularly me. She would have been disappointed."

Becca winced. He squeezed her hand, not wanting her to feel bad about it. It was the simple truth, and though there were still moments of deep shame, Tyler chose to rejoice in healing. In God's faithfulness to him and to his family in spite of his rotten failures. *New mercies every morning* was a constant first among his grateful list.

He brought Becca's knuckles to his lips and then continued. "Apparently what Mrs. Alexander found confirmed to her that the Murphy boys were good men. So she wrote to Mom, asking if she had an available son who would be willing to step in for Megan."

"I can't believe your mom said yes."

A shock to all of them, especially considering the way Mom had struggled so much with Connor's marriage to Sadie a few years back. Perhaps seeing that all come to right had given Mom more confidence in such an idea? Tyler couldn't say. "She didn't—not right away. Think she thought the whole thing was every bit as bizarre as you are thinking it is right now. But the letter kept nagging at Mom, so she started praying about it. Dad did too. A few weeks later they brought it to Brandon. Said they knew it was unusual, and they wouldn't ask him to do it for Megan."

"But?"

"But they felt compelled to present him with it and asked him to pray about it. If anyone was suited for such a task, it would be Brandon the Bold."

"And he's doing it?"

"Yes."

"Why?"

"I don't know."

Brandon had said that he'd felt compelled by the Spirit. Balderdash to anyone who had never felt the specific nudges from God, but Tyler knew Brandon wasn't one to make stuff like that up. If anything, he was one who would snort at such a suggestion as arranged fake engagements and gone on his merry way. He wasn't one to say something he didn't think any more than he was one to withhold much of what he did think.

Men molded by the leading of God. They were working on it—Tyler and each of his brothers.

Becca fell silent. They turned from the dirt road that would begin climbing into the hills if they went much farther, and onto a side avenue that ran parallel to the mountain. The gathering evening grew chilly, and Tyler wondered what Becca would do if he drew her in closer and tucked her under his arm.

"You aren't close with Brandon anymore, are you?"

Ah. The reason for her extended silence. "Brandon and I are good now."

"Are you?" Doubt coated her soft response.

Tyler stopped walking and tugged her into a position facing him. "He and I are good, Becca. There was strain for a while, but not now. But even if we weren't, what happened between my brother and me wasn't your fault." He gripped her shoulders. "Nothing that happened during that time was your fault. I am fully aware of my sole responsibility for all of it. For landing myself in rehab. For Brandon's disappointment in me." With knuckles under her chin, he tipped her face so that she would look at him. "For what happened between you and me. None of it was your fault. All of it was mine."

Her eyes pressed shut.

"Please forgive me, Becca."

A tear leaked from the corner of one eye, and her lips trembled.

"The things I did and said. The way I sent you away. For not coming to apologize to you sooner... I'm so sorry for all of it."

When Becca opened her eyes, he found a look of agony in them.

"I'm so sorry, Becca."

The pain gazing back at him softened, and she gripped the shirt fabric at his shoulder. "I didn't realize how angry at you I've been." Then she pressed her forehead into his chest.

Tyler cupped the back of her head, holding her against him. Waiting on a tight wire, praying for the grace for her to forgive him. "Can you forgive me?"

A tenuous moment passed, and then she leaned back, looked up. "I can," she whispered. Her mouth quivered into a small smile, and something like relief lightened her expression. "I do."

He cupped her neck. Then leaned in, dusting his mouth over hers. "Thank you." He dipped in again, lingering a little longer on her lips.

And this time she kissed him back.

Softly, gently, darkness embraced them. Regrettably, Tyler eased her away. He resecured her hand in his, and together they walked. Their pace became brisk as the mountain air chilled rather quickly, but it seemed too soon once Tyler had her safely at the back door to Just Eat It.

This was it—the final moment. He'd finish packing up tonight and be on the road before sunup in the morning. He'd promised her slowly, but blast it, they'd already lost three years.

Three long, stupid years.

"Rebecca Colson."

Startled, she turned from unlocking the door to look up at him.

"I still love you." There. Now the whole truth was out there. "You can go as slow as you need when it comes to you and me—I'm learning to be a patient man. But here's the truth of it: I still love you, and I'm gonna keep loving you."

CHAPTER TWENTY-FIVE

(in which Tyler worships)

T HERE HAD BEEN A time, not long before, when Tyler had believed that just to hear her voice again would be enough.

Once again he'd been a fool.

No one could frustrate him like himself. He'd waited three years to seek her out. Dumb. Once God had flung doors wide open, literally placing him down the road from her bakery, he'd waited a week to darken her door. Stupid. He'd waited another three weeks to tell her that he couldn't and didn't want to forget her. Cowardly.

And he'd waited until hours before he'd had to leave to tell her he still loved her.

But...it was said. And received. Glory.

From that moment on, he had been sorely tested in that whole *I'm learning to be a patient man* proclamation. A week had gone by, during which he'd talked to her on the phone at least twice a day, which frankly wasn't nearly enough. Seven days of not seeing her intelligent green eyes take in the world around her. Of not watching her love on his nieces and making him desperate to resurrect all their shared plans. Of not losing his breath when she settled her smile on him.

Blast it. *Slowly* was torture. He'd known since he'd been a nineteen-year-old student that he was in love with Becca Colson and wanted her for his wife. There they were seven years later and still not married. And he was still waiting, longing, to hear her say she still loved him.

Please let it be so.

All of it made for a cantankerous mood. Despite his conscious effort to list the gifts of goodness in his life.

Sunrise, warm and pure.

Aching back from work I'm able to do.

Hearing Becca on the other side of the line.

Saying I love you... That one was more sacrifice, as she hadn't said it back.

On the plus side, though, that salty mood, and the desire to see Becca again as soon as possible, had sure lit a fire under his backside when it came to the job Dad had left for him to finish. If Brandon was there, they'd have the whole thing tied up and put down. The thought made Tyler want to growl. What the heck was Brandon doing? Who went off to play pretend fiancée to some spoiled rich girl who had made bad choices?

A Murphy boy, that's who. Should that be an item of praise?

What had Mom and Dad been thinking, putting Brandon up to this?

Trust in the Lord and do good.

Sounded like a verse Lauren would quote at such a moment. There, Tyler inhaled deeply, paused from tossing his tools into boxes and buckets as he cleaned up his work site for the night, and chuckled as he thought on the last conversation he'd had with his sister-in-law before he'd left Pleasant Valley. She'd been up with baby Helene when Tyler had risen early to load out.

"Ty?" She'd sounded tentative.

"Yep?"

"You're not mad at me, are you?"

"No one in this family could stay mad at you for long, Lauren. You're too sweet."

"But you were."

"For a second." He winked.

"I was...worried for both of you. It's not going to make sense, but I was worried that you would go this whole time without telling her how you feel. And I was worried you were going to tell her how you feel and make her upset all over again."

He chuckled. Both had happened, but neither were proving fatal as yet. "We'll figure it out, Lauren." Lifting his ball cap, he scratched his head and then replaced it. "I hope."

"I was reading in Colossians 4 while I was in the hospital. Verse 10 made me think of you."

"Yeah? Why was that?"

Lauren edged nearer, a tender smile on her mouth. "Just read it, Tyler. I think you'll see." She reached to hug him and then lifted Helene toward him. "Kiss your niece, and don't take forever coming back to see the people here who love you."

While warmth flooded him, he'd kissed Helene's soft, fuzzy head, hugged Lauren again, and tucked away that passage to look at later.

Except, he hadn't yet.

Stopping where he stood, a bucket at his feet ready to be placed in the back of his truck, Tyler reached for his phone and pulled up his Bible app.

Colossians 4:10. "My fellow prisoner Aristarchus sends you his greetings, as does Mark, the cousin of Barnabas. (You have received instructions about him; if he comes to you, welcome him.)"

His brow wrinkled as he read it again. This made Lauren think of him?

He finished loading the tools and then pulled away from the nearly completed job. Two more days and he'd be done. Free to head back to Pleasant Valley, to the woman who still held his heart. *All of that!*

Thoughts that should completely free his mind to thrilling joy. What was with that verse though? He puzzled over it for the full hour-long drive and was no closer to an answer when he pulled up at the Murphy family home.

Gert was parked in the long spot beside the garage. Mom and Dad were back.

Setting his stride toward the garage, Tyler hoped he'd find his dad within. Dad had the biblical knowledge one would expect from a preacher —hopefully, he could solve the mystery.

After exchanging the expected *how are you* and *how's the job coming*, Tyler asked about the verse, pulling up the passage on his phone again and handing it to Dad to read. Dad did so and then looked back at him expectantly, pride and joy lighting his eyes, as if this was a delightful discovery.

What had Tyler missed? "I don't get it. Why would this make Lauren think of me?"

Dad's grin spread wide, and he blinked. "Reconciliation, son."

"What?"

"Paul wrote about welcoming Mark. Somewhere between Acts, when Paul had rejected Mark because of something Mark had done on a missionary trip, and Colossians 4, there had been reconciliation. Relationships restored." Dad gripped his shoulder. "Go back and read what happened in Acts, Ty. You'll see it. You'll see what Lauren sees."

Later that night, he did. And it summoned tears. How tender of God to tuck that into the Bible—a quiet, subtle story hidden between a few lines, of relationships made right. *Broken love mended.*

His mind moved to another passage from Paul's pen, this one in 2 Corinthians: *Therefore, if anyone is in Christ, the new creation has come: The old has gone, the new is here!* And then to a promise found at the end of Revelation: *He who was seated on the throne said, "I am making everything new!"*

A promise for things to come, even after things went very dark. God would never lose His grip on any part of life, no matter how ugly and bad things became. Never. And Tyler had this little glimpse of a moment that would confirm that grand promise in the restoration of Paul and Mark. Tyler had confirmation in the restoration he himself had with his parents, with Brandon, and now...

Now—*Lord, let it be so!*—with Becca too.

In place of that petition, a well of praise sprang up from his heart, flooding his mind. The very joy he'd been bending his spirit toward all week now splashed over him like sweet rain to a parched land. Paul's words, found in Ephesians, rang clear and true in Tyler's heart.

Now to him who is able to do immeasurably more than all we ask or imagine, according to his power that is at work within us, to him be glory in the church and in Christ Jesus throughout all generations, for ever and ever! Amen.

To God be the glory for great things He had *already* done. In Paul's life. Throughout history. In the Murphy family. And in Tyler's life.

God had done great things.

Tyler had no reason to doubt that God would continue doing great things. So right there, in the waiting, he gave way to full praise.

To Him be the glory. Amen.

***

Becca checked her watch for the eight hundredth time, it seemed. The week had been ridiculously long. Not bad, but long. But Tyler was on his way back to Pleasant Valley, and hopefully the torture would come to an end.

She had told him she needed time to think, that they needed to go slowly. A week apparently had been more than enough time. Did that make her a fool?

Yes. Becca Colson had been and still was a fool for Tyler Murphy. There was simply no denying it, and stuffing back the truth had nearly suffocated her. She would tell him. Tonight. Or maybe tomorrow. After, it would all come right. Wouldn't it?

Forget that she had worked to create a successful business in Pleasant Valley. Or that Tyler's future didn't seem to have clear definition—and what did seem to be delineated scared her a little.

No, she couldn't forget. What if his new, important friends thought little of her? Becca was no athlete of any sort, let alone the professional kind. What would happen when Tyler measured her against Tessa and found Becca greatly lacking? *He wouldn't...* No. Tyler wasn't the sort.

But what if he fell on a climb? New injuries, more physical therapy, and more prescriptions... Becca rubbed her forehead, attempting to banish such thoughts. She was borrowing trouble.

But what if there was tension between Tyler and his dad? There very well could be—Kevin had been banking on Tyler taking over the business someday. This new direction in Tyler's life could be an issue with them. Where would that put her?

Becca groaned as she pressed her hands to her face. Her tumbling worries made her dizzy. But they could figure it out, couldn't they?

What if Tyler asked her to give up Just Eat It? The life she'd created based on the plans they'd made?

So many worries!

A rise of panic had her pulse running, and Becca checked her watch again. Maybe this was all an impulsive mistake. She'd just missed him too long. He'd just been too...wonderful. But there were real issues they needed to straighten out. Perhaps it would be wiser to pull back a little for the time being. Go slowly...

Trust in the Lord with all your heart and lean not on your own understanding. In all your ways, submit to him, and He will make your paths straight. Proverbs 3:5–6.

Becca pinched the battle card between her fingers. The whirling of her mind slowed.

The slam of a truck door outside Just Eat It jarred her out of her swirling thoughts. Clenching a fist, she stood from her sofa and went to the window that overlooked the back door to her shop. In the shadowy gray of the evening, she could see him walk from his truck toward her back door. Tyler moved with a slight limp.

Had he before? She couldn't recall. Surely she would have noticed, right?

He disappeared from view, and then the door buzzer sounded. Becca's breath stalled, and she felt the same way she had that moment before she had leapt from the platform on the zipline course three years back. The way she had felt the day Tyler had proposed.

Back then she had jumped, choosing to trust that the harness and cable would be her safety. She'd done it scared, and it had been okay. And when it had come to Tyler's bended knee request, that hadn't been a leap at all. She'd said yes without a second thought. Not a single fear.

That memory scrolled through her mind as she descended the stairs and crossed the kitchen. Now she was not leaping into the air and depending on a cable to keep her alive, but this felt just as scary. That seemed unfair, as for the past week she'd been nearly unable to think of anything beyond seeing Tyler again. What was it that was turning her inside out?

Fear. Pure, unchecked fear running loose in her heart. That was not okay.

Trust in the Lord...

She had poured this out before God nearly every waking moment since Tyler had told her he still loved her. Every time she'd replayed that, she wished she'd told him of her own stubborn love. Would that have released her from the bondage of fear?

Love casts out fear. Did that apply here?

Becca paused at the door, and before reaching for the knob, she closed her eyes. She directed her thoughts back to another card containing a verse penned in Lauren's lovely script. One of the first battle cards given. *Do not be anxious about anything, but in everything by prayer and supplication with thanksgiving let your requests be made known to God. And the peace of God, which surpasses all understanding, will guard your hearts and your minds in Christ Jesus. Philippians 4:6-7.*

Below that Lauren had written one simple line: *The Lord will direct your path; trust Him.*

That three-year-old card was taped onto Becca's mirror. Lauren had given it to her when she was deciding whether or not to purchase the small, run-down building that had become Just Eat It and her home. Oh, Becca had agonized over that choice. She was so far from her home in Idaho, and she was on the verge of chasing down this dream that she'd thought to do with Tyler at her side. The building needed so much work, and she would then be carving out a business from nothing. It had been terrifying to do it alone, and she'd nearly folded to the rampant fear telling her it was too hard, too scary, and she was too alone. Too small and insignificant.

Scratching out Just Eat It had been hard—tremendously hard, and there were certainly scary parts. But she'd done it, and the whole way through, God had proven Himself present and faithful. She'd not been alone. In addition to his continuous provision for her daily needs, God had sent her Matt and Lauren, and surprisingly, her parents had supported the plan.

What if she had caved to fear instead?

What if she did now?

Lord, direct my path. And help me to trust You instead of relying on fear to be my guide.

She turned the knob and opened the door. Tyler's brown-eyed gaze fell on her, and he smiled.

CHAPTER TWENTY-SIX

(in which Becca begins a list)

S UMMER'S WARMTH BRUSHED AGAINST Becca's skin with a gentle caress. Early evening stars poked diamond holes in the fading sky, their promise of light and hope needling into the coming darkness. She inhaled, taking in the fragrance of mountain stream and cool pine as it wafted through the valley. She loved Pleasant Valley.

She loved Tyler Murphy too, though in the past weeks as summer eased forward and Tyler spent his time split between working with his dad and visiting Becca on the weekends, she'd yet to speak those words. Two stupid weeks and she still hadn't. If not for the what-ifs that fed her anxieties, she would have said them. He did. Often, and with tender patience. As if he knew the struggles she wrestled with and was giving her space to pin them down. Without frustration or condemnation.

He had said it, hadn't he? Tyler was learning to be a patient man—and so he was. One more attribute about this redeemed version of the man she'd already stubbornly loved that secured her heart to his.

If not for those pesky what-ifs and what-abouts, she'd tell him. Oh, how much she did want to.

But even then, standing on the rooftop where she'd spent many an evening gazing at stars, awing at sunsets, greeting sunrises, and soaking in battle verses, the anxious thoughts swarmed. This evening, as she waited for Tyler to arrive, those thoughts increased by one about tomorrow's climb.

He'd been asked to do another filmed climb, this time at a place three hours from Pleasant Valley. He'd not film tomorrow, but practice, as he'd not done this particular rock, and did she want to go along? She'd meet

Max and Tessa and see him do the impossible thing he did for herself. Yes. She wanted to go, and she'd attempt the climb too.

Tyler had held her with silent study when she'd added that last part. Puzzling. "Are you sure, Becca? You don't—"

"It's not as if I've never climbed something before, Ty," she interrupted. A partial proclamation, as she'd climbed walls in gyms with him. Not rocks out in nature. Though the difference didn't seem notable on the surface, in her heart, there was a very big, scary difference.

Tyler had collected both her hands in his, kissed her knuckles, and then settled that inquiring look on her face again. "I know that, love."

She'd expected him to grin widely. Proud of how brave she was. And while a corner of his mouth curved upward, the small smile loving, it was not as she'd expected. Then with eyes slipped closed, he tipped his face skyward, and that look passed over his features.

She'd seen this often and had wondered at it. It was as if he softened in these sort of moments, transformed into something that she craved for herself. Peace and joy.

What was it?

That question had been yet to be asked, and as she stood near the brick barrier that defined the safety boundary of her rooftop theater waiting for Tyler to come, she tipped her face skyward and shut her eyes, searching for whatever Ty found in this posture.

It was not there for her. Behind her closed lids, instead of peace and joy, Becca smacked up against the loud voices of her fears. The what-ifs and what-abouts.

What about this life of climbing and speaking? How long will that "season" be, and can I even fit into it? What about Tessa—he admires her so much! What if I don't measure up? And what about my life here? What if he asks me to give it up...

Her heart beat so fast, and her breath came hard. Was this a panic attack? Eyes wide open, Becca searched for the baggie of battle cards, which she nearly always had on hand during her rooftop moments. There, on the bricks, waiting.

"The Lord will fight for you; you need only to be still." She spoke the verse from the top card, one copied out of Exodus 14:14, out loud.

The Lord will fight...

She didn't understand why this was such a battle, but it was. But her way of doing it wasn't helping. *The Lord will fight!*

Be still.

In other words...trust Him. *Trust Him. Trust Him!*

Becca straightened the cards, tapping them on the brick ledge before she slipped them back into their baggie. The stack had grown thick. Nearly two inches now. She wished her faith had grown in proportion.

The pop and crunch sound of tires on gravel drew her attention to the vehicle that turned into the parking space below.

Tyler.

Lord, I do love him. And I am afraid. Becca unclenched her rolled fist as Tyler parked, then slid from the driver's seat. He looked up at her and smiled.

She smiled back. Genuine. And determined. This time she would be brave.

***

"You don't have to do this, Becca." Tyler covered her two small, trembling hands as she reached for the harness in the back of his SUV.

Wide green eyes looked up to meet his. This time rather than shrugging her shoulders and saying something like "I want to," which he knew wasn't wholly true, she held his gaze and lowered the harness back to the canvass bag where it lived. The three-hour drive, mostly quiet, and during which Becca had fisted and unfisted her hands so much that Tyler was sure her fingers must be sore by now, had been more than enough to tell him this climbing outing was not a thrill to her. He'd asked her if she wanted to go with him, not expecting that she'd climb, but when she'd suggested it, he'd known a small thrill.

But he wasn't disappointed to discover that she really hadn't ever wanted to climb. Not disappointed in her, at least.

"I feel like I do," she said quietly.

He gripped her hand and lowered onto the open trunk, turning her to face him. There was the disappointment—and it had roots in himself. That he had left with her an impression of something that he didn't expect. "Tell me why."

Becca chewed on her bottom lip. Her hand still in his, Tyler drew her closer, pressing her palm to his heart. "Tell me."

"If I don't, then I'm not brave." She looked down, as if ashamed. "And if I'm not brave, I have no business being with you."

"Brave?" Tyler wrapped an arm around her shoulders, tucking her head against his chest. "You are brave clean through. I don't need you to climb a rock to prove it." Shame on him for ever requiring such.

Honest moments that take courage. There was beauty in that.

Pulling away from him, Becca found his gaze again. Slowly he lifted a hand and trailed his fingers over the loose bits of her hair. Suddenly a tear broke loose from her dark lashes, and she shook her head. "I've spent so much of my life trying not to be afraid. Trying to choose brave instead. Why isn't it working?"

Tyler didn't have sure answers. But he knew she had his heart, and right then he had her pain. She had more than one reason to be fearful of being with him. He'd been an addict, and that would always be part of his story and a lingering danger in his life. He was still a thrill seeker—losing his leg hadn't purged that part of his personality. And now his life had taken an unexpected turn, one toward a more public life than he'd planned. One that, at least at times, would demand more of him than he'd intended to give. He couldn't blame Becca for being leery of that. Especially when he knew she'd worked hard to establish her stable, safe life in Pleasant Valley.

So was he to let her go?

The thought swirled up thrashing panic. Instead of yielding to that, Tyler shut his eyes, tipped his face up, and shifted the direction of his thoughts. Everything in his life was something he could offer back up. Everything. So he did it again.

Beautiful, hard honesty.

Broken love mended, though each stitch pricked.

The chance to die to self.

The chance to trust that You are good.

Fingertips gentle in his beard, Becca's touch came a heartbeat before her words. "You do this often. What are you thinking?"

"What do I do often?"

"Nothing exactly. It's just the look that you get when you're thinking whatever it is that has your mind right now. It's peace and joy and... I don't know. Holy, maybe? What are you thinking when you have these looks?"

He wore that? So plain that she could see it? *Praise!* He gathered her hands, pressed them to his chest. Then gathered the rest of her and pressed her against his heart.

"I'm listing the things in the moment. Giving thanks for them."

"Listing the things? What things?"

"Well, just now..." He shut his eyes again, recalling that list from moments ago. "Honesty, even though it's hard. The chance to die to myself, to trust God. And—" He inhaled, tightening his hold, adjusting his position so that he could whisper to her what he'd cried for to heaven. The line of thanksgiving that was also a plea. "Broken love mended."

Becca held still for a moment, her silence a bit like falling through space. Then she pressed her forehead into his neck, gripping his shirt. "Broken love mended," she repeated.

"Mending," he revised, the longing for it nearly choking him.

She lifted her head, pulling back only enough to gaze up at him. Her fingers raked gently through the whiskers covering his face, then traced the curve over his ear. Finally they burrowed into the thickness that had grown too long over his neck. Every touch sped his heart rate, sending a thrill more exhilarating than any adventure had ever induced.

"How long have you listed moments?"

Could he speak into *this* moment? The one in which the softness of her look held on him confirmed the plea-prayer he'd lifted as praise. It was *yes* and *amen*. It felt sacred.

Words might shatter it.

He swallowed. "Long enough to know that each moment is a gift."

Her expression pinched in question. "Even the bad ones?"

"Those too. You have to look harder though." Tyler searched his mind for an explanation. "Finding the gift is the key, and searching for it leads to peace and joy. Abundant life, because then I see it. It was just right there waiting for me to look."

Her curious study roamed his face, as if she was on a treasure quest of her own. "Your fall?"

"A gift. Because of it, I learned how to stand."

A piece of her skepticism fell away. "The addiction?"

"That was on me. But the gift? I met Ben and Mark, and through them Tessa and Max."

Becca pressed her lips together and nodded. At her next thoughts, she winced. "Me...giving your ring back?"

"That one was"—his voice cracked—"a lot harder." Tyler slowly released a shuddered breath. His hand curved around her waist and gripped the fabric at her back as he allowed the pain of her walking away to reenter his memory.

Would he have become the man he was now if he hadn't forced her to leave?

Would *she* be this woman now?

A clear *no* clanged through his mind. He would have broken her further. Continued the cycle of neediness and begging for her forgiveness, and then angry bitterness targeted at her. They were broken then—but it truly could have been worse. So much.

Both spared from the worst of it. Both pressed deeper into You by the pain.

Fingers curled in his hair, Becca pulled his head to hers. "You call it broken love mended. I have called it stubborn love."

Tyler's eyes flew open.

Tears leaked from hers. "I will start a list too. Because I'm tired of the bondage of fear. I want that abundant life. I want to know that look you wear, in my heart.

"First, *stubborn love*." She moved her hands to his shoulders. "Then you lift it up to God in praise, right? That's what you do when you shut your eyes and look that way, isn't it?"

"Yes." He was breathless.

What was happening? What was Becca saying in this? The hope he'd nurtured in the weeks since he'd first told her he still loved her, froze. Scared to break the long-sought surface, that it might shatter whatever this glorious thing was.

She leaned back, looked up, exposing her neck and tempting his mouth to it. Instead, he moved to catch the expression of her face.

Eyes closed. Her forehead smoothed, etchings of anxiety falling away. Lips eased, lifted. She stayed there, certainly lifting more of the things in the moment than *stubborn love*. Because there were so many things.

Joy found. He lifted that one as she raised hers.

Becca's chin lowered, and her eyes focused on him again. Smiling. "That is quite something, Murphy. How often do you do it?"

"As often as I can. Bonhoeffer said that 'it is only with gratitude that life becomes rich.' Gratitude is the...the antidote. To almost everything, I think. It is proclaiming that God is good and that I trust Him."

Again she tipped her chin heavenward. This time she spoke aloud, eyes open. "Broken man made new." Then she lowered her look on him again.

"That doesn't seem like enough."

"No?"

She shook her head, eyes shimmering again. "No. Not when I've loved that man so much." She traced the curve of his brow and then leaned in to brush the swell of his lips with hers. Warm. Tender. A breath of hope and promise. "When I still love him so very much."

No more words required. Just the praise of his heart lifted toward heaven as the gift of stubborn love filled his arms.

Broken love mended.

Once more added. As it would be again. And again. Every day, for the rest of his life. Amen.

The End

HERE WE ARE AGAIN, my friends. I so hope you enjoyed Tyler and Rebecca's journey! Would you do me the honor of leaving a review for Stubborn Love? Simply click here or go to Amazon (or Goodreads), and share what you thought with other readers.

The Murphy Brothers Stories will continue with Who You Are. Brandon Murphy is the most held back and stern of all the Murphy boys, and as hinted in this story, he's about to step into an arrangement that will challenge the very core of who he is. Who You Are will come out in July of 2021. Please don't miss it!

As always, thank you so much for reading! I'm honored that you'd give me your time.

Dear Reader:

I rarely write these postscripts anymore, as I fear they become obligatory and frankly self-indulgent. I have no interest in either. However, this note, I feel passionately, is the outpouring of where this book has taken me, the sweet living waters to which I've been led and which I joyfully offer. It's not at all about *me*.

As I dug deeper into this story, I found my toolbox for it woefully insufficient. That's a little unnerving—to know you do not possess what it will take to bring something to completion. Who am I do grapple with the hard things? I am insufficient. You'd better know that I prayed double-time when that reality hit.

God's answer? He placed in my hands, at a Bible study, Ann Voskamp's *One Thousand Gifts*. It was literally given to me (as a gift) at the *exact* moment I needed. From there God directed me to Elisabeth Elliot's *Suffering Is Never for Nothing*. (If you've never read this, I beg you, do so. Immediately.) Then to Schememann's *For the Life of the World*. All were immensely rich—not simply for the development of this story, but for the growth of my soul. Know that I am personally submitting to this practice of thanksgiving. It is healing the lingering lacerations in my heart. Cauterizing the seeping selfishness, the greed, the jealousy I have long indulged and yet lamented. It is deepening the trust, worship, and the walking. It is summoning abundant life.

It is literally communion with God, the giver of all the things in all the moments.

I beg you, friend. Do not stop at reading this little fictional tale and wondering *Can gratitude do so much?* Dig in. Read the much wiser, spiritually mature, and deeper people who know much better than I. Then taste and see.

For the Lord *is* good.

Give Him thanks.

Gratefully, with all my heart,

Jen

Printed in Great Britain
by Amazon

59941945R00139